Under Fire

REBECCA DEEL

ISBN-13: 9781717986436

DEDICATION

To my amazing husband, my knight in shining armor.

ACKNOWLEDGMENTS

Cover design by Melody Simmons.

CHAPTER ONE

Someone had been in her house. Delilah Frost fought back the panic threatening to overwhelm her as she stared at the almond milk carton on her counter, the almond milk she hadn't used that morning. She listened for any sounds that might betray the continued presence of an intruder and didn't hear anything. Maybe the person had left already.

Should she go further into the house? Only if she wanted to be the too-stupid-to-live woman in a B-grade movie. Besides, she could destroy any clues the police might gather to catch the person who broke in. Delilah set her bags of groceries on the kitchen counter and turned toward the door.

She had to get out of this house. Now. The person could still be here. Hand shaking, Delilah reached for the door knob, intent on escaping and calling the police.

A heavy footstep sounded behind her.

Heart racing, she grasped the knob. Before she could flee into the yard, hard hands shoved her into the door. Delilah's head slammed against the panel hard enough to edge her vision with black.

She fought the darkness as she slid to the floor. If she lost consciousness, Delilah wouldn't be able to defend herself. Not like she'd done such a great job to this point. Awake, she had a chance to fight back if he tried to haul her out of the house or kill her.

She heard a siren in the distance and a frantic whisper. A low growl preceded a kick to her side. Delilah yelped and curled into a ball to protect her ribs. The man cursed, kicked her away from the door, yanked it open, and fled.

Gasping with her hands pressed to her side, she scooted toward her purse in slow motion. That creep kicked like a mule.

Delilah snagged the strap and tugged her bag close enough to thrust her hand inside and find her cell phone. She called up her contact list and called the one man she knew could save her. As soon as his voice greeted her, she dragged in a painful breath and said, "Help me."

Adrenaline poured into Matt Rainer's veins at Delilah's words. "Where are you?" He gave a hand signal to his teammates from Bravo unit that had all of them grabbing their gear and slipping into battle mode.

"Home."

"Are you sick?"

"Intruder."

Matt raced from the main building on the campus of Personal Security International and sprinted toward his SUV. His best friend, Cade Ramsey, caught up with him and held out his hand for the keys.

He didn't argue, just tossed them to his friend. "Is the person still in the house?"

"Gone." Delilah wheezed in a breath. "Hurts."

Cade cranked the engine and threw the SUV into gear. He peeled out of the parking lot followed by the rest of Bravo in their SUVs.

"Did you call the police?" Matt's hand tightened around his cell phone.

"Only you. Coming?"

"I'm on my way, but I'm at PSI." He was five minutes out which was five minutes too long in his book. Depending on how bad she was injured, Delilah might bleed out on him before he reached her. His gut knotted. He didn't want to lose her.

Matt glanced at his friend. "Call the cops and send them to Delilah's place. Somebody broke in and, from the sound of it, roughed her up." Someone who would pay when Matt caught up with him.

He turned his attention back to the woman on the phone. "How bad are your injuries?" he asked as Cade talked to the dispatcher for the Otter Creek police department.

"Don't know. Shoved me into a door and kicked me."

Rage blinded him for an instant before the medic side of him surged to the forefront. "How is your vision?"

"Blurred."

Possible concussion. "Where did he kick you?"

"Side. Ribs. Black boots hurt."

Bruised or cracked ribs, he though as he gave a short bark of laughter. "Yeah, they do." He'd had enough booted feet strike his body to know firsthand how much they hurt. "We're three minutes out, Delilah. Bravo is with me. Just hold on."

"Hear sirens."

"Good." He wanted to be the one to help her, not Otter Creek's finest. "When the police arrive, leave the call to me active. Tell the cop not to move you until the EMTs arrive." If something more happened before he got there, Matt wanted to know so he and his team would be prepared.

Seconds later, a male voice identified himself as law enforcement and relayed to dispatch a request for a detective and an ambulance.

Matt heard Delilah's voice as she answered the cop's questions, but not her exact words. The phone was too far away from her mouth. Patience, he reminded himself. He'd get all the information once Delilah was checked by a doctor. He didn't care if she protested. The woman was going to the hospital. She might have internal injuries.

As soon as the SUV stopped in front of Delilah's house, Matt threw open the door and sprinted up the walkway. Inside the house, he called out, "Delilah."

The cop stepped into the living room, hand on his weapon. He relaxed when he saw Matt. "In the kitchen. Ambulance is two minutes away."

Matt recognized the rookie as one of his students in a first-aid for first-responders class Ethan Blackhawk, Otter Creek's chief of police, was having his officers take. "How is she?" he asked Cooper.

"The intruder whaled on her, but I've seen worse."

Matt pushed past him and entered the kitchen. Delilah was on the floor on her side, her breathing shallow. He dropped to his knees beside her.

"Matt."

"Let me take a look at you." He brushed her long, dark tresses away from her face. She had a large goose egg on her forehead. Looked like she might need stitches where her delicate skin split from the violent contact with the door.

Cade walked in with Matt's mike bag. "What do you need?" he asked as he squatted next to him.

"To clean the blood from her face and get a better look at that injury."

Bravo's EOD man dug out the medical supplies Matt needed.

Matt frowned. Yeah, she needed a few stitches. He applied a pressure bandage to stop the bleeding.

"Delilah, I'm going to roll you to your back. Let me do the work." Between them, Matt and Cade shifted Delilah to her back with minimal discomfort for her.

Despite hearing the ambulance sirens coming closer, he ran his hands over Delilah's arms and jeans-clad legs. No obvious breaks. He turned his attention to her torso. "Where did this clown kick you?"

Cade scowled when he heard that.

Delilah indicated her right side.

With a gentle touch, Matt pressed lightly on her rib cage, focusing on one rib at a time. When she hissed with pain, he froze. "Here?"

She nodded.

He explored the rib carefully. "I don't feel a break in the bone. The kicks might have cracked a rib."

"Still painful."

"Unfortunately."

The EMTs hurried into the kitchen with Cooper on their heels. "What do we have, Matt?" asked Jay Rogers, an EMT who had taken classes from Matt and Rio, Durango's medic.

"Head injury that needs stitches. Probable concussion, possible cracked ribs and internal injuries."

"No hospital," Delilah murmured.

"You don't have a choice." Matt pinned her with his gaze. "Either you go with Jay and Harry or I'll take you myself."

"Can't you treat me?"

"I could, but I specialize in battlefield medicine." He brushed the compression bandage with a light touch. "Gets the job done, but you need someone with better technique so the scar is minimized."

Cade patted Delilah's hand. "Better heed his advice. We all have the scars to attest to his medical skills."

When he glanced at his friend, Cade just grinned at him. Whatever. As long as Delilah went to the hospital, he'd take the razzing from his teammates.

"Listen to Matt," Jay said as he knelt by Delilah's left side. "He knows what he's talking about. If he says you need to see the doc, you can take that to the bank."

She gave a slight nod.

Excellent. Matt squeezed her fingers. When he loosened his grip, Delilah grabbed his hand to hold him in place. Matt's gaze flicked to hers. While Jay and Harry checked Delilah's vitals and reported to the hospital, she held his gaze.

Probably needed reassurance, Matt concluded. Delilah hadn't hinted at feelings for him beyond friendship. That was something he hoped to change in the near future. Bravo team had to stay home long enough for him to actively pursue a dating relationship with the candle shop owner.

If she would give him a chance. Delilah might not be into him or willing to involve herself with a man who chased terrorists for a living. Not exactly the safest job on the planet.

"We're ready to transport," Jay said to Matt. "You riding along?"

He glanced at Delilah. "Yeah, I'm going with her." He refused to stay behind while she was injured and vulnerable to attack.

"I'll follow in your SUV," Cade said. "That way you'll have wheels when Delilah is released."

"Thanks."

Delilah squeezed his hand. "My groceries are on the counter. Some of it needs to be refrigerated."

"I'll take care of it before I come to the hospital," Cade said.

The EMTs shifted Delilah to the gurney they'd brought in and rolled her from the house with Matt on their heels, his mike bag slung over his shoulder. He never left home without it.

He climbed into the back of the ambulance with Delilah and Jay and forced himself to act like a friend instead of a medic. As they drove away from her home, Matt wondered who had broken in and roughed up his beautiful friend. Would he return to finish the job?

CHAPTER TWO

Matt leaned against the wall across from the exam room where Dr. Anderson was checking Delilah. He willed the old country doctor to move faster. If the exam took much longer, Matt would hunt down his team leader's wife and have her check on Delilah. Grace St. Claire worked as a nurse at Memorial Hospital and was currently working in the ER. She'd passed him a few times rushing from one place to another.

Just as he pulled out his phone to text Grace, Dr. Anderson walked out. Matt shoved the phone into his pocket. "How is she, Doc?"

"Your assessment was correct, Matt. Delilah has a concussion and cracked ribs. No internal injuries."

"And the cut?"

"Required eight stitches. I think the scar will be minimal. I was careful."

Matt clapped Otter Creek's favorite doctor on the shoulder. "I never doubted that. Can I see her?"

"She's been asking for you."

His heart skipped a beat. She'd been asking for him? A comfort thing, he reminded himself. Didn't mean she saw him as more than a friend no matter how much he wanted her to.

"I'll admit her for the night. Provided she doesn't have complications, Delilah can go home tomorrow morning."

Oh, man. Delilah wouldn't be happy about the hospital stay. "Thanks, Doc."

"I assume you and one of your friends will be staying with her tonight."

He grinned. The doctor was familiar with PSI and their security measures. "Yes, sir."

"See that she rests, but let the nurses do their jobs. You're here as her friend. When she rests, I suggest you take the opportunity to do the same yourself."

He didn't bother to argue with the physician, but Matt was on guard duty until Delilah was safe.

"The orderly will be here soon to take her to her room."

When Dr. Anderson left, Matt entered the exam room. Delilah reclined against a pillow, her eyes closed and skin pale. He stopped at her side and wrapped his hand around hers.

She stirred and opened her eyes. "Hi."

"How do you feel?"

"Not that great," Delilah admitted. "The headache is pretty bad."

Matt released her and crossed the room to turn off the lights. "Better?"

"Much. Thanks."

He returned to her side and was surprised when she clasped his hand. "Are you nauseated?"

"How did you know?"

"Common side effect of a concussion along with light sensitivity. Depending on how bad the concussion is, you could be plagued by headaches for a while."

She winced. "Great. When can I get out of here?"

"Tomorrow morning. Dr. Anderson wants to make sure you don't have any problems overnight."

A light tap on the door had Matt swinging around, his hand resting on the grip of his Sig. He relaxed when his team leader, Trent, walked in.

"I hear you're going to be a hospital guest." Trent stopped at the end of the bed and patted Delilah's foot. "Grace is working tonight. She'll check on you during her breaks."

"Gives me something to look forward to." Delilah gave Bravo's leader a wan smile.

A brisk knock on the door and the orderly pushed a wheelchair into the room. "Super express transport to the sixth floor," the man said, a smile spreading on his face. "How you doing, Ms. Frost?"

"I'm okay, Carlos, considering. My injuries could have been a lot worse than a bump on the head. How is your wife?"

"Benita is great. She's planning to stop by Wicks later in the week. Our Marisol is turning sixteen in a couple weeks. Benita wants special candles for the cake and tables."

"If I don't have what Benita wants, I'll make the candles for her."

Carlos beamed at her, his smile broad.

While the orderly locked the chair's wheels, Matt helped Delilah sit up and shift to the edge of the bed. She groaned, hand pressed to her stomach.

Matt grabbed a plastic tub from the counter nearby. "Stay with her," he told Trent. He went to the nurse's station. "I need an ice pack for Ms. Frost." A moment later, he returned to the exam room and placed the ice pack against the nape of her neck.

Delilah drew a shaky breath. "Thanks."

"You'll be more comfortable in your room. Hold the ice pack, Trent." Matt lifted Delilah from the bed and placed her in the wheelchair, then took over holding the ice pack in place. "I'll get you a second ice pack when you're settled."

"We need to go, Carlos." Delilah's voice was shaky as she clutched the plastic bin with a white-knuckled grip.

The orderly got them moving. "If you need to stop, let me know."

Matt kept a close eye on Delilah. The trip to her assigned room left her paler than ever. Her face was beaded with sweat by the time he scooped her up and laid her in the bed with the covers draped over her. "Trent, go to the nurse's station and ask for an ice pack and ginger ale. No substitutes on the soft drink. If they don't have it, find a vending machine."

While Trent was gone, Matt found a washcloth, doused it in cold water, and pressed the cloth to Delilah's forehead. His teammate returned a few minutes later and handed over the cold pack and soft drink and straw.

"Turn off the overhead light." He popped the tab on the ginger ale and dropped the straw in the opening. "Sip this," he told Delilah. "The ginger will help settle your stomach." If the soft drink and the ice packs didn't help, Matt had a few more tricks he used to help his teammates when they were nauseated, including a patch for nausea if he couldn't convince the nursing staff to provide one.

"Thanks." Delilah settled back against the pillow.

"Did Doc Anderson give you anything for pain?"

"The nurse is supposed to give me something."

"I'll be on watch in the hall until midnight," Trent said to Matt. "Let me know if you need anything."

"You don't have to stay. I've got this." He wasn't leaving her to someone else's protection, not even his teammates.

Trent raised an eyebrow. "I'm staying. Not like it's a hardship. I'll have the chance to see Grace for a few minutes on her break. Simon will take the next shift. You focus on Delilah. We'll handle security." He left the room, taking a chair with him.

"You should go home, Matt. You must be exhausted."

He shook his head. "I'll leave the hospital when you do."

"But, Matt . . ."

He pressed his fingers to her lips to stop her words. Her lips were as soft as silk and he longed to press his mouth to hers. "You're important to me, Delilah. I'm not leaving you here." Matt lifted his fingers and trailed the tips over her cheek.

A light tap on the door and Trent stuck his head in the room. "Nurse is here."

Matt dropped his hand and nodded. The nurse moved past Trent and pulled up short.

"Matt, what are you doing here?"

He wrapped his hand around Delilah's. "Good to see you again, Cheyenne. It's been a while."

A hard smile formed on Cheyenne's mouth. "Looks like you've been busy." She turned her attention to Delilah. "Ms. Frost, I'm Cheyenne, your night nurse. Dr. Anderson prescribed a mild pain medicine to help with the headache."

Seeing the ginger ale on the rolling table, she handed Delilah the small paper cup with the pain pill and held the soft drink for her to sip. "Sleep when the meds kick in. It's the best thing for you right now." She inclined her head toward Matt. "Don't let this one talk your ear off."

Matt's cheeks burned with a bite of temper. "I'm not a chatterbox." Unlike the pretty nurse.

"Oh, that's right. You don't talk at all about what's important." She turned her attention back to Delilah who watched the interchange with a stunned expression on her face. "If you need anything, press the call button." Without acknowledging Matt, she turned and sailed from the room.

"I guess you two know each other."

"We went on two dates. I thought we parted ways as friends." He dragged his attention away from the empty doorway to Delilah. She watched him with unasked questions in her eyes. If he had any chance with Delilah, he'd have to explain the obvious hostility from Cheyenne.

"You know I work for the bodyguard training school outside of town. My teammates and I are also sent on missions by Fortress Security as well. The operations are classified. Cheyenne didn't like the secrecy. What little information I gave her she spread all over town by the next morning. I can't risk my life or the lives of my teammates by dating a woman who can't be trusted."

"Your work is dangerous?"

"It can be. We train long and hard to be prepared for anything." A wry smile curved his lips. "Trent doesn't cut us any slack." Would the added information scare her away? Man, he hoped not.

"What kind of missions are you involved in?"

"We run the gamut of simple bodyguard duty all the way to hostage rescue operations." He grabbed a chair and moved it to the side of her bed. "Bravo is one of the best teams I've ever worked with. We cover each other's backs and don't take unnecessary chances."

"How long have you done this kind of work?"

"Since I joined the Army at 18. They trained me as a medic. When I mustered out, Fortress hired me and added to my training."

"Have you considered being a doctor?"

Matt stilled. Would Delilah be able to handle his job? "I thought about it, but I'm not ready to stop going on missions with my teammates. We don't take as many since our boss assigned us permanently to PSI. Once Bravo stops taking active missions, I'll talk to my boss about going to med school and serving as a Fortress physician."

"You've been gone a lot in the past few weeks."

"Josh Cahill's team is on leave because of the birth of Alex and Ivy Morgan's daughter and the imminent birth of Josh and Del's baby. Once they're back on mission rotation, Bravo will deploy once or twice a month."

Another knock on the door. This time, Detective Rod Kelter walked into the room. His grim expression had Matt on alert. Something was wrong.

"How are you, Delilah?" Rod dragged out his notebook and pen.

"Concussion and cracked ribs. You drew the short straw on my break-in, huh?"

"This isn't a simple burglary."

CHAPTER THREE

Delilah stared at the red-haired detective. She had to have heard him wrong. Ice water ran through her veins. Her grip on Matt's hand tightened.

"Who wants to hurt you, Delilah?"

"Until the man attacked me tonight, I would have said no one." Was Rod right? Did someone want to hurt her? Based on the attack and the snakes, she had to consider that possibility.

"Tell me what happened tonight. What time did you leave work?"

"I closed the shop at six like normal. I stopped at the grocery store." She wouldn't have bothered with the groceries except that Matt had been on her case to take better care of herself. "When I got home, I went into the house through the back door. At first, I didn't notice anything. Then I noticed the almond milk on my counter."

The detective was silent a moment. "You're sure you didn't leave it out yourself?"

She shook her head, hissing when the pain in her head increased exponentially. "I didn't have time for breakfast this morning so I didn't use the almond milk."

Matt scowled at that.

"I bought breakfast from That's A Wrap," she assured him. "The wrap was my breakfast and lunch."

He squeezed her hand in silent approval.

Yeah, he took his medic duties seriously. Although Delilah loved the fact that he cared about her, she didn't want to be of medical interest to him. Oh, who was she kidding? There was no way Matt Rainer would be interested in her. With his looks, he could have any woman he wanted on his arm. What would he want with her?

"What did you do when you noticed the almond milk?" Rod asked.

"I set my grocery bags down and turned around to leave the house. I planned to call Matt to see if he could check the place for me."

"Why not the police?"

"And tell them someone moved my milk while I was at work? No, thanks. I didn't want to face the officer who responded. After Matt searched the house and told me it was intruder free, I would have gone through the place and then thought more about calling the police if I found more items out of place."

"What happened when you turned to leave the house?"

"I heard heavy footsteps behind me. Before I could open the door, strong hands shoved me into the door so hard I almost lost consciousness."

"Concussion with eight stitches as a result of the shove," Matt murmured.

"I slid to the floor," Delilah continued. "The guy cursed and kicked me in the ribs a couple times."

"Did the intruder leave at that point?"

She nodded.

"Did he say anything else aside from cursing?"

"No. I don't know if I would recognize his voice if I heard it again. He spoke in a whisper."

"Did you see his face?"

"I only saw his feet. He wore black boots like Matt's."

Rod's head whipped toward Matt.

"I was at PSI with my teammates until Delilah called me for help. We had just finished a training session with the bodyguard class. Aside from an unshakable alibi, I would never hurt Delilah. PSI also doesn't have a lock on the black combat boot supply in Dunlap County. Anyone could have worn boots like ours. We order them in bulk from a supplier who also sells to the public nationally."

"I guess you've worn your combat gear in and around Delilah's house."

Matt inclined his head. "So have my teammates. We've grilled a few burgers at her place and mine the past couple months."

"He also repairs stuff around the house every time he comes over," Delilah added. She felt guilty when he did, but Matt said he liked doing it.

Rod eyed him, amusement dancing in his eyes. "Is that right? I have a few repairs around the house I'd be glad to hand off to you."

Matt's eyes narrowed. "Ha ha. You're on your own, buddy."

"Can't blame a man for trying." The detective returned his attention to Delilah. "No enemies, you said. What about an angry boyfriend?"

Her cheeks burned as she felt Matt's gaze on her face. "No boyfriends."

Rod was silent a moment, his gaze assessing. "Ever?"

Oh, man. Did he have to point out how pathetic her social life had been? Delilah shook her head.

"What about disputes with neighbors or relatives?"

Pain speared her heart at the mention of relatives. "No one."

"Any problems with customers? Someone dissatisfied with the candles or think you charged too much for the product?"

She shook her head slightly, fighting to stay awake.

"What about his clothes? Did you notice your attacker's clothes?"

"Black. T-shirt like Matt wears. Jeans, not camouflage pants or cargoes like PSI uses."

"Gloves?"

Delilah frowned. "Don't know. Didn't see his hands. I only felt them on my back for an instant."

"He didn't strike you with them?"

"No."

"You sure didn't see his face?"

"I was too busy protecting myself from kicks to look at his face. Besides, it was dark inside the house." Another frown.

"What is it?"

"I always leave the light on over the stove and the living room to give me enough light to see. The living room light was off and it shouldn't have been. Maybe the bulb blew."

"Or maybe the clown who hurt you turned it off," Matt said.

"What about scents?" Rod asked. "Do you remember any scents on his clothing or person?"

She was having trouble focusing. What did he want to know? Oh, yes. Scents. "A musky scent. Maybe a cologne." Just the thought of that scent made her stomach churn.

"Let's go back to the men in your life," Rod said. "Anyone angry because you turned him down for a date?"

"Rod, she answered your question," Matt said softly.

Without taking his attention from Delilah, the detective said, "Don't interfere, Rainer, or I'll have to ask you to wait in the hall."

"Not happening."

Delilah squeezed his hand. "It's okay. A few men have asked. When I turned them down, I was careful. None seemed to have hard feelings."

"Have any been persistent in trying to change your mind?"

Beside her, Matt stiffened.

"Two. I told them last week I was interested in someone else."

"How did they take the news?"

"Disappointed." Her eyelids grew so heavy, Delilah gave up the fight to keep them open.

"One more question, Delilah, then I'll leave you to rest. What did you do after the man who attacked you left?"

"Called Matt for help." Her words came out slurred.

"I stayed on the phone with her," Matt said. "We need to let her rest. The nurse gave her pain meds a few minutes ago. Delilah won't be able to answer more questions."

"I have questions for you as well."

"No problem. Let's go to the hallway." She felt Matt's warm breath on her ear as he spoke softly to her. "Delilah, I'm sending Trent in to stay with you. If you need me, send him to get me."

She sighed. "Okay."

The darkness closed in.

CHAPTER FOUR

Once Trent was inside the room with Delilah, Matt folded his arms over his chest and eyed the Otter Creek detective staring at him. "Ask your questions, Rod. I don't want to be away from her for long."

Rod's lips curved. "Does she know how you feel about her?"

"No, and you're not going to tell her." He'd take care of that himself soon and pray she didn't turn him down.

"Better not wait too long, man. The single men in Otter Creek are circling the lady like sharks."

Matt scowled. He'd figured that out while listening to her answer questions. If he waited much longer for her to become comfortable with him, another man might slip in and capture her interest. "What do you want to know?"

"Tell me what happened from the time Delilah contacted you. What did she say?"

Knowing the detective needed every detail he could get, Matt related his conversation with Delilah verbatim.

"She didn't mention a second intruder in the house?"

Matt's jaw tightened. "No. You found evidence of a second person?"

"That's what it looks like to me."

He couldn't imagine any person disliking Delilah enough to hurt her. She was the sweetest woman he'd ever known. "How did they get in?"

"Broke a window in her bedroom. She doesn't have an active alarm system." He glared at Matt.

"I've been encouraging her to let me arrange an installation with Fortress. Delilah Frost is one stubborn lady. She's been saving up for the alarm system."

"If she were mine, I would take the decision out of her hands after this attack."

"Brave words from a man whose wife would chew him up and spit him out if he pulled a stunt like that."

A subtle flinch from his friend. "Yeah, she would. Still, I'd take advantage of the situation and insist. Her home is a crime scene. She won't be able to return home for a couple days at least."

"I'll take her to my place."

Rod's eyebrows soared.

"One of my teammates will stay with us. Don't want the old biddies in town to go into a frenzy. Can you have Stella pack a bag for Delilah and bring it here? She'll need clothes and toiletries tomorrow morning and however long she stays with me." Stella Armstrong was an Otter Creek detective and married to Durango's EOD man, Nate.

"I'll call her on the way back to Delilah's place. I assume you and your teammates will provide security for Delilah until I arrest the clown who's responsible for her injuries."

"As long as I'm in town. If Bravo is deployed, Durango will make sure she's safe until we return."

"Let's hope I get this wrapped up soon. If you and Delilah remember anything else, contact me immediately." He clapped Matt on the shoulder. "Take care of your girl. I'll be in touch." The detective walked to the elevator.

Matt tapped on the door to Delilah's room. "It's Matt. I'm coming in soft." He eased the door open.

Trent stood at Delilah's bedside, weapon in hand. His team leader relaxed his stance when Matt entered alone.

"She been okay?" Matt murmured.

"She's not resting well. Pain meds might be helping, but I don't think they're strong enough to mask the headache symptoms. I'll be in the hall for a few more hours. We'll let you know when Simon takes over."

"Thanks."

With a nod, Trent left the room, leaving Matt alone with Delilah. He returned to his seat beside her bed and wrapped his hand around hers.

Delilah stirred. "Matt?" she whispered.

"I'm here. You're safe. Rest."

And she was out again.

Matt scooted his chair up against her bed and settled back to keep watch over the woman who had fascinated him since the first moment he saw her.

Two hours later, Delilah jerked in her sleep and started to thrash, fighting an unknown assailant.

"Delilah." Matt got to his feet. "Wake up. You're with me. You're safe."

"Hold me."

Stunned, he cupped her cheek. "Are you sure?"

"Please," she whispered, her dark eyes imploring him.

Still unsure if Delilah was awake enough to know what she'd asked, Matt eased one hip onto the bed and gently pressed her against his side. "Are you hurting?"

"The headache is ferocious and making me nauseated."

He grabbed the ginger ale and held the straw to Delilah's lips for her to sip more of the drink. When she finished, he said, "I'll be back."

Delilah laid her hand on his chest. "Where are you going?"

"To get more ice packs. It's too soon for another dose of pain meds. Trent will stay with you. Be back in two minutes," he promised.

Hoping he wasn't pushing too fast, he pressed a soft kiss to temple and left the room.

"What's up?" Trent asked.

"Ice packs. Stay with her for a couple minutes?"

"Sure." He walked inside.

Matt returned to the nurse's station and requested two more ice packs from Cheyenne. Without a verbal response, she left the desk, returned with the cold packs, and slapped them on the counter.

"Thanks." Matt grabbed the packs and left the desk. As long as Cheyenne took care of Delilah's needs, he wouldn't complain no matter how rude she was to him.

As he approached Delilah, he noted her pallor and nearly colorless lips. Matt glanced at Trent and inclined his head toward the door. "Go tell Cheyenne that Delilah needs anti-nausea meds." After his teammate left, Matt laid one pack on Delilah's forehead and slid the other one at the nape of her neck.

She shivered.

"I know," he murmured. "The cold will help."

"You need to leave. I think I'm going to barf."

"I've seen worse. I'm staying."

"Matt, please go." She clamped a hand over her mouth, eyes wide.

He grabbed the plastic container, rolled her to the side, and held her while she puked. When her stomach quit spasming, Matt settled her on the pillow, repositioned the ice packs, and carried the container to the bathroom to clean it. He returned to the room, sat beside her again, and gathered Delilah against his side.

"This isn't fair."

Matt glanced down. "What isn't?"

"I don't want you here as a medic. I don't want you to see me as a patient."

He thought about her choice of words. "How do you want me to see you?" Not as a friend. That just might kill him. The friend zone didn't leave him any wiggle room.

"As a friend."

Oh, man. Disappointment spiraled through Matt. He hated to do this to himself, but he had to know if there was any chance she would change her mind. "Only a friend?"

She turned her face into his neck without answering.

What did that mean? "Delilah, look at me."

A head shake.

His heart rate accelerated. He eased her away from him and raised her face to his. "Can I tell you a secret?"

Delilah's gaze focused on him. "Of course. Anything." A small smile appeared. "I promise not to spread the news all over town by daybreak."

Matt chuckled. "Oh, I don't know. I'm hoping you do tell everyone in town." If she agreed to give him a chance, that is. If not, well, maybe she would be kind enough to not make him a laughingstock. Before he could explain, Trent knocked on the door and peered inside.

"Cheyenne's here with the medicine."

The nurse pushed past the SEAL. She ignored Matt. "Ms. Frost, Dr. Anderson approved an anti-nausea patch to help settle your stomach. Turn your head to the right for me." A moment later, the patch was in place behind Delilah's ear. "If you need anything else, send Trent or press the call button."

Once she left and Trent returned to his post, Delilah nudged Matt. "Spill. What's your secret?"

This was it. Hoping he wasn't making a huge mistake by declaring his feelings this early, Matt cupped her cheek. "My secret is I'm crazy about you. Have been for months. I'm really hoping you want me with you as more than a friend."

"Why?"

Matt blinked. "Which part?"

"Why me?"

"Why not you? You're beautiful, you care about people." He smiled. "You know how to keep a secret. I enjoy your company and I miss you like crazy when I don't see you every day."

"But you could have anyone."

"The only woman I want is you. Would you be interested in dating me?"

"I did a great job hiding how I feel if you couldn't tell I'm crazy about you, too."

All the tension left his body. Thank God.

"Matt, I have baggage. Body image issues the size of Godzilla."

Yeah, he knew. "Understandable considering your history. We'll take this as slow as you need, Delilah. Give me the chance to help you see yourself like I see you."

"How do you see me?"

"As a beautiful, desirable woman with a heart of gold, a spine of steel, and an iron will. You're one of the strongest people I've met."

"You need your eyes examined," she muttered.

He laughed, delighted with her. "Stick with me, my lady, and I'll prove it to you."

"Good luck with that." Delilah shifted closer to Matt. "I'll count every day with you as a blessing."

She didn't expect their relationship to last. Anger burned in Matt's gut. Delilah's family had done a number on her as she grew up. He hoped he had a chance to meet them face-to-face soon. "So will I. How's your stomach?"

"Starting to settle. Thanks for asking for the medicine."

He slid his arm around her shoulders, grateful for the right to touch her at last. "Try to rest. It's the best way to convince Doc Anderson to spring you in a few hours."

After she fell asleep in his arms, Matt kissed her temple and settled back to enjoy holding her the rest of the night. Two hours later, Simon poked his head in the door and nodded at Matt. Shift change.

At five, noise in the hallway caught Matt's attention. Sounded like the hospital employees were stirring. Hopefully, Dr. Anderson would stop in soon and conclude Delilah had improved enough to release her.

Within half an hour, Delilah stirred, opened her eyes, and froze. "Matt. You're still here."

"Good morning, beautiful. How do you feel?"

"Better. When can I leave?"

"As soon as Dr. Anderson signs your release papers. My SUV is in the parking lot so we won't have to wait for a ride."

"Is Trent still here?"

Matt shook his head. "Simon took over at two. Knowing Trent, he's fixing breakfast for Grace."

"Sweet." She looked wistful. "It's obvious they adore each other."

"Are you hungry?"

"A little. I've seen what they serve around here for breakfast. I don't think I can handle Memorial Hospital cuisine."

"A plain bagel and hot tea might settle well. You game to try that?"

"Sounds wonderful."

"Great. Our first official date."

Delilah bit her lip. "I need to go home first. I want to change clothes."

Before he could explain what he'd arranged, a light knock sounded on the door and Stella walked in with a bag.

She smiled at Delilah. "I'm glad you're awake. I thought I'd have to leave the bag without having a chance to talk to you. How do you feel this morning?"

"Better than yesterday." She glanced at Matt, blushing. "Matt's been amazing."

"I'm not surprised." Stella set the bag on the table. "I brought clothes for the next few days plus your tennis shoes and all the toiletries I could find in your bathroom."

"Thanks. Why did you pack so much?"

Stella glanced at Matt who shook his head slightly, then refocused on Delilah. "Your home is a crime scene. You won't be able to enter the house for a couple days. When you're allowed inside, I strongly suggest you have someone stay with you until we're sure you're safe."

CHAPTER FIVE

Shock rolled through Delilah at the detective's words. If she couldn't go home, where would she stay? With the shop barely turning a profit, she didn't have money for a motel.

When she was allowed to return home, who could stay with her? All her women friends were married except Piper, her assistant at Wicks, and Delilah wasn't comfortable asking her to stay with her. She also didn't want to put another woman in danger. "Is asking someone to stay with me necessary?"

"Definitely. Something weird is going on, Delilah. Someone is out to harm you and I don't want to lose you."

"Don't worry about Delilah's safety." Matt lifted her hand to his lips and kissed her palm. "Bravo has her covered."

What did that mean? Security was his business, she reminded herself. Matt knew what he was doing. If he and his teammates had made arrangements, she didn't have anything to worry about.

"I can see that." Amusement danced in Stella's eyes. "Rod and I will work the scene as fast as we can, but we don't want to miss a clue that will help us nail the guys who hurt Delilah."

"Do what you need to. We'll cover Delilah as long as she's at risk."

"I hoped you'd say that." She squeezed Delilah's hand. "Stick with this one. He and his friends will keep you safe. In the meantime, Rod and I will do our best to figure out who these men are and toss them behind bars."

Men? Delilah frowned. Had the detective misspoke? Only one man had attacked her.

"I need to go. I'm meeting my husband at PSI for breakfast before my shift."

Matt's stomach growled. "I'm sorry to miss it."

Stella grinned. "See you later, Delilah." And she left.

"You aren't going to work today?"

"Your safety is my priority."

"Matt, I don't want you to get in trouble on my account."

"I worked everything out with Trent. It's fine."

Still troubled by him missing work for her, she decided to pick her battles. If Rod and Stella didn't have the man who attacked her in custody within a couple days, she would insist Matt return to PSI. He needed to train with his team. Delilah had overheard enough conversations between the Durango wives to know the men couldn't miss many training sessions without affecting their job performance. The last thing she wanted was to be the cause of possible injury to Bravo team, especially Matt. "Have you eaten?"

"Liam brought me a sandwich from Delaney's while you were sleeping. That was seven hours ago, though."

"No wonder you're hungry." With his training schedule, Matt must be starving by now.

The door opened and Grace St. Claire entered the room. "I thought you might like a shower before Dr. Anderson stops by to check you, Delilah. That way you'll be ready to go as soon as he releases you."

Matt stood. "That's my cue to visit with Simon. Call out if you need anything." He dropped a light kiss on Delilah's lips and left.

Grace grinned at Delilah. "Have something to tell me?"

"Matt says he's crazy about me."

"About time he admitted the truth. Matt's a good man. You're going to give him a chance, right?"

"I'm not stupid."

The two women laughed as Grace helped Delilah to the bathroom. Twenty minutes later, she returned to the main room dressed in jeans, long-sleeved t-shirt, and tennis shoes. The headache was down to a dull throb, too. Definite progress. Hopefully, she'd improved enough the doctor would agree to let her leave.

Grace glanced back from the doorway where she talked to the two operatives in the hallway. "Dr. Anderson will be here in a few minutes and I think your handsome protector wants to see that you're still okay."

"Aww, thanks for calling me handsome," Simon said, his lips curving.

The nurse laughed. "Don't pull the tiger's tail. He bites."

Simon chuckled. "Yeah, you're probably right. He's grumpy."

"I'm off to enjoy a breakfast date with my husband. Delilah, I'll check on you this afternoon." With a wave, Grace hurried away.

Matt clapped his teammate on the shoulder. "Go sleep. I've got this."

"Liam is waiting at your place. You need sleep, too. He'll watch over Delilah for a few hours."

Guilt assailed Delilah as she stared at Matt. "You didn't sleep last night?"

The medic scowled at his teammate before turning to her. "I'm fine. Won't be the first time I've gone without sleep."

"Take my word for it," Simon said, mischief in his eyes. "A full eight hours of sleep wouldn't make any difference in his looks. If you want a face the camera loves, you should take mine for a spin."

"Go home, buddy. You're punchy."

After a military salute, Matt's teammate loped off down the hallway to the elevator.

Soon, Dr. Anderson strolled into Delilah's room. "You look ready to leave our fine establishment." The doctor's blue eyes twinkled. "Can't imagine why you want to escape."

"No offense, Dr. Anderson, but I hate hospitals."

He laughed. "You're not alone. Hospitals are for the sick. Looks like you're mending quite nicely. Why don't I have a look at you? Matt, step into the hall for a few minutes."

"Yes, sir." He closed the door behind himself.

Dr. Anderson checked her over and declared her free to leave. "Keep the stitches dry. Drop by my office in a week and I'll remove them." He paused. "Matt is capable of handling the stitches as well. If your ribs are too uncomfortable while they heal, I can tape them to allow more freedom of movement. The nurse will be along shortly with your discharge papers. Come back if your headache worsens or you develop complications. The discharge papers will tell you what symptoms to look for if Matt's not with you." After patting Delilah's shoulder, he left to continue his rounds.

The handsome operative escorted Delilah across the parking lot to his SUV. She breathed a sigh of relief when he closed her inside his vehicle. Thank goodness she was out of the hospital. She hated the smells in that place. The sickness and air of desperation that pervaded the atmosphere always brought back bad memories of when her father was battling cancer, a battle he ultimately lost.

"Glad to be out of there?"

"Aren't you?"

"Hospitals provide life-saving service and treatment. Without them, I would have lost more battle buddies and teammates over the years."

"Battle buddies. That's a military term, isn't it?"

"That's right. I was in the Army."

"How long were you enlisted?"

"Twelve years."

"Do you miss it?"

"I miss my unit, but not the bureaucratic snafus when political bigwigs pulled strings to point spec ops units at favored targets as opposed to the best military strikes. Fortress is better equipped and my boss isn't a dictator. He gives us autonomy in our missions. If the operation is too dangerous, he expects us to retreat or request backup. Bravo team is the best I've ever worked with. I don't regret signing on with Fortress."

"But you work in teams of five. Wouldn't it be safer for you to have more people?"

"If we need more operatives, teams work together to complete the mission. We're well trained, Delilah. Maddox doesn't skimp on our training and preparation. He values us as people as well as operatives."

"Where are we going?"

"To the bakery for that bagel I promised you."

"You know I can't eat a whole bagel."

He nodded. "Eat what you're comfortable with. We'll make sure you have some protein as well as the tea and bagel."

She lapsed into silence for the remaining five minutes of the journey. That was the beauty of living in a small town. Didn't take long to go anywhere.

Matt parked in front of Zoe's Bakery and they walked inside to find the place buzzing with activity.

Delilah breathed in the scent of coffee, sugar, cinnamon, pastries, cupcakes, and cakes. Her mouth watered and the craving for sweets roared back to life. Oh, no. Not good. She shook her head. "I can't do this."

When she turned to dart back outside, Matt grabbed her hand. "What's wrong? Are you nauseated again?"

Several customers in the shop turned to stare at them and the noise level in the shop dropped.

"Matt, please," she whispered, cheeks burning.

"Are you still hungry?"

"Yes."

"Go sit at the table right outside the door. I'll be able to see you while I give Zoe our order. I'll only be a minute." Matt lifted her chin and brushed her lips with his before heading to the counter.

Delilah breathed easier once she was outside in the sunshine. She still felt the gazes of bakery patrons on her. This time, though, the speculation would center around Matt's proprietary kiss. Yeah, they would be the talk of Otter Creek by noon.

She sat at the table and settled back in the chair only to ease up again as pain reminded her she still had cracked ribs. Guess she'd be sitting in chairs and sofas with soft backs for a while.

Matt strode from the bakery with to-go cups in his hands. He set one in front of her. "Zoe will bring our food out here when it's ready. Talk to me, Delilah."

She hadn't wanted to discuss this part of her past now. Her own fault, though. She'd raised his curiosity with that mini-meltdown in the bakery. Delilah swallowed hard, afraid the medic wouldn't see her the same way when he knew the truth.

CHAPTER SIX

Matt wondered at the cause of Delilah's nervousness. Based on their previous conversations, he already knew her mother, stepfather, brother, and two cousins tormented her when she was growing up. Delilah was careful not to give away too much information, a source of frustration for him since he wanted to know everything about her. "You told me about your family."

"Not everything."

The shop door opened and Zoe carried out a tray. "Here you go, guys. Sorry for the delay."

Matt smiled. "No problem. Thanks for accommodating our desire for fresh air this morning."

"It's a beautiful morning." She grinned at Delilah. "You and your escort caused a stir in the bakery. Word's already spreading about that kiss. Be prepared for inquisitions."

"Bring it on." Matt set the plate with Delilah's bagel and egg in front of her. "I want everyone in town to know Delilah's mine. I'll have less men to dissuade from asking her on dates."

Zoe glanced inside the shop. "Wish I could stay and talk, but I have to get back. Let me know if you need anything else."

After the baker left, Matt picked up his breakfast sandwich. "Eat what you can. We'll talk after we eat." He had a feeling whatever she needed to tell him would upset her. He'd been around her enough over the past few months to know she didn't eat when stressed.

To help her, he asked her questions about the shop and her assistant. The more she talked, the more relaxed she became. When half her bagel was gone, Delilah pushed aside the plate.

Matt tapped the cup of tea. "Try this. I think you'll like the taste."

She sipped. Her eyebrows soared. "This is great. What kind is it?"

"Apple vanilla chamomile. Should soothe your stomach."

"Do you give this to your teammates?"

He laughed as his imagination conjured up the probable responses from Bravo if he suggested that remedy. "Not a chance. They'd revoke my man card. If I'm out of anti-nausea patches, my teammates would prefer to puke their guts out to drinking herbal tea."

"They don't know what they're missing."

Matt captured one of her hands and contented himself watching pedestrian and vehicular traffic pass the shop as she finished her drink. When she drained the cup, he squeezed her hand. "Tell me what upset you when you walked into the bakery."

"I need to tell you more about my past so you understand my reaction." Something she was reluctant to do based on her body language.

"Do you want to do that here or at my place?"

"Here is fine. No one is paying attention to our conversation." A smile curved her lips. "They are noticing you holding my hand."

"I want them to notice. I know your family was unkind when you were growing up."

She gave a wry laugh. "They still are. That's why I haven't been home in years. My father was diagnosed with bone cancer when I was ten. Dad fought hard. He lost his battle the day I turned fourteen."

"I'm sorry. That must have devastated you and your family."

"We were close until Dad passed away. After that, Mom turned to alcohol to help her dull the pain of losing her husband. My brother got into trouble at school. He barely finished high school and started gambling."

"Is he any good?"

"Loses more than he wins."

"That's usually how it works." He studied her a moment. "What about you? How did you cope with the loss?"

Her gaze dropped to their clasped hands. "I turned to food for comfort."

His heart literally hurt when he realized what that meant. No one had been there for her. Delilah's mother and brother had been wrapped in their own problems and hadn't bothered to help her. "I guess your cousins weren't there for you, either."

A subtle flinch. "Not even close."

Some of the puzzle pieces fell into place. Oh, man. Although he knew where this story was headed, Matt opted to stay silent and let Delilah tell the tale at her own pace.

"When I was lonely, sad, hurting, happy, any emotion you can name, I ate. The problem became so bad, I was stealing food from the kitchen and hoarding a stash in my room. I can't tell you how much junk food I consumed every day along with soft drinks and juice."

She locked her gaze with his. "I gained weight, Matt. A lot of it. By the time I graduated from high school, I weighed over 300 pounds. I'm only five feet four. Every pound shows."

Holy cow. Though Matt controlled his reaction, he was astonished that she'd managed to carry that much weight on her small frame. Her weight was nowhere near that now. How had she lost all the extra pounds?

"The more I gained, the more my classmates and family made fun of me. I ate more. No surprise to you, I'm sure, that my knees and feet hurt all the time. My blood pressure was through the roof and I couldn't climb a flight of stairs without feeling like I was having a heart attack. I hated myself and my body."

"What made you realize you needed to take control of your body and appetite?"

"I went to college. On my first day in classes, I realized I couldn't fit in the classroom desks or walk across campus without sitting down to catch my breath two or three times. I knew if I didn't take control, I would die young."

"How did you lose the weight?"

"I'm a good researcher. I researched diet and exercise programs. When I narrowed it down to the combination I thought would be safest for me, I made an appointment with a doctor and asked her advice. She approved my choices and helped me implement the program."

"What were your choices?"

"My diet was protein, vegetables, and fruit, berries mostly. No dairy, no sugar, nothing processed. I drank water and herbal tea with no sweetener."

"And the exercise program?"

"Swimming." She flashed him a smile. "I thought I would grow gills I spent so much time in the water."

"How long did it take you to lose weight?"

"Four long years. As a present to myself, I saved up enough money to have surgery to remove the extra skin."

Understanding slammed into Matt. He'd wondered why Delilah always wore long-sleeved shirts and pants, never shorts or short sleeves even on the hottest days. "You have scars from the surgery."

She raised her chin. "Small price to pay for being healthy."

Matt pressed a kiss to the back of her hand. "You amaze me, sweetheart. The scents in the bakery set off sugar cravings?"

Delilah nodded. "I'm addicted to sugar. Indulging too much starts the cravings all over again and I fought too hard to conquer that addiction."

"I understand. I'm proud of your accomplishment."

Her lips curved. "It was the hardest thing I've ever done in my life."

"You still swim, don't you?"

"I use the swim spa every day." Another soft laugh. "I can't afford the alarm system because I'm paying for a spa that costs as much as my car. I know you're worried about my safety, especially after the attack, but I made a choice to keep healthy."

She was incredible. "You haven't told anyone else about the weight gain and loss?"

"My family doesn't even know. You probably think I'm horrible, but after what they did to me, I couldn't make myself go home and face them or the memory of what I was in those years."

"You'll go home when you're ready, Delilah." He squeezed her hand. "When you go, I'm going with you."

Delilah stared at him. "You are?"

"I won't let you face your family or those memories alone. Promise me you won't go while I'm deployed."

"I don't understand why you want to accompany me, but I promise to wait for you. I don't intend to go anytime soon, anyway."

From her expression, her first choice would be to never return home. But plans had a way of changing when you least expected. "Do you want to save the bagel and egg for later?"

"I'd better not. I still don't eat processed food much. In fact, that's the only processed item I've eaten this year."

He extended his hand to her, then gathered their trash, and dumped the remnants of their breakfast into the receptacle. "Can Piper handle the shop alone today?"

"Sure. Why?"

"Take the day off. If you feel up to it, you can go to work tomorrow." He'd work out a security arrangement to keep her and Piper safe at Wicks.

"I slept more than you did last night."

"I'm used to sleeping three or four hours a night. You aren't. You also had nurses waking you every two hours to ask you questions. Not only that, your body is healing. Give yourself a break for today." Matt unlocked the SUV and tucked Delilah inside.

When he climbed behind the wheel, Delilah pulled out her phone and sent a text. A moment later, a chime indicated a response. "Piper had already heard about the intruder and was expecting me to take the day off."

He drove to Delilah's neighborhood and parked in the driveway a few houses away from hers. Liam's SUV was parked in front of Matt's house. When Matt turned off the engine, his front door opened and his teammate stepped out on the porch with a soft drink in his hand. He signaled Matt that all was clear. Excellent.

Matt opened Delilah's door. With her bag in hand, he led her inside his home.

"Wow. This is...nice," she said, glancing around.

Liam burst into laughter. "A bachelor's paradise, you mean."

Matt glanced around, trying to see the place from Delilah's perspective, and mentally shrugged. He didn't have much on the walls. In fact, the only thing was his 60-inch television. Easier to clean. He didn't have to worry about dusting crap scattered on the walls and flat surfaces. One quick swipe and he was done. No muss, no fuss.

Delilah glanced at Liam. "I don't want to take your bed or Matt's."

The sniper shook his head. "I won't be sleeping. When I'm here, I'll be on duty. My job is to protect you while Matt is asleep. When my shift is up, Cade will come over with his wife."

That brought a smile. "Sasha makes the best tea."

"Can't speak about the tea, but her coffee is great." He turned to Matt. "Go rest. I have you and Delilah covered."

Matt held out his hand to Delilah. "Come on. I'll show you where you'll sleep." He ushered her to the bedroom across from his. He'd turned the third bedroom into a workroom.

"Matt, this room is beautiful." Delilah moved past him to scan the room.

It was just another bedroom to him. His mother and sister had chosen the comforter, curtains, and decorations for the walls. Left up to him, this room would be as spartan as the rest of the house. He hadn't purchased items to make the house attractive. Why bother? He didn't have anyone over but his teammates.

He spent money on weapons and medical supplies, and part of that was supplemented by Fortress and PSI. "I'm glad you like it. Will you rest for a while?" Matt didn't want to force her, but she needed the sleep. Despite the bone-deep trust he had in Liam, he preferred to be awake when she was awake.

She looked out the window toward her house. "I should go swim. I always swim in the mornings."

"Not today." He captured her chin in his palm. "One day off won't hurt you. If you feel up to it, you can start back up tomorrow. Hopefully by then your headache will be better. Besides, you need a waterproof bandage to protect the stitches."

"Do you have some?"

He nodded. "I'm holding them hostage for the day. Tomorrow, I'll give you one in exchange for a real kiss."

A frown. "You don't want a kiss now?"

Did he ever. "I definitely do. I won't pursue it, though. I want you to feel good enough to enjoy the first of many kisses with me." No way would Matt be able to stop with just one.

"I'm feeling better than I did last night."

Matt chuckled. "Not today, Delilah." He brushed her lips with his and stepped back. The temptation was strong to linger and give her the real kiss both of them craved. "I promise to deliver on the kiss tomorrow."

"I'm holding you to that, Mr. Rainer."

"Yes, ma'am. Stay in the house and leave the curtains closed. If anything happens, do exactly what Liam tells you to do."

"What about you?"

"I'm trained to sleep light. Liam won't have a problem waking me. If you need me, Delilah, come get me. I want to be here for you, whatever you need." With that, Matt went into his room.

Too tired to do more than take a quick shower, five minutes later, Matt dressed in cargoes and a black t-shirt and socks, his combat boots by the side of the bed. If a problem developed in the next few hours, he'd be ready.

He stretched out on the bed, wondering who wanted to hurt Delilah and when the next attack would occur. As sure as the sun rose in the mornings, he knew the attacker wasn't finished.

CHAPTER SEVEN

Delilah stared at the ceiling, willing herself to sleep. Not happening. She sighed and gave up, too wired to sleep. Hopefully, she wouldn't wake him when she left the room.

She tied on her shoes, turned the knob, and eased open the door. Breathing a sigh of relief when the hinges didn't squeak, Delilah walked toward the living room. Maybe watching television or reading a book would help her settle down enough to take a nap. Doubtful, though. Delilah wasn't a good napper.

When she walked into the living room, Liam turned from where he was watching out the window. His eyebrows rose. "Couldn't sleep?"

Delilah shook her head. "Is there a problem outside?" She prayed there wasn't. Matt needed a few hours to recharge.

"Come here. An SUV arrived forty-five minutes ago and is parked three houses away on the right side. The driver hasn't left the vehicle. Do you recognize it?"

Liam moved back to allow Delilah to take his place. Following his example and staying to the side of the window, she peered through the narrowed curtain opening and stared at the SUV he'd mentioned.

Her muscles relaxed. "That's Tyler Neeland's vehicle. He and his wife, Vickie, are separated. If the town grapevine is correct, she's filing for divorce. Vickie claims he's jealous, obsessive, and possessive."

Matt's teammate snorted.

"Tyler has been parking in different places on the street at various times during the day since Vickie kicked him out of the house for cheating on her."

"Seriously?" Liam sounded incredulous. "He's jealous that she might look at another man when he's sleeping with another woman?"

"That's the rumor. I'm not friends with the Neelands. I usually don't have time to socialize much." Not if she wanted to keep the shop running in the black, something she'd managed to do since her third month of operation.

That was the month she bought the swim spa. Until that time, she'd been making a daily trek to a nearby town with an Olympic-size swimming pool in the local high school that was open to public use at five in the morning. Delilah had been thrilled when her swim spa was installed on her patio. She was able to sleep a little longer in the mornings and still get in her laps.

"Can't imagine what makes a man treat his wife like that." Liam turned away from the living room window. "I need some water. You?"

She followed him to the kitchen. "I'd love some." Sitting at the breakfast bar, she broke the seal on the bottle Liam placed in front of her. "Thanks for keeping watch over me today."

He shrugged. "Not a hardship." Liam guzzled half his water before he set it aside. "Is Piper seeing anyone?"

Surprise and amusement twined inside Delilah. "Not at the moment. If you're interested, you should ask soon."

A scowl. "Why?"

"She's asked to go out frequently, especially by PSI operatives."

"What are they doing in a candle shop?" he snapped.

"Same as you, hoping for a date with a pretty woman."

"Did she go out with any of them?" he asked, his expression dark.

Delilah shook her head. "Piper is choosy. She doesn't want to be a man's flavor of the week."

Liam leaned against the kitchen counter and polished off the rest of his water. "They been pestering you for dates, too?"

As if. "No."

"They're either blind or they noticed Matt's interest in you and backed off."

Delilah shrugged. She didn't attract men from PSI except Matt. Why he was the exception, she didn't know although Delilah was happy about his attraction to her. Hopefully, she wouldn't screw things up and make him lose interest.

"Are you going to ask Piper on a date?"

"Yeah, I am." Liam's eyes narrowed. "Don't tell her. Unlike Cade and Matt, I can handle it myself."

Delilah held up her hands in surrender. "I promise to leave the asking to you." Secretly, she was pleased for Piper's sake. Her assistant was a spunky woman who loved people and was a lot of fun. Delilah was surprised that Piper turned down the string of men vying for her attention. Maybe she'd been holding out hope a certain Bravo member would ask her out.

Delilah's cell phone rang. Afraid her assistant was calling with a problem, she grabbed her phone and glanced at the screen.

Her heart nearly stopped at the name displayed. Immediately, her stomach knotted and her skin crawled. She rejected the call and dropped her phone on the counter, hand shaking.

Liam straightened from the counter. "What's wrong?"

"Nothing." A lie. He never called. Delilah hadn't talked to him or the others in years. Why now? She flinched as the phone rang again. The same name and number popped up on the screen.

Liam looked at her screen. "Who's Randy Holloway and why don't you want to talk to him?"

"My mother's husband, and it's a long story."

"One you don't plan to share."

"Not if I can help it."

Glancing at his watch, he murmured, "I'll be back in a minute." He left the room.

Delilah stared at the phone as though it were a snake ready to bite if she looked away for a second. The ringing stopped. She breathed a sigh of relief for thirty seconds until the phone rang again. Why wouldn't he stop? She didn't want to talk to him.

Matt walked into the kitchen alone and grabbed a bottle of water from the refrigerator. He drained part of it, keeping his gaze on her. When he lowered the bottle, he said, "Answer the call. Let's find out what he wants."

Guilt gripped Delilah. "Liam woke you."

"I was already awake. I told you, I'm used to three or four hours of sleep a night. I got what I needed. Are you going to answer that?"

The ringing stopped. "No."

The phone rang again.

Fear seeped into Delilah. Maybe something was wrong.

Matt sat on the seat beside hers. "Answer it, sweetheart."

Dread swelling in her gut, Delilah tapped the screen and placed the call on speaker. "Hello, Randy."

A pause, then, "Delilah?" His bass voice rolled out from the speaker. "Thank God I finally caught you."

"What's wrong?"

"You have to come home."

"Why?"

"Your mother is dying."

CHAPTER EIGHT

Matt slipped his arm around Delilah's shoulders as blood drained from her face. He thought about the PSI teaching schedule. He needed to call Rio to see if his fellow medic would cover Matt's classes for a few days. He refused to allow Delilah to face her family alone. She'd never go alone again if he had anything to say about it.

Delilah dragged in a shaky breath and leaned into Matt's side. "I talked to her two weeks ago and she didn't mention an illness."

"She didn't want to worry you, but her health has taken a turn for the worse. If you don't come home in the next day or two, you'll be too late. She's asking for you, Dee. She won't say why, insists it's only something she'll discuss with you."

"What's wrong with her?" Matt asked.

"Who are you?"

"Matt. I'm a friend of Delilah's. What's wrong with your wife?"

"Dee?"

"Tell him. Matt's a medic."

"Michelle has liver cancer."

Heavy drinker, Matt remembered. "Transplant?"

"Couldn't find a donor match and now she's too sick. Dee, will you come? Your mother wants to see you before she dies."

Matt pressed a kiss to Delilah's palm. When she glanced at him, he gave her a nod. "You don't want to live with regrets," he whispered in her ear. "I'll go with you."

She shivered. "All right, Randy. Tell Mom I'll be there in a few hours."

"Michelle is in Room 4125 at Mayfield General. See you soon." Randy ended the call.

Matt rubbed Delilah's back with gentle strokes. "Dee?"

"I hate that nickname. Only my remaining family calls me Dee. My father called me Lilah."

"What would you prefer I call you?"

Her cheeks bloomed with color. "I like everything you've called me so far."

Hmm. He'd called her by her given name. That shouldn't have caused the blush. Sweetheart? Satisfaction filled him when he realized she liked the sweet name of affection.

Matt cradled her face between his palms. "I'm sorry about your mother."

Tears glimmered in her eyes. "Me, too. I hate what my family did to me, but she's my only living parent and I still love her."

"Because you love her, she has the power to hurt you more."

"You don't have to go with me. I know you need to train with Bravo. I'll be fine."

Her expression said otherwise, but Matt didn't argue with her. He wouldn't change his mind. "Is there a hotel in town where we can stay?"

"The Lennox Hotel. I planned to stay at my mom's place."

"You need a place to retreat and fortify your defenses. What's the name of your hometown?"

"Harmony. It's three hours from here."

"Go pack while I make the arrangements. We'll leave as soon as I take care of a few things." He needed to inform his teammates and his boss, Brent Maddox, that he would be out of touch for a few days, then call Durango's medic. Matt called Trent first.

"You shouldn't go alone. You'll have your hands full helping Delilah cope with the death of her mother."

"I can handle it."

"Sure, but you need to sleep sometime. You need someone to watch your back and Delilah's while you sleep. It's not a suggestion, Rainer."

Matt scowled.

"When do you leave?"

"In an hour."

"Don't leave until your teammate arrives." Trent ended the call.

Deciding to call his best friend, Cade, on the road, Matt went outside to find Liam and tell him he was off duty as soon as Matt and Delilah left Otter Creek. That done, he called Zane Murphy, the Fortress tech guru operatives depended on for everything from reservations to logistical support on missions.

"Yeah, Murphy."

"It's Matt Rainer."

"I was just thinking about you, buddy. How goes the quest to win the fair Delilah's interest?"

"She agreed to give me a chance."

A soft whistle from his friend. "Nice work, Matt. Congratulations."

"Thanks."

"You don't sound as excited as I expected. What's up?"

"Someone wants to hurt Delilah."

"Talk to me."

He explained about the attack and injuries, then told Z about the call from her stepfather.

"How can I help?"

"Delilah's mother lives in Harmony, Tennessee. For reasons I'd rather not go into, Delilah can't stay in her mother's house. There's a hotel in town, The Lennox. See if there's a suite available. Trent insists on sending one of my teammates with me."

"Not surprising. Your focus will be on Delilah."

"Yeah, I know. Doesn't mean I have to like it." He wanted to keep watch over Delilah and keep her safe himself.

"Understood. I'll take care of the reservations. You need an encrypted cell phone for your lady?"

"I do."

"I'll overnight one to the hotel. Check at the front desk tomorrow morning."

"Will do."

"Anything else I can do?"

"Run a background check on Randy and Michelle Holloway. Delilah also mentioned a brother and some cousins. I want to know what I'm walking into."

"I'll see what I can find out." Zane ended the call.

Matt slid his phone into his pocket as the door opened behind him. He glanced over his shoulder. "All packed?"

A shrug. "Not much to pack since most of my clothes are at my house."

"If you need something specific, I'm sure Stella wouldn't mind bringing it to you." If her mother was as gravely ill as Randy insinuated, she might need clothes to attend a funeral.

Delilah shook her head. "My stepfather exaggerates. I won't know what to believe until I see Mom and talk to her doctor."

Matt didn't press the point. He would take her shopping if she needed something more.

"We can go now."

"I'm under orders to wait for a teammate to arrive. Trent doesn't want us in Harmony without backup."

She frowned. "But the danger is here. The break-in had nothing to do with Harmony."

"Trouble might follow us. Shouldn't be long before we leave. You can pack snacks and bottles of water for the trip while I load our bags into the SUV."

Fifteen minutes later, Matt's doorbell rang. He opened the door to Cade and Sasha. He grinned. "You're my backup?"

"Trent asked if we wanted the assignment. We jumped at the chance to tag along."

Matt bent down and kissed Sasha's cheek. "Thanks for coming. Delilah will appreciate having another woman around."

She laughed. "The testosterone is high when Bravo is together. Besides, Delilah is a friend. I'm happy to be another voice of reason."

"You accusing us of not being reasonable, Sassy?" Cade's eyes twinkled.

"When Bravo is together, it's a tossup who is more alpha, you or one of your teammates."

Matt whistled. "Ouch, man. She has your number."

Cade's eyes narrowed. "You're as alpha as the rest of us."

Sasha moved past Cade and Matt. "Delilah." She hugged the Wicks owner. "Hope you don't mind if Cade and I come with you and Matt."

"Of course not." Despite her words, she looked uncomfortable.

Matt wrapped his arm around Delilah's shoulders and eased her to his side. With his other hand, he dug out his key fob and tossed it to his teammate. "Load your gear while Delilah and I lock up."

After a quick glance at Delilah, Cade said, "Sure." He held out his hand to Sasha and led her outside.

Matt closed the door, wrapped his other arm around Delilah, and pulled her against his chest. "You okay?"

"Not really."

"Aside from your mother, what's wrong?"

She dropped her gaze. "It doesn't matter. Let's just go."

"Hey." Matt lifted Delilah's chin and waited until her gaze locked with his. "I want to know what's bothering you."

"I haven't told anyone except you about my weight problem."

"Cade and Sasha are friends. They'll be as impressed as I am with your accomplishment. You can trust them." He pressed a soft kiss to her lips. "They will understand."

"I'd rather they hear the truth from me."

"You have time to tell them on the drive to Harmony." He set the alarm. Outside, they found Liam talking to Cade and Sasha.

"We'll watch both houses," Liam said. "Trent mentioned assigning PSI trainees to help."

"Good training." Cade tossed Matt his keys.

Matt eyed the sniper. "Let me know if there's trouble at either place."

"Copy that."

Delilah laid her hand on Liam's arm. "Keep an eye on Piper and the shop. I'm worried the man who attacked me might hurt her."

"No problem."

"Time to go." Matt clapped Liam on the shoulder. "Appreciate the help."

"Let us know if you need the rest of Bravo, Matt."

After saluting his teammate, he pressed his hand to Delilah's lower back and guided her to the shotgun seat while Cade and his wife settled into the back. As he drove from Otter Creek, Matt called Rod Kelter.

"It's Matt. Delilah's mother is on her deathbed and asking to see Delilah. I'm driving her to Harmony. If you need to ask more questions, call me."

"Why shouldn't I call Delilah?"

"By tomorrow morning, she'll have a new cell phone number."

Delilah's head whipped his direction, her eyes wide.

"I see. One of the Fortress phones?"

"That's right. I'll let you know the number when I receive the phone."

"Good enough. Check in when you return. Hopefully, I'll have some good news by then."

"A new phone?" Delilah asked when the call ended.

"It's encrypted and safer for us to use to communicate."

"I see." Delilah twisted in her seat to face Cade and Sasha. "I have something to tell you." She detailed her journey from obesity to a healthy woman, and the abuse she suffered at the hands of those who should have been her strongest supporters.

By the time Delilah finished, Sasha's hands were clenched into fists, her eyes alight with fury. "They should have encouraged you to care for your health and searched for a solution, not berate you and contribute to the problem."

"Congratulations on your accomplishment, Delilah," Cade said. "You have amazing willpower to change your life so drastically."

Matt glanced at the woman by his side and saw tears glimmering in her eyes. He entwined their fingers.

"Thanks."

The rest of the drive to Harmony passed with more pleasant topics. At the three-hour mark, Matt drove into the Harmony city limits. Delilah's hand tightened around Matt's. Silently, Matt vowed to protect Delilah from her family and anyone else who meant her harm.

CHAPTER NINE

An invisible band tightened around Delilah's chest the closer Matt drove to downtown Harmony. She wasn't a hurting teenager anymore.

Her lips curved. Instead, she was a grown woman with the terrified teenager lurking deep inside. She could endure snide remarks and contempt when she was alone, but she didn't want Matt and the Ramseys to witness what she'd dealt with all those years.

By the time they parked in front of The Lennox Hotel, Delilah was trembling.

"Delilah."

Matt's callused hands cupped her face and turned Delilah his direction. "Look at me."

When she complied, she noticed Cade and Sasha were walking toward the hotel entrance. "I'm sorry," she murmured. "I didn't think I would fall apart like this."

"What you feel is understandable. The woman who once weighed 300 plus pounds and changed her life and body to weigh a healthy 120 soaking wet is the strongest woman I've ever met. You can face your family and this town, Delilah. You've managed to revolutionize your life, a feat most people can't accomplish. Hold your head high, celebrate your strength, and know I will always have your back."

The invisible band around her chest loosened and Delilah could breathe again. Matt was right. She could do this. Facing her family and this town couldn't be as difficult as losing almost 200 pounds.

She closed the remaining distance between them and kissed the handsome medic. "Thanks."

He smiled. "My pleasure. How do you feel?"

Puzzled at the abrupt change in subject, Delilah said, "I'm fine. The headache is nearly gone. Why?"

His gaze grew more intense. "Excellent. That means tonight I can deliver on my promise."

The promised kiss. "Oh, yeah. You're definitely going to fulfill that promise." Delilah pressed her forehead against his. "I want that kiss, Matt Rainer."

A chuckle. "I'll try not to disappoint you."

"You couldn't."

"You're killing me, sweetheart. We need to store our gear in the hotel room before we head to the hospital, and all I want to do is hold you and kiss you senseless."

"I wouldn't argue against that plan."

After a laugh and a quick kiss, Matt circled the SUV to open her door. "Let's go before my control slips."

They met Cade and Sasha in the hotel lobby. Once Matt had the suite key cards, he and Cade escorted Delilah and Sasha to the room on the sixth floor, then returned to the SUV for their bags.

"Are you okay?" Sasha asked.

Delilah turned from the French doors. "I am. No matter what is said, I'll be fine." She wouldn't allow anything different. She'd fought hard for control over her life. No one could wrest that from her unless she gave them control.

"Good." Her friend rubbed her hands. "Please tell me there's a good hamburger place in this town. I have a craving for an old-fashioned cheeseburger."

Delilah's stomach clenched, a ball of ice settling in the depths. "There's a fast-food joint with the best hamburgers in town."

"But?"

"I need a different kind of restaurant." Junk food junkie that she was, Delilah didn't want to put herself in a situation where she might compromise her diet.

"Choose a place that serves cheeseburgers and whatever fits in your diet. Cade and Matt eat anything that doesn't eat them first."

Laughter melted the ice. "Sounds like a good plan. I know just the place."

"After you visit your mother, we'll eat."

Matt and Cade returned to the suite with their bags in hand. Matt turned toward the room on the right. "Delilah, I'm placing your bag in this room. Cade and Sasha will use the other one."

"Where will you sleep?"

"Couch. I'll sleep better if I'm near you."

"We'll regale you with tales of our weird sleeping arrangements on missions over dinner." Cade dropped a quick kiss on his wife's mouth. "You'll never sleep in your own bed again without feeling sorry for us."

When the newlyweds left to store their belongings in their room, Delilah cupped Matt's cheek. "Let me sleep on the couch. You'll be more comfortable on the bed."

"I'll be fine. Do you want to see your mother before we eat?"

"It's the only way to know if Randy is telling the truth."

"All right. Hospital first, then dinner. Choose a restaurant you're comfortable in."

Ten minutes later, Delilah gave Matt directions to the hospital. The operative parked near the entrance to the hospital. He turned off the engine and twisted to look at her.

"Ready?"

Never. Delilah nodded. The four of them entered the medical facility and walked to the elevator.

At the entrance to her mother's room, Sasha clasped Delilah's hand and squeezed. "Cade and I will wait in the hall. We'll be close if you need us." She and her husband moved to the other side of the hall.

Matt turned to Delilah. "No matter what happens, I have your back. When you're ready to go, we'll leave whether your family agrees or not."

Despite the dread growing in her gut, warmth bloomed inside Delilah at his words. She appreciated that he didn't coddle her or treat her as though she couldn't stand on her own. He believed she was strong enough to deal with her family. And he was right. She would handle anything they threw at her.

She learned a lot about herself during those hard years of gaining control of her weight. She hadn't lacked courage or strength and wouldn't falter now.

Delilah squared her shoulders and knocked on the door. Without waiting for a bid to enter, she pushed open the door and stepped inside the room. Five feet from the door, she cleared the wall blocking her view of the room's occupants.

Her stepfather, Randy, lounged in a chair. No other term for the slumped sprawl of the man her mother had married six months after the death of her father. In his hands, he held a cell phone, his attention locked on the screen. Unless he'd changed since Delilah left home, he was playing a game.

Delilah's attention shifted to the rail-thin woman huddled under a blanket, various tubes delivering fluids and medicine to her mother. Michelle Holloway looked as though a gust of wind would blow her off her feet.

Her heart clutched at the sight. Delilah had never seen her mother looking so fragile. She felt Matt's hand against her lower back, a silent reminder that he was there if she needed him. That small action gave her the strength to move further into the room.

Randy glanced up from his phone. His eyes widened. "Dee?" He rose, his gaze raking over her body in a slow, deliberate sweep. Delilah's skin crawled. "I wouldn't recognize you if I passed you on the street. You had surgery, didn't you?" His eyes glittered. "Where did you get the money for that? Did you con Michelle into paying for it? You'll pay back every penny, I promise you that."

Beside her, Matt stiffened.

She wrapped her hand around his. "How is Mom?"

Her stepfather blinked, glanced at his wife. "Going downhill fast. She wakes up every few minutes and asks for you." He turned back to her and Matt. "I didn't realize you were bringing someone."

Matt held out his hand. "Matt Rainer."

"Randy Holloway, Dee's stepdaddy."

"I'm sure you could use a break, Mr. Holloway. We'll sit with your wife while you stretch your legs."

"I might do that. Been stuck in this room for hours."

Delilah frowned. "Where's Zach? Isn't he spelling you?"

Randy snorted. "He ain't been by in two days. More interested in chasing skirts than he is in seeing to his dying mother." He shoved his phone in his pocket and hitched his pants higher on his ample belly. "Be back in a few minutes." He lumbered out.

Matt moved one of the chairs to the bedside and motioned for Delilah to sit. When she complied and reached for her mother's hand, he turned to the whiteboard on the far wall and studied the notations by the medical staff.

"What can you tell me?" Delilah asked in a voice quiet.

"Your mother is on a high dosage of morphine." His gaze shifted to hers. "They're keeping her comfortable."

The truth of his words hit her like a punch to the gut. Randy hadn't exaggerated. Her mother was dying. Based on Matt's solemn expression, Michelle Holloway would face eternity soon.

She sat in silence, holding her mother's hand and willing the frail woman to breathe. Delilah wanted the chance to give Michelle peace of mind from knowing her daughter had come.

Matt sat in a second chair beside Delilah, wrapped his arm around her shoulders, and settled in to wait with her.

Twenty minutes passed with no sign of Randy's return when her mother drew in a deep breath and moaned. Delilah stood and shifted closer. "Mom? Can you hear me?"

Michelle's eyelids fluttered and lifted. She stared at Delilah a moment, her forehead furrowed. "Who . . .?" She stopped, her eyes widening. "Dee?"

"It's me, Mom."

"You look beautiful."

For a few seconds, Delilah couldn't speak, throat was too tight for speech. Of all the things she'd expected from her mother, this wasn't even on the list of top ten things. "Thanks." Her voice broke.

Matt laid his hand on her back. How had she caught the attention of Matt Rainer?

Michelle's attention shifted to Matt. "Who is he?"

"Mom, this is Matt Rainer."

Matt laid his hand over her mother's. "I'm honored to meet you, Mrs. Holloway."

"You and Dee are friends?"

"Yes, ma'am. We're dating."

Tears filled her eyes. "I'm glad. She'll need someone when I'm gone."

Distress filled Delilah. "Mom."

"You don't know what's ahead. I don't have much time."

"The doctors can't help?"

A slight head shake. "I know you hate me. I deserve it. Thanks for coming anyway."

"I don't hate you."

"Terrible mother. No excuse."

"You were hurting. It's behind us now. You're getting tired. Randy said you wanted to see me. What do you need, Mom?"

"Forgiveness for the way I treated you after your father died."

"Done. If that's all, Matt and I will let you rest. We'll come back later."

"Wait." Michelle's hand clamped over Delilah's wrist. "I made you executor of my will. Talk to Oliver Shannon. He'll tell you what to do. Copy of the will and funeral instructions are in my safe deposit box. You have the key."

Delilah stared at her mother. "Wouldn't Randy or Zach be the logical choice for executor?"

"Can't trust anyone but you to do what I want with the money."

Money? What money? "Mom, I don't understand."

"You will. I love you, Dee. Be careful." Strength at an end, Michelle drifted back to sleep.

CHAPTER TEN

Matt wrapped his arms around Delilah and eased her against his chest. "You okay?" he murmured, his gaze assessing Mrs. Holloway's shallow breaths.

"This doesn't make sense. My family isn't wealthy. I can't imagine Mom has enough money in an account that Randy and Zach would fight over it."

"Things change." He kissed her temple. "We'll figure it out when the time comes."

"How long does she have?"

His arms tightened around her. "Not long." From what he was seeing, Delilah's mother might not live through the night. "I'm sorry, Delilah. I wish I could give you better news."

She drew in a shuddering breath. "I'd rather have the truth than a pretty lie any day. Thank you for being here with me."

"I wouldn't be anywhere else."

When the door flew open, Matt pushed Delilah behind him, hand reaching for his weapon when Randy walked inside the room. Delilah's stepfather glared at Matt.

"What's up with the jerk in the hallway searching me?"

"He's a friend. We work for a security firm."

"That don't mean he's got the right to prevent me from coming into my wife's room."

"When you could be a threat to Delilah's safety, it does. If you want an apology for being protective of my woman, you won't get one."

Randy's eyes narrowed as he rounded on Delilah. "You're involved with this thug?"

She frowned. "He's not a thug."

"But you're involved with him." A bark of laughter escaped the man, contempt in his eyes. "Should have known you'd be desperate enough to hook up with someone like him. No one but a gangbanger would look twice at you."

Matt felt Delilah flinch. Enough. This jerk didn't have the right to hurt Delilah. Not wanting to get himself and Cade banned from the hospital, he opted to retreat. For now. If Randy continued his verbal assault the next time they saw him, Matt would pull him aside and have a chat with him. His fists might be part of the discussion. "We should let your mother rest, sweetheart."

Randy moved to block the doorway. "Did Michelle talk to you, Dee?"

"Briefly."

"What'd she say?"

"Apologized for the way she treated me after Dad died."

"There has to be more." Her stepfather glowered at her. "What are you hiding?"

Matt eased in front of Delilah. "Move, Holloway."

"This don't have nothing to do with you, boy." He tried to shove Matt aside to confront Delilah.

Between one heartbeat and the next, Matt spun the man around and shoved him face first into the wall, wrenching Randy's arm behind his back. "Delilah, wait for me in the hall."

Pleased when she didn't question his order, he waited until she was out of earshot before leaning close to the cursing man in his grip. "Shut up, Holloway," he snapped. Matt changed the angle of his hold, eliciting a pained gasp from Randy.

"Don't speak to Delilah that way again. You might have bullied her when she was a kid, but you won't get away with it now. She won't put up with that treatment." He increased Randy's pain level with another minute change in pressure. "And I won't allow you or anyone else to treat her with anything less than respect. Am I making myself clear?"

"I can have you banned from this hospital." The words came out as a high-pitched whine.

"You can try. You won't succeed. I have more connections than you can possibly imagine. You're wasting your time trying to intimidate me." Another increase in the pressure brought a pained moan from Randy. "Do you understand how to treat my woman, Holloway?"

A short nod.

"You don't want us to have this conversation again. I won't be as pleasant the next time." Matt released Randy and walked into the hall. Delilah left Sasha's side and hurried to Matt. He caught her in a tight embrace and felt her shudder. "Everything is fine," he murmured in her ear.

"I thought he would cause an ugly scene."

"I would have handled it. Come on. I'm starving. We'll come back after dinner and spend a few minutes with your mother." He turned her toward the elevator. "What's the best restaurant for you?"

"A place called Legacy. It's the best steakhouse in town."

And a place where she could choose food on her diet plan. "Sounds perfect."

Fifteen minutes later, they were shown to a table at the back corner of the restaurant. Matt and Cade seated the girls in the corner and shifted their own chairs so their backs were to the walls.

When Delilah tried to limit her selection to a side salad, Matt sent her a pointed look. When she'd been a teenager, Delilah ate because of grief and stress. Now, she automatically cut back on her portions. Delilah's depth of control was great unless she hurt her health.

Cheeks flushed, Delilah amended her order to add grilled chicken.

Cade and Sasha kept the dinner conversation topics light, including Cade's promised stories of their sleeping arrangements while on missions.

"You really slept in a tree?" Delilah asked, her fork hovering near her mouth.

"It wasn't safe to sleep on the ground. Bullet ants and snakes were everywhere. I'd rather be stiff from sleeping in a tree than deal with those critters." Matt polished off the last of his steak.

Sasha frowned. "Why are the ants called bullet ants?"

"The pain of their bite hurts as bad as a bullet wound," Cade said.

"How do you know?"

"Two of them bit me." He grimaced. "Take my word for it. The pain was bad."

The door to the restaurant swung open and a trio of men strolled in, loud and boisterous.

Delilah glanced up and froze.

Matt laid his hand over hers. "Delilah?"

"My brother and cousins just walked in."

He studied the three men, zeroing in on the one most likely to be Zach. From his actions and speech, Delilah's brother had been drinking already this evening. "Do you want to leave?"

"When everyone is ready, not before. No one will make me run again."

Cade looked at her with approval before turning to look at his wife. "Dessert, Sassy?"

After a quick glance at Delilah, the coffee shop owner shook her head. "I'd like an iced tea to go."

Cade caught the waiter's attention and asked for a to-go cup of tea for each of them. After the drinks were delivered and Matt paid the bill, the two couples made their way through the restaurant.

Halfway to the door, Delilah jerked to a stop.

Matt turned to see Zach Frost gripping Delilah's arm, preventing her from leaving. He captured the man's wrist in a painful grip.

Delilah's brother hissed and released her arm. He cursed at Matt. "Who do you think you are? That's my sister." His words were slurred, his eyes unfocused and bloodshot.

"You must be Zach. I'm Matt, Delilah's friend." He slid his arm around her waist, leaving no doubt in anyone's mind that he claimed Delilah as his. A caveman tactic, one he hoped would send a message that he was possessive and didn't like his woman manhandled.

"Where did you dig up this Neanderthal, Dee?" Zach turned his gaze to Delilah.

"I need to go. We can catch up later."

"Hold on a minute. Let me look at you."

Matt nudged Delilah further away from her brother and cousins. "Delilah wants to spend time with your mother before visiting hours are over."

"What for? The old bat is out of it most of the time. Sit, Dee. I'll even buy you a drink for old times' sake."

"We'll see you at the hospital." Although he doubted the hospital staff would kick them out given the circumstances, Matt would use the excuse of a time limitation to spirit Delilah from the restaurant without causing a scene. He escorted her from Legacy's with the Ramseys close behind.

Delilah didn't say anything on the trip to the hospital. When he parked, Cade said, "Sasha and I will meet you in the lobby." They left the vehicle and walked to the hospital, holding hands.

Matt ran the backs of his fingers gently down Delilah's cheek.

"My brother was drunk."

"People deal with death in different ways."

Delilah flicked him a look. "He's added alcohol to his gambling habit. Zach is in a downward spiral that will cost him everything if he doesn't turn himself around."

"Your brother has to choose. You can't guilt him into changing because it won't stick. He has to want to change his life just like you did. You can encourage him, Delilah. Ultimately, it's up to him."

She leaned close, kissed him, then hugged Matt. When Delilah released him, she gave him a light kiss.

He squeezed her nape and climbed from the SUV. They rode the elevator with Cade and Sasha. As before, the Ramseys waited in the hall while Delilah and Matt went into the room.

Instead of Randy slumping in the same chair, Delilah's stepfather bent over Michelle with a pillow in his hands. Alarms were going off.

Delilah gasped. "Randy, what have you done?"

Matt hurried to Michelle, glancing at the monitors. Flat line. He touched his fingers to her neck to check for a pulse. Nothing. He looked at a wide-eyed Randy. "Does your wife have a DNR order in place?"

"DNR?"

"Do not resuscitate."

"No."

Matt started CPR. Within a minute, medical personnel dashed into the room. As soon as one of them took over CPR, he led Delilah into the hall at the bidding of the doctor. Randy belligerently refused to leave.

Matt wrapped his arms around his girl and pulled her tight against his chest.

"What's going on?" Cade asked.

"Michelle coded."

They waited in silence until the medical team left the room. From their body language, Matt knew the result of the battle for Michelle's life and his heart ached for the woman in his arms.

The doctor left the room, his gaze zeroing in on Delilah.

"How is my mother?"

"I'm sorry. We did everything we could, but Mrs. Holloway is dead."

Matt wrapped his arm around Delilah's waist. "Do you plan to do an autopsy?"

"She had liver cancer. It was only a matter of time before she lost the fight."

Holding the doctor's gaze, Matt said, "Delilah, you should request an autopsy."

"Why?"

"I don't think your mother's death was from natural causes."

CHAPTER ELEVEN

Delilah's breath caught at Matt's words. Someone had murdered her mother? Her mind flashed back to the moment when she and Matt had entered her mother's hospital room. Randy standing over his wife with a pillow in his hand and the alarms signaling an alert. Did Randy kill her mother?

Why bother? All Randy had to do was wait a few more days. From Matt's careful phrasing when Delilah asked how long her mother had to live, the medic believed her mother had hours to live. Looked like he was correct.

Delilah drew a deep breath. "Do an autopsy. I want to know what killed my mother."

The doctor frowned. "Very well. I'll see that it's taken care of immediately." He strode off, his back ramrod straight.

She'd ticked off the local doctor. Tough. Delilah trusted Matt. If he said something was fishy about her mother's death, she would follow up on it.

Matt cupped her cheek with his palm. "Do you want to spend a little time with your mom?"

She nodded, grateful he understood her need to see her mother one more time before the autopsy.

Sasha squeezed Delilah's hand. "I'm so sorry, Delilah."

Cade patted her shoulder. "We'll do what we can to help."

"Thanks." She wanted to say more but couldn't speak past the knot in her throat. They were good friends.

Matt returned to the room with her. She braced herself for an ugly scene with Randy to obtain a few minutes with her mom, but her stepfather sat in the chair at the foot of the bed, staring at his wife, a dazed look in his eyes.

As objectionable as he could be, Delilah sympathized with him. They'd both suffered a loss today. "Randy."

He didn't respond.

She laid her hand on his shoulder. "Randy."

He blinked and slowly turned his head toward her. "Did you say something?"

"I want to sit with Mom for a few minutes."

"Okay." He struggled to his feet and headed for the door. "I didn't think she'd be gone today, you know? I thought we had more time."

"Did she have funeral arrangements planned?" Matt asked.

"No arrangements necessary. Michelle didn't want any kind of service. She left instructions to cremate her remains immediately and get on with our lives. I guess I better call the funeral home."

"The hospital won't be releasing the body for a day or two," Delilah said.

Randy stopped, his hand on the door frame. "Why not?"

"I requested an autopsy."

A scowl as her stepfather turned to face her. "She died of cancer. You're causing trouble for everyone."

"I need to know exactly what caused my mother's death. You already said she didn't want a service. It shouldn't matter if the funeral home is delayed by a day."

"What gives you the right to waltz in here and screw everything up?"

Screw what up? There weren't any arrangements for her to disrupt. "She's my mother. I need to do this for my peace of mind."

"What about my peace of mind? Michelle was my wife. I want closure. Now."

Delilah stared. Was he heartbroken and needing to end this nightmare or was there something else behind his desperation for closure?

"Go make your calls, Holloway," Matt said. "You'll have closure soon."

Randy looked as though he would argue until Matt took a step in his direction. Her stepfather hurled a curse at the medic and stormed from the room.

Matt turned to Delilah. "I'll wait in the hall."

Delilah sat in the chair beside her mother, letting the good memories of her mother flood her mind. Their relationship might have taken a nosedive after Delilah turned 14, but she still loved the woman who had given birth to her.

Tears burned her eyes and she let them fall. There would be a time later for strength. Now was Delilah's time to grieve in private. When the storm of weeping passed, Delilah took a moment to compose herself. She touched the gray strands of her mother's hair. "I'll do what you asked, Mom. I don't know the reason for your caution, but I'll take care of everything."

Delilah left the room and walked into Matt's open arms. He pulled her close and just held her. Although she hated the fact she'd taken him away from training with his team, Delilah appreciated his presence now more than ever.

"I guess you'll be leaving town tomorrow." The flat words came from her stepfather.

Delilah faced Randy. "I'll be here for a few days."

"Your mama is gone. You gave her peace in her last hours, a small enough favor for the woman who loved you. Go back to your life. You ain't been around for years. You want them autopsy results? I'll let you know what they say. Zach and I don't need you."

The coldness of his gaze seeped into Delilah's bones. "I have some things to do first." Not the least of which was settling her mother's estate. "Have you told Zach Mom is gone?" Her voice broke on the last word.

"I called him. Didn't seem too broke up about it." Another dark look from Randy. "You kids should have had more respect for your mama."

When Matt stirred, Randy backed up two paces. "You're drifting into dangerous territory," Matt murmured. "Are you ready to leave, Delilah?"

She nodded. "I'll be in touch soon, Randy." She wouldn't have a choice. Looking into her stepfather's hate-filled gaze, Delilah wondered what Randy would say when he learned of her mother's request? She shivered. Yes, Matt being here was a good thing, indeed.

Matt led her to the elevator with Sasha and Cade at their backs.

As soon as the elevator doors closed, Cade muttered, "Mr. Holloway is a piece of work."

Delilah's lips curved. "That's the truth."

"What's the plan, Matt?"

The medic looked at his friend. "I have some phone calls to make. I'll be staying in Harmony as long as Delilah is here. Bravo can't afford to be down two members. You and Sasha should return to Otter Creek."

A snort from the other operative. "Are you kidding? Nate Armstrong can cover for me without a problem if Bravo is deployed. I'm not leaving you without backup."

Conversation stopped until they were enclosed inside the SUV. Matt glanced over his shoulder at Cade. "I'll talk to Trent and the boss to see what they can work out. In the meantime, keep an eye out for Holloway."

"Any particular reason?" Sasha asked.

"When Delilah and I walked into the room earlier, the alarms were going off and Holloway was standing over his wife with a pillow in his hands." He drove away from the hospital.

"Do you think he killed Mom?" Delilah asked.

"It's possible. Since you asked for an autopsy, hopefully we'll find out what caused her death."

"At least I know Zach didn't kill her. He was at Legacy's with his friends."

"Doesn't prevent him from hiring someone to do his dirty work," Cade said.

A raw laugh escaped Delilah's throat. "My brother probably doesn't have two cents to rub together."

Matt placed a call a moment later.

"Talk to me," Trent said.

"You're on speaker with Delilah and the Ramseys. Delilah's mother passed away a few minutes ago."

"Oh, man. I'm sorry for your loss, Delilah. How can we help?"

"Allowing Matt to be with me is enough."

"When is the funeral? The rest of Bravo would like to be there for you and Matt."

"According to my stepfather, Mom didn't want a service."

"Interesting. Matt, what do you need?"

"To be off with Delilah as long as she's in Harmony."

"Done. What else?"

"It could be a few days, Trent."

"We'll handle it."

Cade spoke up. "I need to stay as well."

"Expecting trouble, Matt?"

"Maybe. Delilah requested an autopsy. We found her stepfather in the hospital room, standing over her mother with a pillow clutched in his hands."

"He killed her?"

"Don't know, but Randy Holloway's behavior is odd. He doesn't appear upset about losing his wife."

"Keep me apprised of any developments. You talk to Maddox yet?"

"I planned to call him after I returned to the hotel."

"Let me know if he doesn't want you and Cade to take off a few days."

"Yes, sir."

Matt drove into the garage under the hotel and parked near the elevator. Back in their suite, he said, "I'll take the first watch, Cade. You and Sasha rest."

A nod. "I'll relieve you in four hours." Cade threaded his fingers through Sasha's and led her to their room.

Delilah followed their progress, heart aching.

"Something wrong?"

She turned. "No, just the opposite. Watching them makes me long for a relationship like theirs."

"What kind is that?" Matt cupped her nape and drew Delilah to him.

"A relationship of deep, abiding love, mutual respect, and joy in each other's presence. That kind of relationship is rare."

He was silent a moment, thumb brushing over her bottom lip. "I want a similar relationship with you. I respect you and love being with you, even during stressful times like this."

The butterflies in Delilah's stomach took flight. "I feel the same."

A soft, lingering kiss on her lips, then, "I could easily fall in love with you, Delilah."

"Matt."

He pressed his finger to her lips to stem the flow of words. "Shh. There's no pressure and no hurry, sweetheart. You needed to know the truth. I've wanted to be with you for a long time. I don't intend to lose you by holding back now."

Lose her? Fat chance. She'd pined after him for months. "You won't."

A slow smile curved his mouth. "Excellent. I need to call my boss. Are you ready to go to bed or do you need more time?"

"I can't sleep yet." Too much sadness.

"Would you like to drink tea on the balcony with me?"

She glanced at him, skeptical. "You drink tea?"

Matt chuckled. "Not a chance. I'll make coffee for me. I brought tea from Otter Creek. I thought you might need some because of the concussion." He slid her a glance. "You haven't said anything in a few hours. How do you feel?"

She grimaced. "Since my crying jag by Mom's hospital bed, my headache and nausea are worse."

"Understandable. Grab a blanket and go to the balcony. I'll be there in a couple minutes."

Delilah found a blanket in her closet. The early summer evening was cooler than normal and the fresh breeze felt good against her skin.

On the outdoor couch, Delilah draped the blanket across her lap. Although she heard traffic in the distance, nothing within eyesight moved except trees swaying in the breeze. The scene appeared unaffected by the raw pain of her loss. How could life march on as though nothing momentous shifted Delilah's world an hour ago?

A moment later, Matt sat down and handed Delilah a mug along with a couple capsules. "Over-the-counter headache medicine."

"Thanks." She popped the capsules into her mouth and washed them down with a sip of tea.

After consuming half of his coffee, Matt set his mug on the table and grabbed his phone. He called and reported to his boss, Brent Maddox.

Delilah found the conversation fascinating. He and his boss used military codes and terms. If she wasn't aware of the situation already, she wouldn't have been able to follow the gist of the conversation. Considering the jobs of Matt and his teammates, that was a good thing. Less chance of spreading information to hostiles.

When the call ended, Matt slid his phone away and gathered Delilah against his side.

"Your boss didn't object to you staying in Harmony for a few days?"

"No. He promised to assign missions to other teams until Cade and I return to PSI."

Relief rolled through her. Thank goodness. Yes, she could handle everything without him. Having Matt with her gave Delilah a sounding board as she dealt with her mother's estate.

She finished her tea and leaned down to place her mug beside Matt's when a crack sounded and glass shattered.

CHAPTER TWELVE

Reacting on instinct, Matt tightened his grip on Delilah and rolled her off the couch, twisting so he hit the floor first. He flipped their positions and covered her body with his, weapon in his hand and tracking, looking for the shooter between the wrought-iron rails of the balcony.

The woman underneath him gave a soft moan.

"Are you hurt?"

"Ribs."

Realizing his weight was putting pressure on her cracked ribs and causing pain, Matt shifted his weight to his forearms.

"You guys okay?" Cade called from inside the suite.

"No injuries. You?"

"We're good. Spot him?"

"Not yet. Delilah, I'm going to move in front of you. Go to Cade and Sasha's bathroom. You and Sasha climb inside the tub and lay flat. It's the safest place."

"What about you?"

"I'll be fine. Go fast and stay low." He shifted to a crouch, keeping his body between Delilah and the shooter.

Matt's blood ran cold at the thought of how close he'd come to losing her.

Cade plucked Delilah off the floor, nudged her toward the suite, then took up position beside Matt to block the shooter's view of her. Seconds later, Cade's phone signaled an incoming text. "The women are in the bathroom. What do you want to do?"

"Hunt."

A quick grin from his friend. "Go. I'll protect your woman and mine."

Matt sprang up and raced inside the suite. He holstered his weapon, and sprinted downstairs to the garage. Based on the terrain and angle of the shot, the shooter had chosen the hill at the back of the hotel. Bush cover and enough height to get a decent line of sight on their balcony made that location perfect.

Furious with himself for allowing Delilah out in the open, Matt vowed to be more cautious in the future. He hadn't believed the danger from Otter Creek would show up here. He'd been wrong. He wouldn't make that mistake again.

Matt circled to the right, using cover to conceal his approach. Although he suspected the shooter was long gone, he kept his steps silent. He climbed the left side of the hill. As he crested the top, Matt scanned the area. No shooter. He grabbed a small, powerful flashlight and aimed the beam at the ground.

Near the bushes, Matt found evidence a person had been here recently. He studied the scuff marks and tread in the dirt. Whoever had been here wore combat boots.

As he studied the area, the flashlight beam glinted on something metal. Matt crouched and pushed bush limbs aside. Brass for a .308. Much as he longed to bag the evidence and send it to the private lab Fortress used, he left the hardware for Harmony's police to collect and process.

He returned to the suite to find two uniformed officers inside along with a detective. The three cops swung around to stare at him, hands resting on their weapons.

Delilah launched herself into his arms.

Matt pulled her tight against his chest. "You okay?" he murmured into her ear.

She nodded. "Are you?"

"Now that I have you in my arms." He kissed her temple and turned to face the men watching them. Matt held out his hand to the detective. "Matt Rainer. I'm with Fortress Security."

The detective's eyebrows rose. "That outfit from Nashville?"

He nodded. "My friend, Cade, and I are based out of Otter Creek now."

"Is the police chief a man named Ethan Blackhawk?"

Matt smiled. "You know Ethan?"

The detective's hand moved away from his weapon. "We were in the same Ranger unit. Name's Miles Russell. How is Ethan?"

"Taking to small-town life like he was born to it."

"I hear he's married."

"To a beautiful chef. They have a six-month-old son."

A grin. "Blackhawk always had the best luck. Tell me what went down here?"

Still holding Delilah tucked against his side, he gave Russell a rundown of events and ended with the news of the shell casing on the hill.

"Show me." The detective turned to the uniform officers. "Barker, with me. White, take statements from the other three."

Matt dropped a quick kiss on Delilah's mouth. "I won't be long. Stay with Cade." He looked at his friend, who gave a short nod. Knowing Cade would protect Delilah with his life if necessary, Matt led Russell and Barker to the hillside, following the same path he'd used before. He crouched and aimed the beam of his flashlight at the shell casing.

Tugging on rubber gloves, Russell dropped to his haunches and studied the casing. "A .308. Rifle with a scope." He glanced at the hotel in the distance. "Around a six-hundred-yard shot. You're lucky to be breathing, Rainer. Did your enemies follow you to Harmony?"

"You think I have enemies?"

A snort from the detective. "You're a member of a black ops group that routinely takes on the worst of the worst around the globe. Somebody at home drops a word in the wrong place and your enemies will know where to find you and yours. Is that what's happening here?"

Matt rose, gut churning at the possibility the attacks on Delilah might be connected to his job. He'd contact Zane to make sure his name and location hadn't been leaked. "It's possible. More likely this is related to my girlfriend. She grew up in Harmony. Delilah was attacked in Otter Creek last night."

Barker stirred. "I went to high school with her. She looks different than the last time I saw her. I didn't recognize her at first."

"She worked hard to change her life." Matt looked at Russell. "I want to check on Delilah. Need anything else from me?"

"Contact information."

He gave the detective the main number for Fortress. "Leave a message. I'll call you back."

Irritation lit Russell's eyes. "We're on the same side. I won't post your number on my Facebook page."

"I'd be surprised you had one. It's a precaution all Fortress operatives take. We don't pass out our contact information. As long as your questions are answered in a timely manner, a slight delay won't matter."

"What about Ms. Frost? Will I have the same roadblock with her?"

"Delay, not roadblock, and yes, you will. She's mine to protect. I take my job seriously."

"How long will you be in town?"

"Unknown. Delilah's mother passed away a couple hours ago. She has responsibilities to fulfill before we return home."

"I'm sorry to hear about Mrs. Holloway." Russell looked at Barker. "Rope off the scene while I call in the crime techs."

"Yes, sir."

"Rainer, drop by the police station tomorrow. I'll have your statements ready to sign."

When Matt returned to the suite, Delilah looked relieved. Bemused, he sat beside her on the couch and wrapped his hand around hers. He could get used to having Delilah worry about his safety. The question was, could she handle his job and erratic schedule?

Man, he prayed she could. Losing Delilah Frost now would gut him.

Two hours later, the police left and the hotel manager arrived to offer them a new suite. Matt considered taking the new accommodations since Delilah was still reeling from losing her mother and the shooting, but their security had been compromised and he wouldn't risk her life.

Matt shook his head. "Have our bill ready in fifteen minutes."

The manager looked troubled. "Do you have another hotel in mind? I can call ahead and make reservations for you."

"I'll take care of it."

"I'm sorry your stay was unpleasant. There's no charge for the suite. When you drop your key cards by the desk, I'll have a complimentary basket with snacks and drinks waiting for you."

After the manager left, Matt squeezed Delilah's hand. "I'm sorry to move you again."

"Not your fault." Delilah stood, hand pressed to her ribcage. "I'll be ready in five minutes."

"I'll go pack," Sasha said and left.

Cade looked amused.

"What's funny?"

"Sasha didn't unpack anything. She's giving us a chance to discussion the situation."

"I should call Zane. We need another hotel."

"Not one in Harmony."

Matt agreed with him. They should find a place outside Harmony, close enough to be convenient, but far enough away to make tracking them down a hassle.

He called his friend as the suite's in-house phone rang. Cade answered the hotel phone.

"Yeah, Murphy."

"It's Matt. I need a favor."

A pause, then, "Go."

"I want another hotel with a suite available, preferably in a town outside Harmony. Use one of my aliases to make the reservation."

"Trouble?"

"Oh, yeah." He summarized the events of the evening. "I also need you to find out if my identity has been compromised. I know you have bots scour for mention of our names on the Net, but I need to be sure my work isn't the cause of Delilah's problems."

"Everybody okay?"

"No injuries. Scared Delilah on top of losing her mother."

The sound of the keyboard clicking could be heard on the phone's speaker. "West Fork is forty minutes from Harmony. I've reserved a suite for you at River's Edge Hotel. Room's reserved in the name of Mark Ross."

"Thanks, Z."

"Yep. Want me to reroute Delilah's phone to the new hotel?"

Cade handed him a note and left the suite.

He scanned it. "The package just arrived at the front desk. Perfect timing, Zane."

"Huh. That was faster than the courier service promised. I'll make a note of it. If they're always this good, they may become our exclusive courier. I sent information on Delilah's family to your email. Look at the files when you have a chance."

Cade returned to the suite, a small box in his hand. Matt pulled out a phone identical to his aside from the cover. His lips quirked. Where had Zane found a phone cover decorated with candles?

Delilah's door opened and she walked out with her bag in hand. "I'm ready."

"I'll check on Sasha," Cade murmured.

Matt took Delilah's bag and set it next to his bags. "Zane sent your phone." He checked her contact list and had to smile. "He's already added my number and the rest of Bravo's numbers along with his and Brent Maddox's."

Her jaw dropped. "Why would he include phone numbers for him and your boss?"

"You're part of my life now and Fortress supports those we care about. If you need anything and you can't reach me, start down the list of my teammates. If they can't be reached, call Zane or Brent. They'll help you."

"I don't know what to say."

Matt handed her the phone. "Check out the cover Zane found for you."

A smile curved her mouth. "That's perfect. Where did he find this?"

"He has a stash of different ones." His cheeks burned. "I might have mentioned you a few times in casual conversation." More like every time he talked to the SEAL.

"Would Zane mind if I sent a text to thank him?"

"Of course not."

Delilah typed a message to Zane and sent it. "Thanks for arranging this, Matt."

He saw the moment she remembered the loss of her mother. Matt hugged her close and held her until Cade and Sasha returned to the living room. When he released Delilah, she brushed tears from her cheeks.

Matt hoisted his Go bag and duffel to his shoulder while Cade grabbed the mike bag with Matt's medical supplies. "We'll take the stairs. I'd rather not be boxed in if there's another attack."

At the front desk, Matt turned in their key cards and accepted the complimentary basket from the hotel manager.

Delilah held out her hands. "I can handle the basket along with my bag. You're loaded down."

Though he hated she had to carry anything, Matt acknowledged that she was correct. If trouble found them again as they left the hotel, he needed to have his hands free.

He pressed his hand to Delilah's lower back and guided her toward the garage stairs with the Ramseys close behind. Once the women were inside the SUV, he and Cade loaded the gear.

A minute later, Matt drove from the garage and headed out of town. "Do you know how to get to West Fork?" he asked Delilah.

"Yes. Why?"

"Zane reserved a suite for us at the River's Edge Hotel."

Delilah's face lit. "I heard the River's Edge is really nice."

"Worth the inconvenience of another move?"

She nodded.

The trip to West Fork was uneventful. They arrived ninety minutes after leaving Harmony because of Matt's detours. He couldn't alleviate Delilah's grief, but he was determined to give her an undisturbed night of rest.

Tomorrow, all bets were off. Matt would pursue every avenue of investigation to find the culprit and stop the attacks on Delilah, no matter what it took.

CHAPTER THIRTEEN

Matt registered at the River's Edge Hotel and picked up the key cards. According to the desk clerk, their suite was on the fourth floor with a view of the river. Since they hadn't been followed from Harmony, Matt felt confident Delilah was safe for the moment.

They climbed the stairs to the fourth floor. Matt opened the suite door and understood why Delilah had been excited about staying here. Oil paintings on the walls, a grand piano in the corner of the living room, a fireplace with gas logs, plush carpet, and overstuffed leather furniture along with a large-screen television. This was going to cost him. Worth it, he reminded himself. Anything to keep Delilah safe. Besides, he had the money to cover the suite charge. Brent Maddox demanded a lot from his operatives but paid them well for their service.

While Delilah and Sasha explored the suite, he and Cade returned to the SUV for their gear.

"We're in the room on the left," Sasha told Cade when he reentered the suite with Matt.

Matt set his bags against the wall next to Delilah's room, carried her belongings inside, and placed them on the queen-size bed. "Do you like the room?"

"It's great." She sat on the bed gingerly, hand to her ribs. "I still feel guilty for making you sleep on the couch, even if the couch is worth more than all the furniture in my house combined."

"I'll rest better if I'm close to you and positioned to hear if someone breaks into the suite." He crouched in front of her. "Ribs still hurt?"

Delilah nodded.

"I'm sorry I hurt you."

"It's better than being shot."

"Do you mind if I check your ribs?" Matt wanted to make sure he hadn't injured Delilah.

"It's fine. I trust you."

He kissed her gently. "Thank you."

"You owe me a real kiss."

That made him smile. "I do. Before you go to sleep, okay?"

"Promise?"

"Yes, ma'am. I've been looking forward to that kiss all day." He placed his hands on her ribcage and felt for breaks in the bones. Finally, he sat back. "No breaks. Tell me the truth, Delilah. Is the pain subsiding at all?"

She shook her head.

"I can support them with athletic tape. You'll be able to move more freely with reduced pain. I use the tape on Bravo. You'll be able to shower with it on. In a few days, the tape will loosen enough to pull off. Go slow and make sure the tape is wet. Otherwise, you'll remove a layer of skin along with the tape. Will you let me tape your ribs?"

"You think it will help?"

"I know it will."

"Okay."

He squeezed her knee and rose. "I'll be right back." Matt left the room and picked up his mike bag. Figuring Delilah would be more comfortable with a woman in the room, he turned to Sasha. "I need you for a minute."

She turned from the French doors. "How can I help?"

"I need to tape Delilah's ribs. Will you keep her shirt elevated enough for me to work? Should take a couple minutes."

"Sure." Sasha followed him inside the second bedroom.

Matt unzipped the mike bag and plunged his hand inside to grab the athletic tape. "Black or blue? Sorry, no girly color like pink. My teammates would never let me hear the end of it if I had that color."

"Blue, please."

When Delilah's voice quivered, Matt's gaze locked on her. She sounded nervous. Why? "This won't take long," he assured her. "Two minutes, tops."

"Okay."

Unsure what the problem was, Matt feared he'd make matters worse if he didn't get busy. "Which side, sweetheart?"

"Left."

"Show me where it hurts." After she complied, Matt glanced at Sasha. "Lift the shirt to the bottom of Delilah's bra and hold it there." He tore a strip of the blue tape. He turned to Delilah and noticed she wouldn't look at him.

Jaw clenched, Matt bent to apply the tape to her skin and froze. Oh, man. No wonder she was upset. She didn't want him to see the scars left from her surgery. He placed several strips, then nodded at Sasha to let go of the shirt. "Thanks."

"No problem. I'm going to check the room service menu." She left the room, closing the door behind her.

Matt took a minute to close his mike bag, then sat on the bed beside Delilah. He waited a moment for her to look at him. When her gaze remained glued to her hands, he cupped her chin and raised her head. The woman refused to look him in the eyes. "Delilah, look at me."

When she complied, her cheeks were flushed.

"Every inch of you is beautiful to me. Those scars are evidence of your courage and determination."

"They're ugly," she whispered.

He shook his head. "I don't see scars. I just see you, a woman with the strength to change her life, a beautiful woman I want more than my next breath. I am in awe of you, Delilah Frost." He only knew one way to show her the scars didn't deter his attraction to her.

Matt stood and helped Delilah to her feet. He wrapped his arms around her and brought her against his body. Bending his head, he captured her mouth with his own.

He teased her with soft butterfly kisses until she wrapped her arms around his neck and increased the pressure of her mouth against his in silent demand for more. Matt edged closer and traced her lips with his tongue, asking for permission to deepen the kiss. His heart skipped a beat when she instantly complied and he indulged in his first taste of her. Warm honey, the inside of her mouth as soft as silk.

Oh, yeah. He was a goner, all right. No other woman would do for him from this point forward. If she rejected him, he didn't know if his heart would survive intact.

The kiss spun on and on as he changed the angle by degrees until the fit was perfect. He paid attention to every catch of her breath, every moan, learning what Delilah liked, what made her shiver with delight.

When his control was razor thin, he broke the kiss.

"Not yet. Please."

He pressed his forehead to hers, his breathing rough. "Shh." Matt pressed her face into his neck. "Let me hold you for a few minutes and bring my heart rate out of the stratosphere. Your kisses are addictive and potent."

She laughed softly, her warm breath brushing against his skin. "Back at you."

When they had both calmed, he released her. "Let's see if Cade and Sasha decided what to order from room service."

"I don't know if I can eat anything. I try not to eat between meals."

"You can order something light along with tea."

"Sounds good."

He dropped a quick peck on her lips, resisting the burning need to dive into a deep kiss, and went to the living room with her. "Did you decide what to order?" he asked Cade.

"Sasha's in the mood for ice cream. What about you, Delilah?"

She looked torn. "I shouldn't but ice cream sounds great."

Comfort food. "A treat once in a while won't hurt you." Matt placed their order a minute later. He turned to the others. "I need to call Rod Kelter and give him an update. Maybe he'll have information for me."

He unlocked the French doors, stepped out on the balcony and made the call.

"Kelter."

"It's Matt."

"Perfect timing. Tell Delilah we're finished with her house. Will you be in town soon or should I arrange to have someone watch the place?"

"PSI has the house covered. We'll be in Harmony for a few more days. Delilah's mother died earlier this evening."

"I'm sorry. Please give her my condolences."

"Thanks. Do you have updates?"

"Keep an eye on Delilah. We found evidence of two men in the house, and a roll of duct tape and a syringe in her bedroom. Before you ask, I don't know what was in it.

We sent the syringe to the lab to be analyzed and, like always, they're backed up."

Not a simple burglary, then. Had the men planned to abduct Delilah or kill her? Knowing the contents of the syringe would help him decide their intent. "No further trouble in town?"'

"No. Why?"

"Someone fired a rifle at Delilah a few hours ago."

A quiet gasp made him turn. Delilah's face was pale, her eyes huge. Matt motioned for her to come to him. When she did, he tucked her against his chest. Things had been so chaotic since the shooting, he hadn't told her she was the target of the new attack, not him. He tapped the speaker button so Delilah could hear the conversation. "You're on speaker with Delilah, Rod."

"Are you all right, Delilah?"

"I'm fine, thanks to Matt."

"He's a good man to have at your side. Matt, did you report the incident to the local cops?"

"Yeah. Detective Miles Russell is handling the case. By the way, he's a Ranger buddy of Ethan's."

"Yeah? I'll be sure to pass that information along. Tell me what's been going on since you arrived in town. Don't leave anything out."

Between the two of them, Matt and Delilah brought the Otter Creek detective up to speed.

"Incredible. I want regular updates, Matt. I don't like the sound of this. I'm afraid trouble followed you to Harmony. I'll touch base with Russell." Rod paused. "Might be better if Ethan contacted his buddy. The detective could be more forthcoming with details if Ethan talks to him. In the meantime, be careful. I know you and your team think you're bulletproof. You aren't."

"I hear you. Thanks for the warning." Matt ended the call and wrapped his other arm around his girl.

"You should have told me."

"No time. I didn't plan to keep the news from you. You would have known the truth before you went to bed tonight."

"Did Rod share any information before you put him on speaker?"

"He found evidence of two men in your house. They left behind duct tape and a full syringe in their haste to get away from Bravo."

Delilah stared. "Duct tape and a syringe. What does that mean?"

"They didn't break in to steal. Those men came for you."

CHAPTER FOURTEEN

Delilah frowned. "I don't have enemies." Had she seen something she shouldn't? She wracked her brain and couldn't come up with one single thing to explain why she was the target of these attacks.

"Come on. We shouldn't let the ice cream melt."

Delilah allowed Matt to lead her from the balcony although she wasn't sure she could eat the treat after all. If not, she would enjoy drinking her unsweetened iced tea.

They joined Sasha and Cade at the table. The half hour passed with laughter as the others kept the conversation light. When the treat was gone, Matt sent Cade to rest with the promise to wake him in four hours.

Alone with the handsome medic, Delilah helped him stack the dishes and glasses on a tray and place them outside the suite door.

"Would you like to go for a walk?"

Dreading being alone with her thoughts, she nodded. "Do you think it's safe?"

"We're registered under assumed names. The shooter hasn't had time to discover what hotel we're in and I know we weren't followed. We're safe enough for now."

"I'd love to go for a walk. I'm not used to being inactive. I miss my swim spa."

Matt threaded his fingers through hers and headed for the stairs. "I saw a walking path beside the river. How does that sound?"

"Perfect."

They descended the stairs in silence. By the river bank, Matt kept pace with her. "Tell me some good things about your mom."

Delilah's throat grew thick. She was grateful he didn't push, seeming content to let her share what she could. As she waited for the emotional surge to recede, Delilah thought back to her childhood, the fun memories of outings and vacations, her early disastrous cooking attempts, and her initial interest in making candles.

She began to talk, the sweet memories flooding her mind as she related funny stories from her childhood. Throughout her recitation, Matt remained silent aside from the occasional encouraging comment or a chuckle.

By the time they returned to the hotel and the suite, the turmoil inside Delilah had subsided. Temporary, she knew. Still, she'd take a reprieve from the horrible sense of loss.

At the door to her bedroom, Delilah turned into Matt's arms. "Thank you."

He leaned down to kiss her, long, soft, and sweet, the caress a balm to her aching heart. "If you can't sleep, come to me. We'll watch a movie." Matt smiled. "I'll count the walk as our first date."

She grinned. "A moonlit walk beside the river is definitely romantic."

"You forgot one thing."

Her brows knitted. "What?"

"A moonlit walk beside the river with a beautiful woman."

A warm glow suffused her. "You're quite the charmer, Mr. Rainer."

Matt's smile faded. "Only with you, Delilah. There is no one else for me."

She searched his eyes, stunned to realize he meant what he said. Did that mean what she thought? She needed to get a grip on her emotions. It was too soon for him to declare that he loved her. Wasn't it? She must have misunderstood what he was saying.

Delilah leaned up and kissed him. "Good night, Matt. Try to rest." She slipped into the bedroom and closed the door, her heart racing. Good grief. Matt Rainer was a dream come true. His touch and kiss were dynamite to her system.

She readied herself for bed, climbed under the covers, and prayed for sleep to take her fast. Delilah woke three hours later. The first thought to hit her was the death of her mother. The pain of loss stabbed her heart and Delilah knew she wouldn't be able to sleep more.

Glancing at the clock, she wondered if Matt was still on watch or if Cade had taken over. She longed to go to Matt but was loathe to interrupt his sleep. He hadn't rested much since she had been injured.

She debated with herself, then huffed in aggravation. Might as well make herself some tea. Maybe she'd be able to nap once she finished the drink.

Delilah opened her door and walked into the living room. The lights were dim and a man stood at the French doors, staring outside. Matt? No, the shoulders were wrong. Cade.

The operative turned. "You okay?" Cade murmured.

Delilah shook her head.

"Come here, Delilah." Matt sat up on the couch and placed his feet on the floor. He patted the cushion beside him.

"I don't want to disturb you."

"You aren't." He held out his hand. "Let's find a movie."

"You need to sleep. Please, Matt."

"You watch the movie. I'll hold you and nap. Deal?"

Cade chuckled. "Might as well give in. He's relentless when he wants something." He grinned. "Or someone."

Cheeks burning at Cade's gentle teasing, Delilah realized Matt would sleep sooner if she stopped protesting and curled up beside him. She sat down and found herself tucked against Matt's side, a blanket spread across her legs.

He grabbed the remote. When he found a Perry Mason film she liked, he propped his feet on the coffee table and settled deeper into the cushion, urging Delilah to lay her head against his chest. "This okay?"

She nodded.

"Relax and let me enjoy holding you."

"Go to sleep, Matt."

"Yes, ma'am." After kissing her temple, Matt rested his head against the couch and closed his eyes.

For a while, Delilah let the movie take her mind off her loss. Eventually, the blanket and Matt's body heat worked to make her drowsy. She doubted she'd sleep, but it wouldn't hurt to close her eyes.

Sometime later, Delilah woke to sunlight streaming into the living room of the posh suite. The Perry Mason movie had morphed into the morning news and the scent of coffee filled the air.

Still deliciously warm, she hated to move. Matt couldn't be comfortable, though. Delilah tilted her head to look at the warrior holding her tight against his side.

He glanced down when she moved. "Good morning, beautiful. Sleep well?"

"I'm surprised, but I did. Did you rest?"

Matt captured her lips for a leisurely kiss before answering. "I feel great this morning. Turns out I need to hold a certain gorgeous woman to keep nightmares and flashbacks at bay. Thank you for letting me hold you."

Delilah marveled at his ability to turn something that benefited her into a favor for himself. She glanced around. "Where's Cade?"

"With Sasha. I took over the watch two hours ago. Cade will sleep another two hours. Hungry?"

Her stomach lurched. "Not really."

"What do you normally eat in the mornings?"

"A banana. Sometimes an egg."

"Go get ready. I'll call in an order. By the time you're finished, the food should be here."

She started toward her bedroom. At the doorway, she paused and twisted. "Thanks for holding me, Matt." Delilah hurried inside and closed the door before he replied.

As she showered and dressed, Delilah considered the tasks she had ahead of her today. A trip to the bank followed by a visit to her mother's lawyer. She should call to set an appointment with Oliver Shannon.

Delilah remembered again her mother's odd statement about not trusting Zach and Randy to handle her estate. Maybe Michelle had a few personal items to give friends.

A few more hours and she'd have the answers to her questions. After dragging a brush through her hair, she tied her tennis shoes and left the bedroom.

Matt turned from the French door, coffee mug in hand. "You look good enough to nibble on."

Wow. Charmer, indeed. "Thanks. Do you have more packets of tea?"

He inclined his head toward the kitchen counter. "I made your tea while you were in the shower. Should be ready now."

"You're one in a million."

A chuckle as he turned back to the window. "I hope you still say that when I do something stupid and tick you off."

"You're sure you'll need to get back in my good graces?"

"I'm human. I'll screw up at some point. I hope you're in a forgiving mood when I do."

Delilah sipped her tea and sighed. Perfect. "Don't worry. I don't hold grudges. Is it safe to sit on the balcony?"

"I haven't seen anything suspicious. It's a beautiful morning. Do you want your banana? Breakfast arrived a few minutes ago."

She selected one of four bananas on the tray and joined Matt on the balcony's outdoor couch. They sat in silence until their mugs were empty and her banana eaten.

Matt glanced at Delilah. "What do you need to do today?"

"Go to the bank to check my mother's safe deposit box."

"Wouldn't your stepfather do that?"

"He can't. Only Mom and I have keys and she kept hers hidden."

"What's in the box?"

"Her will. I don't know what else might be in there. I also need to call Oliver Shannon and set an appointment."

Matt glanced at his watch. "The bank won't open for another hour."

"Neither will the law office. I should call Piper."

"Need privacy for that?"

She shook her head and pulled the cell phone from her pocket. After four rings, her assistant picked up.

"I don't know who this is, but do you have any idea what time it is?" Piper groused.

"It's Delilah. I have a new number. I apologize for calling so early."

Muffled thuds and covers rustling. "Sorry, Delilah. I'm not a morning person."

"Could have fooled me. You're always cheerful."

"That's because by the time I arrive at Wicks, I've consumed a full pot of coffee. Caffeine does wonders for my attitude and mental clarity."

Delilah laughed. "I guess I need to buy a coffee maker for the break room at the shop."

"You just made my day. Thanks, boss. Now, why did you call me at this ungodly hour of the morning?"

"I'll be out of town longer than I anticipated. Can you handle the shop alone?"

"Sure. What happened?"

Delilah explained about the loss of her mother and her new responsibility. "If you have trouble or anything makes you uneasy, contact Liam McCoy, Matt's teammate."

"That's not a hardship. Liam is a hottie. How long do you think you'll be gone?"

Delilah grinned at hearing her assistant's assessment of Liam. Looked like the operative wouldn't have much trouble convincing Piper to go out with him. "I'm not sure. I don't know what's involved in settling Mom's estate. I won't be here longer than necessary." Being in Harmony brought back painful memories.

"No rush. I'll be fine. I'm sorry about your mother, Delilah."

Her eyes burned. "Thanks." After a few minutes discussing shop supplies and orders, Delilah ended the call. She leaned her head against Matt's shoulder. "Can we stay out here for a while?" Watching the water drift past the hotel and pedestrians wander along the walkway beside the river was peaceful. She couldn't do anything proactive for another hour. She'd like to enjoy just being with Matt until Cade and Sasha made an appearance.

"Sure. I need to check the files Zane sent me before we leave the hotel. I'll read them after I shower."

An hour later, the door to the second bedroom opened.

Matt stood and held out his hand to Delilah. "I don't want you out here alone in case of trouble. Call the lawyer's office and set an appointment while I shower. After I finish reading Z's files, we'll go to the bank."

Delilah followed the medic into the suite, mentally gearing herself up for a long and difficult day.

CHAPTER FIFTEEN

While Matt's computer booted up, he poured himself another mug of coffee. "What did you find out from Shannon?" he asked Delilah.

"We have an appointment at 11:00 this morning. That should give me enough time to empty out the safe deposit box and see what Mom wanted me to take care of for her."

"Give me a few minutes and I'll be ready to go."

Delilah glanced at the computer. "What if the files Zane sent are large?"

"If we need to leave, I'll finish reviewing the files later." He set down his coffee mug and studied her face. "You need more tea?"

"How did you know?"

He winked at her. "A beautiful, but very pale face. Have a seat and I'll fix you another cup."

"Do you mind if I read the files with you?"

"You may see things you won't like."

"I'd rather know the truth than believe a lie."

He slid the mug of water with a tea bag into the microwave and started the heating cycle. "Under normal circumstances, I wouldn't let you read the files. Since you're at the heart of this mission, I can justify the protocol breach."

"Will there be many things you can't tell me?"

Matt's insides knotted. "Most things. Fortress and PSI are in security, and our missions are confidential. Some have national security implications. The level of secrecy would be the same if I was enlisted in the Army and part of a Special Forces unit." He set her mug by his computer and dropped into the seat beside hers. Would she accept his limitations?

"You were in a Special Forces unit?"

"Rangers."

"Did you like it?"

"Most of it."

"What didn't you like?"

"The brass. They had objectives and insisted we go on missions even when the intel was bad and they knew it." Matt's hands fisted. "One of their screw ups cost the life of a good friend, a man I'd grown up with. We enlisted together, trained together, and eventually made it into the same Ranger unit. We lost Jacob and four others on that mission."

Delilah's soft hand wrapped around his wrist. "I'm sorry, Matt. Is that why you don't sleep well at night?"

Smart lady. "That mission and others still haunt me. The soldiers I couldn't save, the lives I had to take in the line of duty."

"Thank you for telling me."

"You have a right to know what you're getting into." He slid her a look. "Now is the time to walk away, Delilah. The longer I'm with you, the harder it will be to let you go if you change your mind." He already knew it would be nearly impossible to watch her leave. Delilah Frost was fast becoming necessary to him. Knowing the truth would likely scare her to death.

To his surprise, Delilah brushed his lips with hers. "It's already too late."

Matt stared, unsure what to make of her statement and afraid to push. Was she claiming him temporarily or permanently? He knew which one he voted for. Unwilling to box her in, he changed the subject. "After we scan Zane's report, I'll grab a quick shower and we'll go."

Delilah wrapped her hands around the tea mug. "Shower now, Matt. I'll drink my tea while I wait for you to finish. We'll read Zane's files if we have time."

"You sure you don't mind?" He hated to make her wait alone. Matt knew well haunting thoughts could creep into a person's mind when all was quiet. Today would be difficult enough for Delilah without starting her day with tumultuous thoughts.

"Positive. I promise not to get a head start on the report."

He grinned. "The computer is password protected and the files encrypted. You wouldn't have much luck breaking through either of them."

"Go shower."

"Stay inside the suite and away from windows." He pointed to the chair near her bedroom door. "That's the safest place. If anyone knocks or tries to get into the suite, come get me. I won't be longer than five minutes."

Matt grabbed his duffel and went to Delilah's bathroom. One deep breath froze him in place. The fresh, breezy scent of citrus filled his lungs, a scent he always associated with Delilah.

Wrenching himself into gear, he zipped through his shower, leaving off shaving this morning in favor of returning to Delilah's side sooner. The beard made him appear to have a dangerous edge.

He almost laughed at that thought. He did have a dangerous edge. If the beard stubble scratched her skin,

Matt would take a couple minutes after his teammate woke and scrape off the stubble.

When he returned to the living room with his bag in hand, Cade was standing in the kitchen, leaning against the counter with a mug of coffee in his hand, an amused smile on his face. His friend's relaxed stance told Matt the suite was secure.

Cade turned. "About time you showed up. Thought I'd have to save you from drowning."

Matt rolled his eyes. "Took me six minutes."

His friend's smile widened. "Used to take you three. Guess you're out to impress your girl." Cade picked up another mug and started toward the second bedroom. "Sasha and I will be out soon. Don't leave without us."

Delilah frowned. "They don't have to come. I feel bad dragging them from place to place."

"If we need him, Cade won't do us any good from West Fork. Besides, Sasha always visits coffee shops for ideas to improve Perk." He sat in front of his laptop and typed in the passwords necessary to log into his Fortress account.

Matt clicked on the report Zane prepared and shifted the computer for Delilah to view the screen easier. As he read, Matt's astonishment grew. According to Z, old Randy was a hound dog. While married to Michelle, he'd had one mistress after another. Randy had also quit his job four years earlier and hadn't worked a day since. According to his financials, though, Randy spent a lot of money each week. The jewelry store, flower shop, restaurants, and several hotels in towns outside Harmony benefited from his generous spending.

Matt frowned. If Randy didn't work, where was he getting the money to pay for all the extravagances?

Setting aside those questions for the moment, he scrolled to the next part of the report dealing with Zach, Delilah's brother. Z's research showed that Zach blew through more money each week than his stepfather. The gambling habit had grown worse and Delilah's brother ran a sizable tab in the town's three bars.

A quiet sniff drew his gaze from the screen to Delilah. Tears trickled down her cheeks as she read the report.

Matt wrapped his arm around her shoulders and drew her against his side. "Hard to read, isn't it?"

"Heartbreaking. Zach's life is spiraling out of control and he doesn't even realize it." She grabbed a nearby napkin and blotted her face dry. "Where is he getting the money for the lifestyle? Zane didn't mention my brother winning a big pot of money at a casino to fund the spending spree."

Matt clicked on the second report Z attached to the email. "The money came from your mother."

"That's not possible."

"Your brother has been receiving a generous allowance from your mom for nearly four years." Matt frowned. "So have Evan and Shane Frost. Your mother was supporting them all. Zane couldn't find an employer for your stepfather, brother, or your cousins."

"Your friend at Fortress is thorough."

"Details keep us alive on missions." He squeezed her shoulders. "Where would your mother come up with enough money to support five people?" The fact she hadn't offered to send Delilah money hadn't escaped him. Why wouldn't Michelle be as generous with Delilah as she was with her no-account husband, son, and nephews?

"I don't know. Mom was an interior decorator. When she was sober, she did all right for herself, but she didn't earn enough to support the lifestyle in this report."

"If we can't figure out where the money came from, I'll ask Zane do an in-depth run on your mother's finances." Might still do that anyway. Something was hinky with this arrangement.

Cade and Sasha returned the living room. For the first time in months, Matt's heart didn't hurt watching the deliriously happy couple and he didn't feel like a third wheel despite the Ramseys' assurances that he was always welcome to spend time with them. The difference was Delilah.

"Please tell me we have time to eat before we leave." Sasha lifted the cover from one of the plates. "Oh, nice. Waffles. My favorite." She smiled at Matt. "You remembered."

"How could I forget? Cade talks my ear off all the time about you."

Bravo's EOD man narrowed his eyes. "Who drives me crazy talking about a certain candle shop owner?"

Delilah motioned them to the other side of the table. "We need to leave in a few minutes. I have to stop at the bank before we go to the lawyer's office."

When the couple finished their meals, Matt shut down his computer. "We'll carry the gear to the SUV and be on our way."

"We're not staying another night?" Disappointment filled Delilah's eyes.

"I'm not checking us out. If there's a problem and I think our location has been compromised, I don't want to return to retrieve our belongings. I'd rather just disappear and assume another identity at a different hotel in another town."

"Told you," Sasha said to Delilah.

"Good thing I paid attention to your advice." She turned to Matt. "My bag is ready to go."

"Excellent. Let's roll."

Minutes later, their gear was loaded and they drove away from the hotel. Almost an hour later, Matt parked in front of First Harmony Bank and glanced over the seat at the Ramseys. "Delilah might appreciate more chamomile tea if you two want to visit the coffee shop beside the bank."

Sasha turned, her face lighting up. "It looks great. Do you mind, Cade?"

"I can always use more coffee." He eyed Matt. "You sure you don't need me to watch your back?"

"Not at the bank."

A nod. "I'll buy drinks for all of us while Sasha looks around the coffee shop."

Matt escorted Delilah into the bank and waited by her side while the assistant manager finished a phone call. "Do you recognize any of the employees?"

She nodded. "I went to high school with two of the tellers and the assistant manager."

"Did I tell you that you look breathtaking today?"

Delilah smiled. "No but thank you."

Footsteps heralded the approach of the assistant manager. "Sorry to keep you waiting. I'm the assistant manager, Cindy Kenworth. Please follow me." Once they were in her office, Cindy waved them to the chairs in front of her desk. "What can I do for you?"

"I'm Matt Rainer and this is Delilah Frost. We need access to a safe deposit box."

Cindy's gaze swung to Delilah, her eyes wide. "Oh, my goodness. I didn't recognize you, Delilah. You look fantastic."

"Thanks."

"Does your mother know you're in town?"

"I saw her last night. I need to open Mom's box."

"What's the number?"

She told Cindy the information she needed. "You'll hear before the morning is gone. Mom passed away last night."

"I'm so sorry. Your Mom was a nice woman." Cindy stood. "I'll grab the key and we'll get you on your way. You must have a million things to do." She left the office and returned a moment later with a card in her hand. "Sign here."

That done, they followed the woman down a long hall. Cindy veered to the right and opened a secured room. She slipped her key in the lock of the correct box and motioned for Delilah to do the same with her key. Together they unlocked the box. "I'll make sure you aren't disturbed. Take your time, Delilah." The assistant manager left the secured room.

Taking a deep breath, Delilah lifted the lid and goggled. Inside the box was a letter-size envelope and bundles of cash.

Matt whistled. He glanced at Delilah for permission and picked up one of the bundles. After thumbing through the bills, he said, "All one-hundred-dollar bills."

Delilah dropped into the closest chair, envelope in hand. She tore open the flap and scanned the one-page document inside. After a few moments, Delilah looked at Matt.

"What is it?" He crouched beside her chair and sandwiched her hand between his.

Instead of answering verbally, she handed Matt the letter. He unfolded the paper and read. By the time he finished, his teeth were clenched. Michelle Holloway had placed a target on her daughter's back.

CHAPTER SIXTEEN

Despite her mother's instructions to take all the money in the safe deposit box, Delilah didn't feel comfortable carrying that much cash in her purse. She opted to take $6,000 and still felt as though everyone knew she was a prime target for robbery. She refused to walk around Harmony carrying $100,000 in a handbag.

Matt ushered her into the coffee shop where Cade and Sasha waited. Delilah took the proffered to-go cup of tea from Cade. "Thanks." She turned to Sasha. "Did you find anything useful for Perk?"

"They have amazing croissants. I know a vendor near Otter Creek who has been after me to try his baked goods. Turns out this shop buys croissants from the vendor's franchisee. Same recipe, same service. The customers here are snapping up the croissants. I can stock small individual containers of butter and different flavors of jam in one of the display cases. What do you think?"

"I'm ready for one now," Matt said, eyeing the windowed cabinets around Harmony's coffee shop. "We have a few minutes before Delilah's appointment with the lawyer. Anybody else want something? I'm buying this round."

Cade opted for a croissant and Sasha chose an orange muffin. Delilah scanned the menu and chose iced blueberry tea in lieu of food not on her diet plan. Matt was right. A treat once in a while was fine. However, indulging two days in a row began a pattern of eating processed food that ruined her life as a teen. She wasn't about to head back into that miasma. Getting the weight off was too hard to ever let her discipline slide like that again.

After finishing the hot tea from Cade, Delilah sipped the blueberry tea as they walked to the lawyer's office. "You should offer this tea in Perk, Sasha. It's sure to be a hit with the customers."

"I'll keep that in mind. I've been thinking about adding several types of tea to the menu. You're not the only one who's been asking for herbal tea instead of coffee."

A minute later, they walked into Oliver Shannon's outer office.

A dark-haired woman occupied the receptionist's desk. She smiled as they approached. "May I help you?"

"I'm Delilah Frost. I have an appointment with Mr. Shannon at 11:00."

Her smile dimmed slightly. "Have a seat. I'll tell Mr. Shannon you're here." Her gaze shifted to Matt and Cade, a gleam in her eyes.

Delilah frowned. Shannon's assistant was drop-dead gorgeous and knew it. Couldn't she see that Cade and Sasha were a couple? Their wedding rings gleamed in the overhead light.

She glanced at Matt, expecting him to be enamored of the bold assistant. Men always paid attention to beautiful women when they were with Delilah. To her surprise, his attention was fixed on her. His lips brushed over hers, making Delilah's heart skip a beat over the sweet gesture.

Sitting in the waiting area, Delilah studied the office space. The design looked familiar. When she noticed the bonsai tree, she understood the familiarity. Her mother had decorated Shannon's suite of offices. The bonsai tree was her mother's signature. The knowledge brought a smile.

Matt squeezed her hand, his eyebrow raised in wordless inquiry.

"Mom decorated the office. I recognize her handiwork."

The outer office door opened again and four men walked inside. Dread knotted Delilah's stomach. Walk might not be the right term to describe the four men. Randy looked sober. Delilah couldn't say the same for her brother and cousins. They stumbled through the doorway, bleary-eyed with sour expressions on their faces.

Her stepfather spoke to the receptionist who gestured to the waiting area. The four men turned and scowled when they spotted Delilah and her friends. She wasn't happy to see them either. Too bad the lawyer or his assistant hadn't indicated her family would be attending this meeting as well. She would have been more prepared.

"Should have known you'd show up with your hand out," Randy said to her, a sneer on his face. "Your mama ain't been gone more than a few hours and you're showing your true colors."

Zach dropped into a chair across the sitting area from Delilah. "I guarantee you won't see a penny if I have anything to say about it. You're nothing but a gold digger."

That was rich coming from a man with no job who'd been living off his mother. Matt stiffened, fury burning in his eyes. Delilah tightened her grip on his hand. When he swung his gaze to her, she shook her head. Punching out her stepfather and brother wasn't worth Matt ending up in jail. Her family was vindictive enough to press assault charges and anything else they could come up with. In a few minutes, she'd have larger battles to fight when her family learned about the will.

The inner office door opened and Oliver Shannon stepped out. "Oh, good. You're all here. Please, come in. I'm ready for you."

Matt gave a hand signal to Cade, then walked into the office with Delilah.

"Get out." Randy glared at Matt. Lingering fear spoiled his effort to appear strong and in control. "This ain't none of your business."

Delilah threaded her fingers through Matt's. "He stays."

"He's not family," Shane spat out.

"Yet," Matt said evenly.

Delilah barely managed to hide her surprise at his statement. Did Matt mean that or was he trying to force her family to back off?

A scowl from her stepfather. "You're engaged to this thug, Dee?" His gaze dropped to her bare left hand. "No ring."

The medic bared his teeth in a semblance of a smile. "Coming soon."

"Let's get started, please," Shannon interrupted. "I have another meeting in less than an hour and a court appearance after lunch." He retreated behind his desk, opened a file folder, and scanned the document inside. Tension in the room built by the second.

While her family huffed and fidgeted, Delilah relaxed against Matt's side on the couch in Shannon's office. His thumb caressed the back of her hand, his gentle reminder of his presence and support raising goosebumps along the surface of her skin.

Randy broke the silence. "Can we get on with this? I have a lunch appointment."

Shannon removed his reading glasses and laid them on top of the file. "First, I'm sorry to hear of your wife's death, Randy. She was a fine woman and a good friend. As for her will, Michelle left very specific instructions."

A scowl from Randy. "What are you talking about? We made our wills at the same time four years ago. I'm the executor and get everything except our agreed upon amount for the boys." He waved at Zach and the cousins. "No provisions were made for Dee since she left Harmony and didn't return."

"Michelle made a new will six months ago. The terms changed." The lawyer glanced at Delilah. "Were you able to speak to your mother before she passed?"

"Yes, sir."

"Then you know what your responsibilities are?"

She nodded.

"Responsibilities?" Zach turned a suspicious gaze on Delilah. "She's been out of our lives for years. Why would Mom ask her to do anything?"

A frown from the lawyer. "On the contrary, Zach. Your mother and sister spoke regularly on the phone."

Delilah's family stared at her.

"How much money did you sponge off her?" Zach's face turned beet red. "You're paying back every penny, Dee. You had no right to ask for money."

"No money changed hands," Shannon insisted. "If you'll be quiet, I'll explain the terms of your mother's will. It won't take long if I'm not interrupted."

"Go on, then," Randy said. "Keep your trap shut, Zach."

"Yeah, yeah. Get on with it, Shannon. The sooner you finish, the sooner we can break whatever crazy will Dee talked Mom into signing."

Evan and Shane chimed in with their agreement for the lawyer to get down to business.

With a scathing glance at the four men, Shannon said, "The terms of the will are simple. Michelle named Delilah as the executor of her estate."

Four hostile gazes swung Delilah's direction.

"The will stipulates that Randy, Zach, Evan, and Shane are to receive $50,000 a year for a period of five years. After that time, no more money will be forthcoming."

Stunned silence filled the room, and Delilah prepared for a verbal explosion. She wasn't disappointed. Seconds later, Randy jumped to his feet and slammed his palms on the desk. "This is outrageous. Michelle is worth hundreds of millions of dollars. She can't cut me off with that measly amount of money for five years and then leave me high and dry. I'm her husband. There must be some mistake."

Shannon was already shaking his head before Randy finished his rant. "I'm sorry. There is no mistake. This is what Michelle wanted."

Ghostly white, Zach dragged a hand over his face. "Who gets the rest of the money?"

"You!" Evan shot to his feet and stalked toward Delilah. "She gave the rest to you, didn't she?"

Matt was on his feet in an instant, his body blocking Evan's access to Delilah. "Back off."

"Or what?" Her cousin placed his hands and shoved. The medic didn't budge which inflamed Evan further. Another shove, and this time Matt wrapped him up in a hold her cousin couldn't break.

As Evan cursed and raged, struggling ineffectively against Matt, Shane leaped to his feet to go to his brother's aid.

"Chill." Matt adjusted his hold enough that a pained expression crossed Evan's face. "Sit down," he ordered Shane.

To Delilah's amazement, although her cousin cursed softly he obeyed Matt.

"Let me go, you oaf." Evan tried to lurch away again only to stop with a groan as the medic shifted his hold.

When his detainee ceased struggling, Matt said, "If you come after my woman again, I'll take you down, hard. This is your only warning, Frost."

"Who are you?" Zach spat out.

Matt inclined his head toward Delilah. "Hers." He shoved Evan toward his seat. "Act like an adult or I'll boot you out of here."

Randy scrubbed his face with his hands. "What's Dee supposed to do with the rest of the lottery money?"

"Delilah can do almost anything she wants with the money. Michelle included a few suggestions in the will."

Zach's eyes narrowed. "Then she can split the money between the five of us."

"I'm afraid not." Shannon grimaced. "According to the terms of the will, if she attempts to distribute more than the allotted amount, the rest of the money will be split between four charities and you will receive nothing further. If you contest the will, you will be cut off immediately and the five years of payouts will go to Delilah."

"This is insane," Shane snapped. "Aunt Michelle must have been out of her mind when she made that will. You should have stopped her, Shannon. Doesn't that will have some statement about my aunt being of sound mind? She couldn't have been when she made that. We'll sue you for every penny you're worth."

The lawyer stiffened. "You're free to pursue that option if you choose. The rule of law is behind me. No court in the country will side with you. If you want to waste what little money Michelle allotted for you this year, then by all means go ahead and find another lawyer."

Randy dropped heavily into his chair. "Why? Why would my wife do this to me? After all I did for her over the years. Why would she stab me in the back this way?"

Delilah wanted to blast her stepfather for his lavish spending and infidelity but refused to waste her breath.

Randy wouldn't listen anyway. Instead, she turned to Shannon. "Do you have their account information?"

He nodded. "I've been distributing money to their accounts since the lottery payout."

She turned to her family. "You will receive your first year's allotment by the end of the week."

"What happens to the money if Dee dies or is incapacitated?"

Shannon looked troubled. "In that event, after Delilah's expenses have been covered, the money will be distributed to her heirs."

Delilah stilled. According to her current personal will, her heirs were the remaining members of her family. Oh, boy.

"Is that all?" Zach asked the lawyer. "Did Mom leave any other instructions or bequests?"

"You know it all. Everything goes to Delilah." He sent an apologetic glance toward Randy. "Including the house. According to the terms of the will, you have twenty-four hours to vacate the premises. You are to take only your clothes and personal belongings."

Delilah almost felt sorry for Randy. Almost.

Her stepfather rose to his feet. "I want a copy of the will. I'll warn you right now that I intend to have another lawyer look at the document."

Shannon stood. "I'll have Ms. Walters make you a copy. Follow me, please." He stalked from the room followed by Zach, Evan, and Shane.

Her brother stopped at the threshold and glared at Delilah over his shoulder. "You won't win this battle, Dee. Accidents happen all the time. Sometimes those accidents are fatal."

CHAPTER SEVENTEEN

Rage filled Matt as Zach Frost slammed the office door behind himself. Was Delilah's brother responsible for the attack in Otter Creek? One of her family members could have found out about the will and planned to kill Delilah before Michelle passed away so the will would favor the four men.

Delilah leaned her head against Matt's shoulder. "Are you sorry you came to Harmony?"

"I'm glad I was here. Are you all right?"

"I have to be. Mom asked me to do this. Based on what Zane found, Mom was right not to trust Zach or Randy with the money. I can't imagine how much money they would have blown through in the next few years."

"Sounds like Michelle wanted to wean them off being dependent on her." He suspected Michelle's actions came too late. The men hadn't worked in years and their spending habits were set. They were either going to flourish or crash and burn. His money was on the second choice.

"They'll hate me."

He pressed a kiss to her temple. "You hold the purse strings, and they wanted free reign with the cash."

"I can't imagine what Mom was thinking. She should have given Randy and the others the full five years of allowance, then given the rest to charity without involving me at all."

"You don't care about the money for yourself?"

"My shop is doing well enough to pay the bills and support a few extras every month. I'm happy."

"Maybe that's why she chose you for this task." He wished Michelle had thought this through. Delilah already had her hands full with Wicks without this added burden.

The door opened and Shannon entered the office. "Where are you staying, Delilah? I'll have the papers drawn up, giving you signing rights to your mother's accounts, and send them to your hotel."

"Why don't you tell me when to stop by your office? Matt and I have several things we need to take care of and won't be in the hotel much."

The lawyer frowned. "Leave a phone number where I can reach you."

Matt gave him the main number for Fortress. "Leave a message for Delilah. She'll call you back when she has a chance."

"Surely Delilah's phone number isn't a secret."

"I'm in private security, Mr. Shannon. We don't pass our phone numbers around. I'll be notified within minutes of your call."

"Private security, you say? What exactly does your company do?"

"We specialize in hostage retrieval and training bodyguards."

Shannon's face took on a pinched look. "I see. Stop by this evening about six. I should have your paperwork ready."

A knock sounded on the door and Ms. Walters peered inside. "Mr. Shannon, your 11:30 is here."

"Send him in, Cynthia. Delilah, I am sorry about your mother. I'll help you in any way I can."

Matt escorted Delilah to the outer office where Cade and Sasha waited. Sasha pressed Delilah's iced tea into her hand. "Take a few sips. Looks like you need a boost."

"If I was a coffee drinker, I'd be guzzling by the gallon."

"Bad?" Cade asked in a low voice.

"Worse than I imagined."

Matt noted Ms. Walter's avid interest in the conversation. "Let's go. We have other things to take care of."

The beautiful assistant intercepted them. She smiled at Matt. "Is there anything else I can do for you? I'll be happy to help in any way." With a manicured hand on his arm and her bold gaze eating him up, she left no doubt as to the lengths she would go to satisfy him. Disgusted with her boldness, Matt shifted away from her touch. "No." He ushered Delilah from the office without another word. Rude? Maybe. Matt hoped he made his point without being blunt. He preferred not to have more interaction with her. He didn't like the uncertainty growing in Delilah's eyes.

On the sidewalk, Delilah turned to Matt. "What else do we have to do?"

"Lunch first. Your banana is long gone by this point." He got her moving toward a restaurant he'd noticed coming into town. The diner looked like a good option for everyone.

He also wanted her off the street. Matt's skin was crawling with an awareness of at least one person watching them. As he passed a hardware store, he slowed as though to admire the power tools, his gaze scanning reflections in the glass.

Cade moved up beside him. "Problem?"

"Eyes."

His friend was silent a few seconds. "Alley between the bank and the coffee shop."

Matt searched the shadows. There. A figure lurking in the darkness shifted just enough to draw his attention. "Can you make out if it's one of Delilah's family?"

"No. Once we're inside the restaurant, I'll go out the back and circle around behind the alley. Hopefully, he'll stay in place long enough for me to snap his picture."

With a nod, Matt slid his arm around Delilah's shoulders and urged her toward the restaurant.

"What's going on?"

"We spotted someone watching us. Cade will try to snap a picture of the guy."

When Delilah started to turn around, Matt propelled her forward. "We don't want this guy to know we're aware of him. He could rabbit before Cade's close enough to see who it is."

"Go with him. It could be the hotel shooter."

He tucked her closer to his side. "Trust us to do our job. This is what we do and we're good at it. Believe me when I say Cade can handle anything this clown might try."

"I don't want you or Cade hurt because of me."

"Everything will be fine." He opened the door to Baxter Family Restaurant and led Delilah inside. He requested a table at the back of the restaurant against a wall. Although the hostess gave him a strange look, she grabbed four menus and led them to a suitable table.

Cade leaned down and kissed Sasha before walking to a hallway to the left. The signs for the restrooms were visible. Anyone watching the operative would assume he was going to use the facilities.

The expression on Delilah's face conveyed her worry for Cade's safety. Matt covered her hand with his on the tabletop. "Check the menu to see if they serve the right food for you. If they don't, we'll go somewhere that does."

She dropped her gaze to the plastic-covered menu and perused the list of dishes available. "I'll be fine. How long will he be?"

Matt appreciated her discretion in lowering her voice although he didn't believe the precaution necessary with the lunch-time crowd carrying on multiple conversations. "As long as he needs."

The waitress arrived. "Welcome to Baxter's. I'll take your drink orders while you decide on your meals."

Once she wrote the choices on her pad, Matt said, "We're ready to order our meals, too." If Sasha didn't know what to order for Cade, Matt would take care of it. He'd been friends long enough to know the EOD man's preferences.

"Okay. Shoot."

At that moment, gunfire erupted from the street and the front windows of Baxter's exploded.

CHAPTER EIGHTEEN

Matt wrapped his arms around Delilah and Sasha and dragged them to the floor. "Stay down," he ordered as the restaurant erupted in chaos. Some patrons jumped and ran for the exits. Others dropped to the floor, screaming. One man fell to the floor, clutching his chest. A second man tackled a woman running in a panic into the line of fire. He rolled to his side, moaning as blood pooled beneath his leg.

Matt flipped the table onto its side, making sure the women were blocked from the shooter's view. He laid his hand on Delilah's shoulder and squeezed gently as he rose to a crouch. "Don't move from here until I tell you it's safe."

"Where are you going?"

"To help the injured." Unfortunately, his mike bag was in the SUV. He'd have to make do with the supplies at hand. Matt rushed to the guy with the leg wound as gunfire peppered the restaurant.

Matt assessed the wound. A through-and-through. Without other options, he took the man's belt and cinched the leather around his upper thigh. The man hissed. "Keep this tight."

Two more shots sounded from the street and then all was silent. Sirens drew nearer.

Matt shifted his attention to the man with the chest wound. The victim was losing too much blood. If the ambulance didn't get him to the hospital within the next ten minutes, he wouldn't make it.

He yanked the cloth from the next table, wadded it up, and pressed hard against the man's bullet wound. The front door slammed open and Cade ran inside with Matt's mike bag.

His friend laid the bag next to Matt, his gaze scanning the dining room, no doubt searching for his wife. "Sasha?"

"Behind the table." Matt inclined his head to where he'd left the women. "She's fine. Take care of the shooter?"

A grim look settled on Cade's face. "Both of them."

Two shooters. "Recognize them?"

"Nope. Took pictures and sent them to Z before I grabbed your bag."

"Matt, is it safe for us to come out now?" Delilah asked. "Sasha and I want to help if we can."

He longed to tell the women to stay put, but he believed the danger was over for now. "Go to the right side of the room. Stay away from the windows."

When restaurant patrons started to leave, Matt raised his voice to be heard over the growing din of conversation. "Everybody needs to stay in place. The cops will need your statements."

He turned to Cade. "Take over here. Don't let up on the pressure." When his partner took over, Matt returned to the leg wound with his bag. He thrust his hand into the mike bag and pulled out two pressure bandages. "Hang in there. Help's almost here."

Matt ripped the pant leg, used gauze to clean off the blood, and applied the bandages to the front and back of the bullet hole.

"How bad?" the man asked through gritted teeth.

"You'll be fine. Bullet went through muscle. Doesn't look like the slug hit the bone. You'll be good as new in a few weeks and have a scar to wow the ladies with."

A huff of laughter was the man's response. "You a doctor?"

"Medic."

The man's gaze sharpened. "Military?"

"Army. You?"

"Navy."

"Matt Rainer."

"David Montgomery."

"Good to meet you, David. Wish I could give you something for pain, but you should be at the hospital in a few minutes." He shifted his attention to the cut on his forehead. Blood was dripping into Montgomery's eye.

The injured vet grinned. "Can't say I like being shot, but this injury will keep me from attending a wedding tomorrow afternoon."

"Doesn't bother you to miss the festivities, huh?"

"Are you kidding? I hate weddings. I'm only in town because a brother-in-arms asked me to attend. Now I have a good excuse to beg off. How long will I be down?"

"Depends. What do you do for a living?"

"Cop."

"About 8 weeks. You'll be able to return to light duty in 3 weeks if you follow the doc's instructions."

Sharp eyes studied him a moment. "Do you always carry your mike bag?"

"Oh, yeah. Never know when I'll need to treat injuries or be deployed."

"You still active duty?"

"I'm with Fortress Security now."

Montgomery whistled. "Tough company to get into. Maddox still CEO?"

"You know the boss?"

"Know of him. He invited me to apply for a job."

Huh. "Why did you turn him down?"

"Needed to be home. Family crisis. Anyway, thanks for the help."

Matt pulled a card from his pocket and handed it to Montgomery. "If you change your mind about applying, call me. I'll put in a good word with Maddox." He clapped the vet on the shoulder and scanned for more injuries. At the next table, a woman had a napkin to her forehead to staunch the flow of blood from a cut. He knelt beside her chair. "I'm a medic. Let me see if I can help."

After examining the wound, he bandaged the cut. "You'll need to go to the hospital for a few stitches. You hurt anywhere else?"

"No. Thank you for helping me."

"Yes, ma'am."

The local law rushed into the restaurant, weapons drawn.

"We need the EMTs," Matt said. "Two gunshot victims, one critical."

"You a doctor?" the nearest cop said.

"Medic. The shooter never entered the restaurant."

One of the policemen went to the restaurant entrance and called out for the EMTs to bring two gurneys. A moment later, the medical personnel arrived.

Matt pointed at the man with the chest wound. "He's critical. You need to get him out of here." He directed the second set of EMTs to Montgomery. "Leg wound. A through-and-through. He's lost a lot of blood."

More EMTs spilled into the restaurant, and Matt went from table to table, assessing injuries while keeping tabs on Delilah and Sasha. Thankfully, the rest of the injuries were minor cuts and scrapes. Amazing considering the number of shots fired into the building.

By the time he finished the impromptu triage, Cade had seated Delilah and Sasha at the corner table with filled glasses in front of them and stood in front of them, blocking the women from view of anyone on the street.

Matt cleaned his hands, then carried his mike bag to the table. He sat beside Delilah. "Are you sure you're all right?"

"I'm not hurt. What you did here was amazing to watch."

He shrugged. "I'm trained for this."

"Still, I'm impressed."

At that moment, Miles Russell walked in. He zeroed in on the four of them and weaved through the tables to them. "You folks hurt?"

Matt shook his head.

"I guess you're the medic treating the injured and organizing the chaos."

"Guilty."

"Your aid was invaluable. Restaurant patrons and EMTs alike are singing your praises. Thanks for the assist." His eyes narrowed. "Now that the niceties are done, I have you four once again at the heart of an attack. My officers tell me there are two men dead on the street, one shot, center mass for each. You know anything about that?"

Cade slowly placed his Sig on the table. "You'll need this for comparison."

"You took down both shooters?"

"Yes, sir."

"Why didn't you wait for law enforcement to arrive?"

"Those clowns were shooting into a restaurant where my wife was sitting."

A frown. "I would have liked to question at least one of them."

Cade shrugged. "Training and too many civilians in the line of fire to draw out the confrontation. I won't apologize for protecting innocents, especially Sasha."

"Do I need to ask if you have a permit for the weapon?"

Again, the EOD man reached into his pocket. He pulled out his wallet and tossed his carry permit on the table.

Russell gave it a cursory glance. "Considering the trouble dogging you boys, do you have a backup weapon?" A smile was his answer. The cop snorted. "Should have known." He glanced over his shoulder to the knot of cops at the entrance. "I'll be back in a minute."

As soon as he was out of earshot, Delilah said, "This wasn't a random attack?"

Matt shook his head.

"I feel like this is my fault. The Baxters are a nice family. They were some of the few people in town who didn't make comments about my weight problem. They shouldn't have to suffer because of me."

"First, it's not your fault you have someone wanting you dead. Second, even though this isn't your responsibility, you have the resources to do something to alleviate the financial burden of repairs now if that's what you want to do."

Delilah stared. "Yes, I do, don't I?" She leaned closer. "I don't want people to know about the money. I have enough on my plate as it is without fending off people with their hands out every day."

"Send Zane a text and tell him what you want to do. He'll take care of the details anonymously."

As she tapped out a message to Zane on her phone, Russell returned, dragged a chair to their table, and sat. He took out a notebook and pen. He pointed at Cade. "I'll start with you."

Cade glanced at Matt who nodded. Russell needed as much information as they could provide. While Cade began his part of the story with the visit to the coffee shop, Matt stayed alert for more trouble. Aside from the speculative glances their direction, no one paid undue attention to them.

The detective turned his attention to Delilah. "You're next, Ms. Frost." And so it went until the cop was satisfied he'd gleaned all possible information from them. He eyed Matt. "Cops don't believe in coincidence."

A smile tugged at his lips. "We don't, either. Based on the angle of the shots, the shooters were aiming for us."

"I was afraid of that. What kind of trouble did you bring to Harmony, Ms. Frost?"

CHAPTER NINETEEN

"Do you know who the shooters were?" Delilah asked Detective Russell. She doubted he would have decided questioning witnesses was more important than seeing bodies at the crime scene.

"Two brothers. Ace and Cage Randolph." The cop's dark eyes observed and cataloged her shock. "I see you recognize the names."

"They're friends with my brother and cousins. They were at my house all the time when we were growing up."

"Any reason they want to hurt you?"

"I didn't have anything to do with them in school and haven't seen them in years."

His gaze assessed the others of their group. "What about the rest of you?"

"Never met them," Cade said.

"You have a personal stake in this, Matt. Any chance one of those boys was behind the attempt to shoot Ms. Frost last night?"

"You'll have to test their rifles."

His gaze sharpened. "How do you know they used rifles?"

"After years in the military and five in private security, I know the difference between shots fired from a rifle and a handgun."

"If you found out one of them was responsible for the attack on your girlfriend, would you act on that knowledge?"

Matt's expression darkened. "What do you think?"

Russell stood. "I guess that's all for now. Stop by the station tomorrow sometime." A wry smile curved his mouth. "I'll have your statements from last night's incident and this afternoon's ready to sign. You're free to go for now."

After the detective strode away, Matt stood, hauled his mike bag to his shoulder, and extended his hand to Delilah. "We'll find a restaurant close to the hotel or order room service."

Soon, Delilah was back in the SUV. Matt drove them out of town, taking many detours on the route to West Fork. Ninety minutes later, he parked in front of a steakhouse.

Her stomach knotted at the thought of eating after the carnage in Harmony.

"Side salad and at least four ounces of protein, sweetheart," Matt said quietly. "No matter how you feel right now, your body needs the fuel to function."

Delilah knew he was right. Didn't make her stomach any happier. She needed a gallon of chamomile tea and that might not be enough to rid her of the sick feeling in her stomach.

How did Matt handle casualties all the time? He didn't act as though the attack and the aftermath bothered him. That made her wonder about his military service and his job at Fortress.

The steakhouse hostess seated them once again in the corner of the restaurant. This time, however, Matt requested the corner away from the windows. After taking their orders, their waitress hurried off to give their choices to the kitchen.

"So, the Randolph brothers are friends with your family." Cade leaned against the cushioned back of the booth, his arm around Sasha. "Any of your relatives better friends with them than the others?"

"All five of them hung out together along with Sebastian Norris. They were thick as thieves back in the day." She spread her hands. "I have no idea if that is still true."

"We'll find out." Matt covered her hand with his. "Gives us a starting place."

When the waitress brought their food and drinks, Delilah managed to choke down her meal of a chicken breast and a side salad. Although she hated to admit it, she felt better when she walked out of the restaurant. At least, she wasn't as weak. Her stomach was still unsettled. Thankfully, the horrid shaking had stopped while Matt was driving to West Fork.

With a full stomach and feeling relatively safe again, fatigue weighed down her eyelids. Matt drove them to the hotel and Delilah soon found herself back in the suite.

When the door closed behind them, Matt drew her into his arms and held her tight. "Go rest for a few minutes. Adrenaline dump can leave you exhausted. You should be good to go in a couple hours."

"I can barely hold my eyes open."

He kissed her. "You're safe, Delilah. I'll make sure you stay that way."

When she woke two hours later, Delilah heard a rumble of voices in the living room. She put on her shoes, dragged a brush through her hair, and opened the door.

To her surprise, the rest of Bravo lounged around the living room. All but Liam, she corrected herself. He was at the French door, scanning the area for trouble.

The men turned at her entrance. Matt scanned Delilah's face. "You look more rested. How do you feel?"

"Better." She joined him on the couch. "What are you doing here?" she asked his teammates.

"Heard the action was here," Simon said. "Didn't want to miss out."

Delilah frowned. "How are you able to leave PSI? You're covering for Durango."

"Adam Walker's team needed to train for a mission. They agreed to cover for us at PSI while they train. If Maddox needs them, they'll deploy from Otter Creek," Trent said.

"We're a team and best friends," Simon added. "We have each other's backs. Matt's and Cade's priorities are protecting you and Sasha. We're here to help them and support you."

Liam glanced over his shoulder. "Because you're with Matt, you're one of us now. We take care of our own."

"I don't know what to say."

"You don't have to say anything." Trent turned to Matt. "We secured rooms across the hall. We'll coordinate the security watches to allow you and Cade more time to recharge. Tell me about this latest incident."

Between the four of them, they detailed the events at the restaurant and the aftermath.

"Classmates," Simon said, his voice thoughtful. "Did you have trouble with them in school, Delilah?"

Did she have to go into everything she'd been through in high school? The idea of baring her soul and weight issues to a bunch of super fit men filled her with dread. Matt wouldn't be happy that she hadn't told him and Detective Russell everything. Her cheeks burned with remembered embarrassment and shame.

"Delilah." Matt's soft voice brought her gaze to his. "There's something more?"

She nodded.

"Tell me what happened." His fingers entwined with hers.

"I've already told you the Randolphs and Sebastian Norris were close friends of my brother and cousins. You know how my family treated me during high school. Ace, Cage, and Sebastian were as bad as my family with their comments."

"Comments?" Trent rested his forearms on his knees as he leaned forward to hear Delilah better.

Delilah turned his direction.

Matt captured her chin between his thumb and forefinger and angled her head toward him. "Look at me." Although his gaze remained locked with hers, he addressed his team leader. "After the loss of her father, Delilah developed a weight problem. Since high school, this amazing woman has lost almost 200 pounds."

He stroked his thumb over her jawline. "Don't look anywhere else, just at me. Tell me the rest."

Man, she didn't want to talk about this, especially not in front of Matt's teammates.

"Every piece of information could be critical to figuring out who's targeting you and stopping them. You had the courage to totally change your life. A few sentences among friends who care about you is nothing compared to that."

He was right. Two minutes of discomfort was nothing compared to the degradation she'd suffered at the hands of the terrible trio of boys. She dug deep for that courage Matt insisted she had. "I stayed after school one day in the spring of my senior year. I tutored a girl who was failing English. Our session ran long and by the time we finished, the school was empty except for the janitorial staff. At least I thought it was empty."

Delilah closed her eyes a moment. "Ace, Cage, and Sebastian were still at school. They saw me walking toward the exit, cornered me, and shoved me into the bathroom. They said some ugly things." Her throat closed up at the memories flooding her mind.

Matt brushed his lips over hers in a brief caress. "Finish it," he whispered. "I need to know everything."

She dragged in a ragged breath and spilled the secret that had been hiding in the darkness since she was eighteen. "They stripped me to the skin and put their hands all over me, slapping, poking, and pinching, all the while making lewd remarks."

Rage filled Matt's gaze though his hold on her hands remained gentle. "Did they rape you?"

She shook her head. "I was afraid they would. Just before they left me crying on the floor of the bathroom, they said I was too fat and ugly for them to rape."

"Did you report them to the police?"

Another head shake. "I was mortified and wanted to forget the whole incident. I told my mother the bruises were from a fall at school."

"Did they ever touch you again?"

Delilah hesitated. "No."

"But?" Matt prompted.

"They threatened to if I told anyone. They said they'd tell everyone I begged them to touch me. It would have been their word against mine. Who wouldn't believe the sons of wealthy, prominent citizen leaders in Harmony over me?"

"They are part of the reason you didn't go back to Harmony after you left for college."

"A small part. I was too busy getting my degree, finding work in candle shops, and losing weight. I made a life, Matt, a good one. I might have been a victim at eighteen." Her chin lifted. "I'm not now and won't ever be again."

"Good for you, Delilah," Trent said, his voice rough and deep.

The medic slid his hand around her nape and pulled her against him. With her face pressed to his neck, Delilah couldn't see his reaction, but she could feel Matt's tense muscles even as his hand cupped her back of her head. "I know that was difficult. Thank you for telling me."

"It's a good thing the Randolphs are already dead." This from Liam, his voice ice cold.

"That still leaves Norris," Simon muttered.

Matt tightened his grip around Delilah. "He's mine."

CHAPTER TWENTY

Rage flooded Matt. The Randolphs and Norris terrorized the woman who was his heartbeat. No man should treat a woman with disrespect. For those clods to have touched and humiliated his woman was unacceptable. The Randolphs were out of his reach. Norris wasn't.

"Matt, no." Delilah raised her head to look at him, distress evident. "You can't. His father is the mayor of Harmony. The police chief is in Charles Norris's pocket. I don't want you in jail."

"We know how to scare people without leaving a mark," Simon said. "By the time Matt's finished with Norris, he won't forget he messed with the wrong woman."

"We have to talk to him." The pad of Matt's thumb brushed over Delilah's bottom lip. "He could be targeting you." His mind was made up. No one hurt his Delilah and got away with it.

"Don't expect me to bail you out of jail."

Amusement punched a hole in Matt's anger. "Understood." He turned to his teammates. "Have you eaten dinner yet?"

"We wanted a sit rep first," Trent said. "You have a suggestion?"

"The Blackwood Grill on West Main," Delilah said. "It's family run and serves great home-cooked meals."

"Sold." Simon rose. "Let's go. I'm starving."

Liam rolled his eyes. "When aren't you starving?"

"You aren't any better. Who wakes up at three in the morning to rummage through the refrigerator?"

Darkness filled Liam's gaze despite the smile. "I'm a growing boy. I need my calories because Trent runs us into the ground every day."

While the rest of Bravo ragged on the sniper in good-natured fun, Matt noticed the same concern in their eyes he felt himself. Something dark was eating at Liam, something haunting him deep in the night and in his dreams. They'd all been there and each of them dealt with the night demons in different ways. If Liam couldn't find a way to exorcise those demons, Bravo would lose him, either to the darkness or an enemy's bullet.

Delilah laid her hand on Matt's arm. "Do you think it's safe for us to go as well? Dad used to take me to the Blackwood Grill for my birthday every year."

Matt glanced at the sniper. "Liam?"

"I haven't noticed anything suspicious." He turned away from the French doors. "I'll check around the hotel."

"I'll go with you. We'll cover territory faster between the two of us." Simon followed his teammate out the door.

Within minutes, Matt received a text with the all-clear. In light of the attack at Baxter's, the operatives drove the two blocks to Blackwood Grill. This time, they ate their meal without incident.

After returning to the hotel and setting up watch shifts, Trent and Liam returned to their rooms. Simon took the first watch, sitting on a cushioned chair on the balcony.

"Sasha and I are going to turn in. I have the watch in four hours." Cade left with his wife.

"Wow. The room cleared fast." Delilah moved into the circle of Matt's arms. "What are you planning to do? I can watch a movie in my room if you're ready to sleep."

"I'm overdue to check in with Rod Kelter. After that, I planned to research Norris. You're not tired?"

"Not after a two-hour nap."

Matt also suspected she wasn't ready to be alone with her thoughts after the shooting at Baxter's. "Stay with me. I'd love your company." He could research Norris after Delilah went to bed.

She stepped back. "Let's call Rod. We don't want him in the dark."

They settled on the couch and called the Otter Creek detective.

"I was just getting ready to call you, Matt," Rod said. His voice sounded grim.

"Why?"

"Nick is working a vandalism call at Wicks."

Delilah stiffened. "Is Piper all right?"

"She wasn't at the store."

"How much damage?" Matt asked.

"Brick thrown through the front window. Knocked over several candles in jars, too. Spray paint on the bricks in front of the building."

"No one saw anything?"

"Afraid not. Wicks isn't on the town square. The rest of the businesses in the area had closed for the night and that section of Otter Creek is a ghost town after six o'clock. A teenager who took a shortcut home saw the damage and called it in. Nick will look for security footage in the area, but that will take a while. Our tech pool isn't as deep as the one at Fortress."

"Want me to run the search through Fortress?"

"We have to follow the letter of the law. However, we can't stop you from doing your own research."

Matt chuckled. "You want the results?"

"My brother-in-law would appreciate all the help he can get. Since Wicks is one of Madison's favorite shops, this one is personal for him."

"What about my shop, Rod?" Delilah gripped Matt's free hand. "When will I be able to reopen?"

"Day after tomorrow. You need to replace the display window. Right now, Nick and the crime scene team are in the shop. When they leave, the shop won't be secured."

A phone call to a senior trainee would fix the problem temporarily. "I'll take care of that." Matt frowned. "Do you think bored teens or kids caused the damage?"

"We haven't had vandalism reports in several weeks. I wouldn't rule it out, but it seems unlikely."

"Does Nick know when the vandalism occurred?"

"Between eight and ten o'clock. What do you have to report?"

The detective listened in silence as Matt and Delilah gave him the latest news. "How much money did your mother win from the lottery, Delilah?"

"According to her letter, $216 million. She took the lump sum payout and invested the money after paying off the house, all the bills she and Randy accumulated as well as my brother's and my cousins' debts. Mom's letter said within a month of settling everyone's bills, the four men racked up twice as much debt as she'd paid off. That's when she realized they couldn't be trusted with the money and started paying them a large allowance each month. Six months before her death, she changed her will to give me responsibility for the money."

"If you die, who gets the money?"

"It's divided between the four men."

A soft whistle from Rod. "That's a lot of incentive to come after you."

"I know."

Matt hated the fear in her voice. As long as he had breath in his body, no one would harm Delilah again.

"Matt, have your tech people at Fortress dig into Oliver Shannon. Watch your back, my friend. That amount of money makes people desperate."

CHAPTER TWENTY-ONE

After he ended the call to Rod, Matt wrapped his arm around Delilah's shoulders. "Doesn't sound like the damage to Wicks is too extensive."

"I need to be in Otter Creek." She laid her head on his shoulder.

"Let me make a couple calls. We'll have Wicks open for business as soon as Nick gives the okay."

"I have to call my insurance agent. He'll want to take pictures of the store before the damage is repaired. I don't know how long it will take for the company to approve the repairs. Then I have to find someone willing to take it on. You know how busy the remodeling experts are right now."

A fair point. Otter Creek was in the middle of a building boom and construction crews in the area were stretched thin. "I'll cover the cost of repairs. You can repay me when the insurance company ponies up the funds. Don't worry about finding someone to do the work. I have a friend at PSI who can do it. Leave a message on your agent's phone. If you want to talk to him, give him the Fortress number."

"Won't my number show when I call?"

Matt shook his head. "The screen shows a blocked caller, and Zane's program prevents the agent from seeing the number to return your call."

Delilah glanced at her watch. "It's not that late. Gene is a night owl. I'll call him at home." She tapped in her insurance agent's number from memory.

How well did she know this guy and how old was he?

"Gene, it's Delilah. Sorry to call you at home. I need your help." She explained about the vandalism and the police presence at her store.

Matt listened to her side of the conversation without saying a word or moving a muscle until Delilah's breath caught and her body tensed.

"Dinner Friday night? It's sweet of you to ask, but I'm dating someone. I don't think he'd appreciate me having dinner with another man." Gentle humor colored her voice. "Matt Rainer, a trainer at PSI." A pause. Her gaze locked with his. "Yes, it's serious."

Definitely serious. Matt brushed his lips over hers in a light caress.

"I appreciate you taking care of the paperwork as fast as possible. Contact Detective Nick Santana to set up a time to take pictures tomorrow. Friends of Matt will be repairing the damage to the store."

When she ended the call, Delilah slid the phone into her pocket, still watching him.

"He's been interested in you for a while."

A nod.

"Have you gone out with Gene?"

She shook her head. "He's good looking, wants a large family, works a steady job, is involved in his church, and loves Cajun food. Most would say he was perfect."

"Why did you turn him down?" Matt hadn't given her a reason to pass up a date with another man, a fact he would regret for a long time.

"He wasn't you. I haven't wanted anyone except you since you moved to Otter Creek."

Unable to resist, he pulled her tight against his chest and kissed her, long and deep. Matt came up for air minutes later and was gratified to note Delilah's breathing was as erratic as his own. Nice to know he wasn't the only one skating the edge of control.

Mindful of their centralized location, Matt eased her back to his side and grabbed the remote.

"You're not going to research Sebastian."

He chuckled. "Wouldn't do me any good right now, Delilah. The chemistry between us is off the charts. I need to clear my head first."

He found a mystery series Delilah liked and gave himself time to slow his racing heart and calm his rioting emotions.

By the thirty-minute mark, the woman in his arms was sound asleep. Moving carefully, Matt carried Delilah into her room and tucked a blanket around her. He left the bathroom light on so she could see if she woke in the middle of the night again. He expected her to awaken in a few hours. Nights were the worst for him because his mind was unguarded. Memories held at bay during the daylight hours resurfaced and slammed into him with a vengeance when he slept.

He returned to the living room and glanced at the clock. Liam would want to know about the vandalism at Wicks. Hoping the other man was asleep, he sent his teammate a text with the details.

Within seconds, Liam responded that he would check on Piper immediately. His friend had it bad for Delilah's perky shop assistant.

Matt messaged Zane, asking him to run deep background checks on Oliver Shannon, Sebastian Norris, and Ace and Cage Randolph, and for him to hack into the security and traffic cams in the area around Wicks. That done, he booted up his laptop to do his own research.

By the time Cade entered the living room to take over the watch from Simon, Matt had unearthed some interesting tidbits of information about Norris and the Randolphs.

"I thought you'd be asleep by now." His friend strode to the kitchen to pour coffee into a mug.

"Too much on my mind."

Cade sat on the arm of the couch. "Something happen while I was asleep?"

Matt told him about the vandalism at Wicks.

After Matt relayed the information about Wicks, Bravo's EOD man scowled. "How much damage?"

"Don't know yet. I planned to call Gator in a few minutes, have him assess the damage so I can take care of the repairs." Gator was a trainer at PSI, a former full-time operative at Fortress who'd suffered a leg injury on a mission that prevented him from returning to the field. His family owned a contracting business specializing in remodeling homes. Gator had worked in the family business from the time he was ten years old until he joined the police force and ultimately the FBI, then Fortress. He'd know what materials would be needed for the Wicks repairs.

Cade's eyebrows rose. "Won't her insurance cover the cost?"

"She needs to be open for business before the insurance paperwork clears. I can help her do that." Anything to take pressure off Delilah was worth the cost of repairs to him.

"Your woman is loaded, Matt. The repairs to Wicks won't even put a dent in her account."

He grinned. "I know. She's forgotten that fact."

"Gator will do the repairs himself if you ask."

147

"That's the plan. Didn't think he'd be awake until about now." Gator didn't sleep much after midnight.

Cade stood. "I'll relieve Simon."

Matt closed his laptop and grabbed his cell phone. A moment later, the PSI instructor answered. "It's Matt. I need a favor."

"Name it. I'll get it done."

"Wicks was hit by vandals earlier tonight. Swing by the shop, assess the damage, and, take care of the repairs. I'm out of town with Delilah or I would do it myself."

"Cops give you an idea of the damage?"

"Brick through a display window, broken jars, and graffiti on the brick facade outside the shop."

"I'll take care of it. Deadline?"

"Santana should release the scene sometime tomorrow. Wicks needs to be ready for business by Friday morning."

"That's doable. I'll contact the detective for permission to measure the display window. Got a friend who works at the glass company outside Otter Creek and owes me a favor. If the cops are finished processing the scene outside the shop, I'll power wash the graffiti from the exterior tomorrow after work. I need access to the shop to replace the window Thursday night."

"I'll get in touch with Piper Reece, Delilah's assistant, and let her know to expect a call from you."

"Good enough. How soon will you return?"

"Don't know yet. There are complications."

A wry laugh came over the speaker. "Aren't there always? Let me know if you need anything else. Later."

Simon and Cade walked in from the balcony. "Everything set with Gator?" Cade asked.

"He's on board." He glanced at Simon. "Have Liam tell Piper that Gator will contact her tomorrow. He needs access to Wicks to replace the display window."

"Will do." A moment later, his teammate left to return to his and Liam's room.

Standing at the French door, Cade said, "Anything else happen while I slept?"

"I researched Norris and the Randolphs. Found some interesting things in their backgrounds. Norris has a sealed juvie record."

"You hack the file?"

"Tried, failed. I'll ask Z to check it tomorrow. Norris had several domestic assault complaints swept under the rug."

Cade turned, a frown on his face. "He beat his wife?"

"And his kids."

"A real prince. Who covered up the assaults?"

"Police chief talked to the judge and convinced him to mandate an anger management class every time."

"Nice." His friend glanced over his shoulder. "Any more on Norris?"

"He's cheating on his wife and girlfriend."

A snort. "Figures."

"He's also a deacon in his church and a pillar of the Harmony community who champions the local pet shelter."

"Regular chameleon."

"Oh, yeah. The Randolphs aren't much better. Ace did a nickel in the state pen for nearly killing a man who cheated him in a game of poker. He was eighteen at the time. He kept in touch with his lowlife cellmates after his release. He had minor skirmishes with the law although there are rumors he was involved with the drug trade. No one pinned anything on him but he never ran out of cash despite a lack of work."

"And Cage?"

"Another prize. He was the guest of the state for three years for embezzling funds from the repair shop he worked for. When he was released, he found work with a lawn care business for a while. Despite the job paying minimum wage, Cage also had plenty of money at his disposal and he wasn't shy about spreading cash around at the bars and with various women. After six months, he quit the lawn care business and never found other work."

"Drug trade?"

Matt shrugged. "He's the one who introduced his big brother to the easy money."

"And the cops never figured out these two clowns were the source of the drug supply in town?"

"They're Sebastian's friends and his father ran interference for them. The Randolphs had a free pass in Harmony."

Cade shook his head. "Ethan Blackhawk would have tossed them in jail and lost the key."

Otter Creek's police chief never turned a blind eye to crime, no matter who was guilty or who asked for favored treatment. Scrupulously honest, the Army Ranger honored his calling to uphold the law.

"Will you have Z look deeper into their backgrounds?"

"Already sent him a text. I didn't want to call in case he was asleep."

"Seems as though Zane is always on duty." Cade retraced his steps to the kitchen for more coffee. "You should rest, Matt. You may not have much time to sleep before Delilah wakes."

Matt set aside his computer and stretched out on the couch, a pillow under his head. "We didn't have a chance to return to Shannon's office tonight."

"I'm sure he'll understand in light of the attack on Baxter's. A few hours won't make much difference."

Turning onto his side, Matt allowed himself to drop into a light sleep, wondering how soon the attacks on Delilah would escalate. He didn't believe for one second the Randolphs masterminded the attacks. He had to unmask the person pulling the strings from the shadows before Delilah paid the ultimate price.

CHAPTER TWENTY-TWO

Delilah woke with a start. Disoriented, she glanced around the darkened room. She remembered watching television with Matt. He must have carried her to bed.

Heart still pounding from a nightmare about the shooting at Baxter's, Delilah checked the time and winced. Three o'clock. Too much adrenaline buzzed through her veins to sleep. Might as well get up.

She swung her legs over the side of the bed, zipped through a shower, and dressed. Delilah opened the door to the living room.

"What's wrong, sweetheart?"

Matt's sleep-roughened voice sent chill bumps surging over her skin. How could he make three words sound sexy? Easy. The words came from Matt. "Nightmare. Go back to sleep. I'll make tea and read or something."

"I take over the watch in an hour." He sat up and held out his hand. "Sit with me."

Feeling guilty for interrupting his sleep again but needing his arms around her to chase memories away, she curled up beside him. "I'm sorry."

"I expected you to wake up about now, Delilah. When traumatic events like the attack at Baxter's occur, our minds replay everything over and over, trying different scenarios to change the outcome. It's a coping mechanism that fades over time."

"Will it disappear?"

"Not totally. Other things will bring the memories back."

"Another attack?" Man, she hoped never to experience something like that again. If Delilah was an operative, she'd never sleep again. She didn't have the personality to be a black ops soldier.

"Not necessarily. Could be a scent or sound. A car backfiring or firecrackers might remind you of those few minutes in the restaurant."

"Fantastic. I'm like a bomb waiting to explode."

Matt kissed the top of her head. "It will improve."

"How do you deal with this all the time? I'd never sleep again."

He chuckled. "I work out. Ask Josh Cahill how many times he rolled up alongside me at three in the morning because memories plagued me."

Durango's team leader was also an Otter Creek police officer who loved to work the night shift. "What I'm experiencing is normal?"

"Absolutely." He picked up the remote.

"You don't have to turn on the television for me. Try to sleep. I'll sit quietly with you."

"White noise stops the loop running in your head. I'll take a nap while you watch something." Matt handed her the remote. "If you need me, promise you'll nudge me awake."

Not unless she had to. "I promise."

The medic shifted her closer, rested his head against the back of the couch, and dropped off to sleep.

Delilah wished she could do the same. With a soft sigh, she turned on the television with the sound low, and found a station running episodes of a favorite cozy mystery series.

Instead of falling asleep, she divided her attention between watching the television and Matt. An hour later, he stirred, tightened his grip on her, and captured Delilah's mouth in a series of long, deep kisses.

"Good morning," he murmured when he eased back. "I like waking this way."

"Scrunched up on the couch?" He couldn't be comfortable.

"With you in my arms." Another kiss. "You're highly addictive, Ms. Frost."

"So are you, Mr. Rainer."

Cade walked in from the balcony, nodded at Delilah, and returned to his room.

Matt went to the kitchen and poured a mug of coffee. "Want tea?"

"Please. Will I distract you if I sit here while you're on watch?"

He winked at her. "As long as you don't steal kisses, I'll be fine."

Delilah smiled. "There goes my plan to pass the time until Sasha's awake."

With a soft laugh, he placed a mug of water with a tea bag into the microwave and started the heating cycle. A minute later, he handed her the mug and took up his watch at the French doors. "Would you like to sit outside with me?"

"Tempting offer. Is it safe?"

"We haven't seen signs our location is compromised."

Delilah carried her tea to the outdoor sofa to sit with Matt. By the time the sun rose, Sasha was in the kitchen pouring herself a mug of coffee and brewing another pot.

She wandered out to the balcony. "I assume nothing happened overnight."

"Wish I could say yes to that." Delilah told her about the vandalism at Wicks.

"Are you going home?"

"I have responsibilities to fulfill first. I hate depending on Piper and Matt's friends to clean up the mess."

Sasha sat nearby and patted Delilah's hand. "Extenuating circumstances. They understand."

For a woman with no friends during high school, the number of friends in her life now was a miracle. Delilah's gaze shifted to Matt. In a million years, she never would have dreamed a man like Matt would be interested in her.

He kissed her lightly. "What do you need to do today besides drop by the lawyer's office and the police station?"

"My stepfather should be out of the house by now. I need to see what I'm facing to prepare the house to sell. Do you want to talk to my brother, cousins, and Sebastian?"

He nodded. "Don't know if we can talk to all of them today."

"Sounds like more than a full day."

A knock sounded on the suite door. Matt stood. "Delilah, you and Sasha go into your room until I know it's safe."

Once they were in place, he eased his weapon from the holster at his back and opened the door a crack. When he swung the door wide, Delilah breathed a sigh of relief.

Trent, Liam, and Simon walked inside.

Matt indicated the room service menu on the breakfast bar. "Order breakfast for all of us, Trent. Delilah and I need to go to Harmony this morning."

"What do you want us to do while you're gone?"

"Surveillance on our primary suspects. We can't cover all five of them, though."

"Go shower, then tell us what happened overnight."

Matt glanced at Delilah. "Okay if I use your bathroom? I don't want to wake Cade."

"Of course."

He grabbed his bag and closed himself into her room.

"All right, ladies." Liam handed them the menu. "Choose what you want. We'll order for the rest of us."

Delilah and Sasha perused the menu, made their selections, and handed the menu to the operatives. In short order, Trent called in their choices.

"Did you talk to Piper last night?" Delilah asked Liam.

He nodded. "She was shaken up by the vandalism." His hands fisted. "I wish I was in town to help."

"We all do," Simon said. "Gator will take care of the repair work and Piper."

That brought a scowl to the sniper's face. "That doesn't make me feel better."

His friend gave an unrepentant grin. "You better step up your game, buddy. You know Gator's a ladies' man."

Liam grabbed his phone and went to the balcony, closing the door behind him.

"And my matchmaking job's finished for the day." Simon slid onto a barstool.

Trent shook his head. "Gator won't be happy if Liam punches him in the nose for moving on Piper."

"Our boy shouldn't have delayed this long. Gator's not the only man from PSI interested in the lady. I'm trying to nudge Liam before he loses his chance."

Trent snorted. "You can't resist interfering. One of these days, that habit will bite you."

Matt returned, dropping his bag by the bedroom door.

Bravo's team leader pointed at the couch. "Park it, Rainer, and give us an update." The rest of his teammates ranged themselves around the room with Liam on the balcony, keeping watch, phone pressed to his ear.

The medic sat with Delilah and summarized what he'd learned about Wicks from Detective Kelter. "I also sent a request to Z for more in-depth research on Delilah's family and Sebastian Norris."

"What's your gut say?" Trent asked.

Matt shook his head. "Could be any of them. I doubt Holloway's involved. Yeah, he's a sleaze for cheating on Michelle. That doesn't make him a killer. He's also in terrible shape to have broken into Delilah's house and hurt her."

"Could have hired someone to do it," Simon pointed out. "Maybe the Randolphs if they were in good enough shape."

Delilah shuddered at the possibility one of the Randolph boys put his hands on her. Matt's hold tightened.

"Their prints are in the system. If they hurt Delilah and left a print or DNA in her house, Rod will find it."

"What about the shop? Who was responsible for the vandalism?"

Matt glanced down at her. "Could still be kids."

"But you don't believe that."

He shook his head. "Hopefully, Nick will find evidence to pinpoint the person responsible for the damage to Wicks."

Simon shook his head. "Wouldn't hold your breath. All he or she had to do was wear gloves. I doubt he'll find anything."

"The traffic and security cams might give us something to go on," Trent said. "If there's anything to find, Zane will get it."

After breakfast, the operatives scattered to their surveillance posts while Cade, Sasha, Matt, and Delilah drove to Harmony. Matt dropped off Cade and Sasha near Sebastian's house to keep watch. Easy enough to do since the man lived in a brownstone across from the coffee shop. The Ramseys would watch his place while they drank coffee and ate a snack.

Matt parked in front of the law office. Ms. Walters looked up when they entered, a smile curving her mouth as her gaze skimmed over Matt.

"Mr. Rainer. Welcome back. What can I get for you?" Her voice came out sultry.

Based on her expression and the glint in the woman's eyes, Delilah had no doubt what Shannon's assistant was offering.

"The forms for Delilah to sign, Ms. Walters."

"Call me Cynthia." She trailed her fingers from her neck to her plunging neckline.

To Matt's credit, his gaze remained locked on the woman's face. "The forms?"

Brows beetling, Ms. Walters rose from her chair. "Wait here." She walked past them, deliberately brushing against Matt as she left the receptionist area.

"I might need a whip and a chair," he murmured. "I feel like a juicy steak in front of a starving lion."

A moment later, Shannon's assistant returned. "Mr. Shannon will see you now."

Giving her a wide berth, Matt cupped Delilah's elbow as they walked to the lawyer's inner office. After a quick knock, he opened the door and ushered Delilah inside.

"Ms. Frost, Mr. Rainer." Shannon gestured toward the chairs in front of his desk. "I expected you last evening."

"We were in Baxter's when shots were fired yesterday," Matt said. "Once the police allowed us to leave, I was more concerned with getting Delilah to safety than signing papers."

Blood drained from the lawyer's face. "Were you injured?"

Delilah shook her head. "We're fine, thanks to Matt and his friend."

"I understand the Randolph brothers were killed."

"They were the ones shooting."

"Why do something like that? There must be some mistake."

"No mistake." Matt curved his fingers around Delilah's. "They deliberately fired into Baxter's several times with rifles. More importantly, those two clowns were aiming for Delilah. You wouldn't know anything about that, would you?"

A scowl. "Of course not. Are you accusing me, Mr. Rainer?"

"I'm asking questions."

"Your questions are highly offensive to me."

"My priority is Delilah's safety, not your feelings."

"Careful. Remember I am a lawyer. I'm not above filing a suit against you."

"If you don't have anything to hide and you're not a danger to Delilah, you have nothing to worry about."

"What possible motive could I have for trying to hurt Ms. Frost?"

"I can count more than $200 million of them. What's your personal financial situation like?"

"None of your business."

"You might want to rethink your stance. Delilah has been attacked four times in the past three days. If you're not involved, you might want to watch your back. Everyone connected to her is a potential target. Tell me, Mr. Shannon, do you know how to protect yourself? Are you aware of your surroundings? If you aren't, you should be for the sake of your health."

"Is that a threat?" Shannon sounded outraged.

"Not from me. But someone is determined to hurt Delilah. I don't think it's a coincidence that she's handed the responsibility for her mother's estate the same week that she becomes a target. If you're not careful, you might become one as well."

CHAPTER TWENTY-THREE

Matt watched the old lawyer swallow hard. Shannon had to know the money might be the source of Delilah's problems. The violent response to Michelle's will was evidence emotions ran hot. "You're positive you don't have anything to tell me, Mr. Shannon?"

"Don't be ridiculous. I know nothing about the attacks on your girlfriend."

"If you think of anything, no matter how small, tell me. Do you have Delilah's papers ready to sign?"

With a frown, Shannon opened the manila folder on his desk. He turned the document around and slid the paper toward Delilah with a pen. "Sign on the bottom, please."

After she signed her name, the lawyer picked up the paper and left the office.

"Nothing like alienating the one person who was glad to see me when I arrived in town."

Matt raised Delilah's hand to his lips and kissed her knuckles. "Better to let him know he hasn't escaped my attention as a suspect. If he's our man, we'll find the evidence and turn him over to the cops."

"What if he comes after us before that happens?"

"I'll take care of him. No one harms what's mine."

Shannon returned with an envelope. "Two copies of the signed document, checks for your mother's main account, account information for the rest of the accounts and investments, and a debit card. Take one of the copies to the bank so they'll know you're taking over the accounts."

"One question," Delilah said as she accepted the envelope. "Does the will stipulate how I pay the allotted money to my family?"

He shook his head.

"What about the timing of the payments? Would it be legal to pay the five years of allotments at one time?"

His eyebrows rose. "I see no reason why you can't. Are you sure you want to? They haven't proved themselves as competent money managers."

"If one of them is responsible for the attempts on my life, I'd rather give Matt and his friends time to identify the culprit." She smiled. "And they will identify the man responsible."

Shannon tossed Matt a look of derision. "You have much faith in a man who hasn't managed to find answers to this point. Perhaps your faith is misguided, Ms. Frost."

"You don't know the resources at Matt's disposal. Fortress never gives up on a mission. These men don't fail. In this case, the mission is personal."

"What difference does that make?" Shannon looked perplexed.

"It means I'm invested in her protection and more dangerous than you can imagine." Matt rose and extended his hand to Delilah. "Expect a forensic accountant to contact your office shortly. You will provide total access to Michelle Holloway's financial records."

The lawyer stiffened. "Are you insinuating I stole money from Mrs. Holloway?"

"Someone is desperate to keep Delilah from fulfilling her responsibilities."

"Perhaps the problem stems from her new home. After all, Ms. Frost hasn't lived in Harmony for years."

"I'm looking into that as well. If you've done nothing wrong, you should have no problem giving full access to the accountant."

The old man lifted his chin. "I'll need the accountant's name before I turn over that volume of sensitive information to him."

Matt smiled. "Her name is Kira Brody. Expect to hear from her within the hour."

"Very well." He turned his gaze to Delilah. "I assume you're in favor of this ridiculous waste of time. If you need anything else, feel free to contact me. Good day to you both."

As dismissals went, this one was civil if cold. Matt escorted Delilah from the office and onto the street. "The police station is two blocks away. Drive or walk?"

"Walk. The weather's perfect and I haven't exercised for days."

He turned her toward the police station. "With cracked ribs, running or swimming will be painful. How is the tape on your side?"

"Starting to peel."

"When the tape becomes annoying, let me know. I'll help you remove it or you can ask Sasha to give you a hand." His cell phone buzzed with a text message. Matt checked the screen and called Zane. "What do you have for me?"

"Can you talk freely?"

"I'm walking to the police station with Delilah."

"Zach Frost is in deep to a bookie from New Jersey. Name's Joey Petrelli. He has a stable of leg breakers he uses to persuade people who owe him money to pay up. All would use Delilah to pressure Zach."

Matt frowned. "Why her? She hasn't contacted him in years."

"None of the women Zach dated lasted more than a few weeks."

"Sounds like he took a page from his stepfather's black book. How much does Zach owe?"

"Fifty thousand."

Matt whistled. "Why did Petrelli let the tab run that high?"

"Good old Zach was good for the cash since Mama was flush. When Mrs. Holloway's health failed in the last three months, Zach made more trips than normal to Atlantic City to escape from Harmony and his sick mother. Petrelli let the tab accumulate because Zach convinced the bookie he would inherit a fourth of the estate."

Had he known about the provisions in Michelle's new will? If he did, that would explain the attack on Delilah before she knew about her mother's illness and will. If they found proof Zach was behind all this, Delilah would be devastated. Treating her with disrespect as a teenager was one thing. Betrayal by a blood relative was a whole different level of pain, especially now that Michelle was gone.

"What else?"

"Holloway is blowing up the Internet with rants about his dead wife and money-grubbing stepdaughter. The gist is he's been cheated out of his rightful inheritance by Delilah. He's the wronged party with a broken heart and an empty wallet."

"Threats?"

"Nothing specific. The usual crap about how she'll get what's coming to her one of these days."

Matt blew out a breath, frustrated with the lack of information from that quarter. "Where did he land?"

Zane chuckled. "I'm glad you asked. He's staying with his current girlfriend for right now. I found rumors of her discontent with the dating arrangement before Holloway moved in. I think she might be interested in someone else but hasn't made a move that direction yet. My guess is she won't put up with Holloway sponging off her for long. He has a few hundred dollars in his account at the moment. Mrs. Holloway died before she authorized the standard monthly allowance for the men in her family."

"That has to hurt."

"What hurts more is he planned to take a cruise around the world when his wife passed away. The plans were made without being booked because no one knew when his wife would die. The arrangements were for two."

"Is the second ticket for the current squeeze?"

"Found her name in the travel agency's computer along with Holloway's. Next on my list of information is Norris. He's something else."

"Tell me."

"I poked around in his juvie file. Norris was arrested for sexual assault and attempted rape four times. Never went to trial because the charges were dropped each time."

Matt growled. "He went after Delilah when she was a senior in high school."

"How did he get away with the assaults?" Zane demanded. "According to the police files, the cops had him cold on the assaults."

"His father is the mayor of Harmony."

"Ah. That explains the reluctance to prosecute this clown. He married his high school sweetheart right after graduation. Had a couple kids. The family relationship is rocky. The cops have been called to his house multiple times for domestic abuse. No jail time if he attended anger management class."

And this creep had touched Matt's woman. His hand tightened around the cell phone. "You said house. Did you mean brownstone? He has a place in downtown Harmony."

"That's because his wife filed for divorce and kicked him out of their home on the outskirts of Harmony."

Matt pressed his hand against Delilah's back as they climbed the stairs to the police station. "We're at the station. Anything else that can't wait until I'm in a more secure location?"

"The Frosts, the Randolphs, and Norris and a man named Donovan Cain all belong to a hunting club. Very exclusive. They also participated in shooting tournaments and won awards."

He scowled. "How did lowlifes like the Randolphs become part of an exclusive organization?"

"Probably their connection to Norris. Watch your back, Matt. The Randolphs might be gone, but that leaves six other dangerous men who have good reason to target your girl."

Matt gave Delilah a summary of the information from Zane, then escorted her into the station and asked for Detective Russell. Within a couple minutes, Russell appeared with a folder under his arm and motioned for them to follow him through the double doors. Instead of stopping at a desk, the policeman led them through the bullpen, down a hall, and into a room with a mirror, wooden table, four chairs, and a camera mounted in the corner of the ceiling.

"You brought us to an interrogation room." Matt seated Delilah before taking the chair beside hers. If the detective thought he would catch them in a lie, he was in for a disappointment.

"Camera's off and the observation room is empty. I checked before I came for you." The detective sat and opened the folder. He handed them their statements and tossed a couple pens on the table. "Read your statements. If they're correct and you haven't thought of anything else to add, sign them."

When they slid the papers back to Russell, the cop withdrew another sheaf of papers. "The ME sent Mrs. Holloway's autopsy report."

The grim expression on the detective's face told Matt the results before he'd said a word.

"Did Mom die of natural causes?"

Russell shook his head. "I'm sorry, Ms. Frost, but your mother died of suffocation."

CHAPTER TWENTY-FOUR

Delilah stared at the Harmony detective after his shocking revelation. She and Matt had walked in on her stepfather standing over her mother with a pillow in his beefy hands. Maybe her first instinct had been correct. Was it possible Randy murdered his wife?

"You need to talk to Randy Holloway." Matt wrapped his hand around Delilah's.

Russell's gaze sharpened. "Why?"

"When we walked into Michelle's hospital room, we found Holloway standing over his wife with a pillow in his hands while the monitors were going off."

"That won't be enough for a conviction. I need proof or a confession, but I'll bring him in for questioning. Maybe he'll have something to get off his chest."

"Check hospital security cams." If Holloway wasn't guilty, the cameras should show who entered the room before Delilah's stepfather.

"I know how to do my job, Rainer." Russell shoved back from the table and stood. "You're free to go. Tell Ramsey and his wife to come sign their statements. If I'm not here, one of the other detectives in the bullpen will have access to them." Russell stalked from the room.

Delilah sat back, dismayed at the final exchange with Russell. "We're making enemies in Harmony."

"I don't care if Holloway and Shannon are angry. Russell, however, isn't used to outsiders making suggestions. Wouldn't matter if we were federal law enforcement. He'd still resent us. It's worse because I'm in private security."

"Even though he knows the quality of Fortress operatives?"

"He's territorial. Can't say that I blame him." A pointed look at her. "I'm territorial about you and your safety. I don't trust the police to keep you safe."

"I want him to find out who killed my mother. Do you think Randy is guilty?"

"It appears that way."

"But you're not satisfied with that explanation."

He shrugged. "Too easy. I think someone is setting up your stepfather for your mother's murder." Matt stood. "Let's get out of here. I'll treat you to a cup of tea, then we'll visit Norris."

Her stomach knotted as she followed Matt from the interrogation room. The last thing she wanted to do was confront the man who played a major role in the worst day of her life.

The coffee shop was bustling with customers again. Sasha waved at them from a corner table. Delilah and Matt weaved through the tables filled with animated customers sipping hot or cold drinks and nibbling on pastries.

"The special today is iced strawberry green tea," Sasha told Delilah. "It's fantastic. I'd love to add this combination to my shop."

"It sounds great."

Matt seated her. "I'll get one for you. Do you need chamomile mint as well?"

How did he know? She must have a flashing neon sign on her forehead. Either that or he was incredibly observant. "Both, please."

He bent and brushed a kiss over her lips, then eyed his friend. "Need a refill?"

Cade nodded. "What about you, Sasha?"

"I want to try the iced green tea with orange."

As Matt walked to the order counter, Cade said, "Everything okay, Delilah? You seem upset."

"In the space of an hour, I've ticked off my mother's lawyer and the police detective investigating her death."

"Takes talent to accomplish that much in a short time."

"Ha ha. By the way, Detective Russell wants you and Sasha to stop by the station to sign your statements. Do yourselves a favor and don't antagonize the man. He's already angry at me and Matt."

"What happened?" Sasha gripped Delilah's hand. "You don't rattle easy and it's obvious something has shaken you."

Delilah leaned closer to her friends to keep from having to speak over the din of the crowd and attract unwanted attention. "Mom's autopsy results are in. She was smothered to death."

Cade frowned. "Your stepfather?"

"Russell is bringing him in for questioning, but Matt doesn't think he's guilty. He says it's too easy."

"He's not the only suspect. Wouldn't be wise to focus exclusively on him."

Matt returned to their table with a tray of drinks. "Delilah tell you the latest?"

"Yeah." Cade shook his head. "Hope the cops look at all the players."

"They have cause to explore further."

"Zane got back to you?"

Matt summarized the information he'd learned.

"You want us to stay on Norris?" Cade's lips curved. "Sasha is becoming good friends with the coffee shop owner so I doubt she'll mind if we stay here."

"Go sign your statements. After that, visit a few shops and strike up conversations. I'd like to know if the Frosts are friends with anyone besides Norris and Cain. Delilah and I will track down Norris."

Cade inclined his head toward the office building across the street to the right. "He went to work twenty minutes ago. He's on the fourth floor, suite 410." He grinned. "Tori, the coffee shop owner, doesn't mind chatting with Sasha between waves of customers."

Matt chuckled. "Guess you won't need to leave the shop to strike up conversations."

"I'll see what I can find out on Tori's next break." Sasha sipped her tea and closed her eyes. "This is another winner. You'll like this one, Delilah."

"I'll have to try that tomorrow."

After she finished her mint tea, she glanced at Matt. "I'm ready to go. The sooner we confront Norris, the better."

Matt swallowed the last of his coffee and gathered empty cups to toss in the trash. When he returned, he crouched by Delilah's side. "If you want to stay here with the Ramseys, I can talk to Norris myself." An edgy smile curved his lips. "I'd prefer to talk to him alone."

She longed to take him up on his offer. Couldn't, though. Not if she wanted to keep her self-respect. "I'm not a scared teenager anymore." She was a terrified adult with a big, bad black ops soldier by her side. No matter what happened, she would handle whatever came. She'd come too far to back down now. Matt wouldn't allow Sebastian to touch her again.

"You're a strong, capable woman. A worm like Norris doesn't stand a chance against your strength of will and courage. You have the right to confront him and I won't take that from you. I'll support whatever you decide."

His belief in her boosted her confidence to another level. She could do this. No, Delilah had to do this. She turned to Sasha and Cade. "We'll return soon."

"Want me to keep your strawberry drink for you?" Sasha asked.

Delilah nodded. "Thanks."

She and Matt crossed the street and entered the red brick building. Matt steered her toward the stairs to the right of the lobby. On the fourth floor, they walked a long, carpeted hallway until they found the right suite.

Delilah's mouth gaped when she saw the sign on the door. Sebastian had founded a charitable foundation for children. Interesting career choice for a man who abused his own children.

"Ready?" Matt cupped her cheek with his palm, his gaze steady on hers.

His rock-solid faith in her ability to handle herself and the situation sharpened her resolve. She nodded.

He turned the knob and pushed open the door. The receptionist's desk was empty though it was obvious the employee had recently left. The computer screen showed a document still open, and a pink mug filled with coffee sat close to the mouse. Matt closed the outer door with an audible click. Still nothing.

A woman's soft, sultry laughter came from behind the closed door with Sebastian's nameplate displayed prominently.

Matt rolled his eyes. "Sounds like he's not missing his wife much."

"What should we do?"

"Break up the party." He strode to Sebastian's door and knocked hard.

The woman inside gasped. "Just a moment," a male voice called. Murmured voices, then male laughter.

Delilah's cheeks burned. Good grief. This was a place of business. Couldn't Sebastian wait until the workday was finished?

Two minutes later, a lock clicked and the door opened to reveal an attractive woman with auburn hair and sleepy blue eyes. Her skirt was twisted and wrinkled, her blouse buttoned wrong. "I'm sorry. We were in the middle of an important conference call."

Delilah's eyebrows rose. Right.

"Do you have an appointment? Mr. Norris is a busy man. His time is valuable."

She wanted to point out the woman had just been wasting Sebastian's precious time as well as her own. "I'm an old friend of Sebastian's." Big exaggeration. "He'll see me."

She pushed past the woman to catch Sebastian smoothing his hair. His tie was crooked and his shirt tail was out.

Sebastian scowled as he tucked his shirt into his pants. "Who are you and what do you want? I don't appreciate you barging into my office when I'm in the middle of business negotiations."

"Wonder what your wife's lawyer would think of your negotiations." Matt pressed his hand to the small of Delilah's back and nudged her further into the room. He closed the door on the nosy assistant.

Sebastian's expression darkened. "Who are you?"

"Matt Rainer. You already know Delilah, don't you?"

Those familiar icy gray eyes swept over Delilah, then settled on her face. He stilled, a light of recognition appearing in his eyes. "You've changed." His gaze trailed over her again, heating as he absorbed the changes in her body.

Matt stepped half in front of her. "Eyes right here, buddy."

"What do you want?"

"I can't have what I want. Yet. I'll settle for a few answers for now."

"Are you threatening me? Do you have any idea who I am?"

"No threat. A promise of things to come. As for who you are, yeah, I know exactly who and what you are. You're a pathetic worm who preys on the innocent, especially defenseless women and children."

"All right. That's it. Get out. Expect to hear from my lawyer by day's end."

"Sit down and shut up, Norris. I'm not intimidated by you, your lawyer, or your daddy. Aren't you a little old to be riding on your daddy's coattails? I know what you did, you little weasel, and I can't be bought off like the people in this town."

"I don't know what you're talking about." The sweat beading on his face and the fast pulse pounding in the carotid artery in his neck said otherwise. Norris's glance flicked to Delilah.

She stared at him. Matt was right. The man she'd had nightmares about for years was a worm. "Feeling a little cornered, Sebastian? Now you know how I felt in that bathroom with you and your cohorts in crime."

He glared. "You want money? You're not getting it. No one would believe you." Contempt filled his eyes. "Why would the captain of the football team have any interest in touching Two-Ton Delilah? You'll be the laughingstock of Harmony. Again."

Before two heartbeats passed, Matt grabbed Sebastian's lapels, hauled him off the edge of the desk where he'd been perched, and slammed his back against the wall. Two framed photographs fell to the floor, glass shattering on impact.

Behind Delilah, the knob rattled but the door didn't open. "Sebastian, are you all right? Sebastian!" The woman pounded on the door.

"Tell her you're fine." Matt's voice was cool in direct contrast to the fury in his gaze.

Sebastian swallowed hard. "I'm fine, Trish. A picture fell off the wall. Go back to your work."

"Are you sure?"

"Trish, do as I told you."

Trish's footsteps faded away as she returned to her desk.

"How much do you want?" Sebastian snapped. "This is about money, isn't it, Delilah?"

"I don't know. You tell me."

A puzzled look. "You want me to buy your silence for that misunderstanding in high school, right? How much do you want?"

Matt growled and shoved his forearm against Sebastian's throat. "Misunderstanding?"

"He's not worth bruised knuckles." Delilah laid her hand on Matt's back, her touch gentle.

He shifted his weight until Sebastian's face reddened, panic filling his gaze. No matter how he twisted and jerked to throw off the operative's hold, Matt didn't budge.

Delilah tried again, concerned Matt would seriously harm Sebastian. She'd never seen him so angry. "Matt."

"Move back."

Understanding his need to protect her trumped everything else, Delilah returned to the far side of the desk, away from Sebastian's reach.

The medic released Sebastian who slid to the floor, gasping for air. "If you insult Delilah again, I'll lay you out. Am I making myself clear, Norris?"

He nodded.

"We want answers to a few questions. If you don't give us what we want voluntarily, we'll get the answers the hard way." A cold smile curved Matt's mouth. "You won't like how I'll learn the information we need, but I'll enjoy watching you squirm in pain. And you will tell me everything I want to know. You won't be able to spill your secrets fast enough."

"Information?" Sebastian's voice came out hoarse. "That's all you want?"

"Unless I have reason to believe you conspired to hurt Delilah recently, that's all." He paused. "For now. Give me what I want and you walk away unharmed."

"Not much of a bargain."

"It's all you're going to get." Although he didn't take his attention from Sebastian, Matt spoke to Delilah. "Ask your questions, sweetheart."

Sebastian's eyes narrowed. "You're her boyfriend?"

"Where were you three nights ago, Sebastian?" Delilah asked.

"With Trish. I spent the night at her place. She lives outside Harmony."

"Didn't want to give your wife's lawyer more ammunition?"

"I answered your question. Leave."

"What do you know about Zach, Evan, and Shane?"

He blinked. "They aren't as close to each other as they used to be. Michelle's illness has been tough on your family. Of course, you wouldn't know that since you haven't bothered to come back to town in years."

"Been busy earning a living. Some of us legitimately earn our wages."

Outrage filled his face. "I work hard raising money for charity which is more than I can say for you."

She gave a nod. "You're right. I don't raise money for charity. I just write them a check every month. Something tells me you haven't spent a penny of your own money to help out underprivileged children."

"Why do you want to know about your own family from me? Ask them yourself."

"I plan to do that, but it's hard to believe what they tell me right now, Sebastian. Someone in my family or their circle of friends wants me dead. Since that circle includes you, you're on the suspect list as well."

Sebastian's eyes widened. "You're crazy." His gaze darted to Matt. "Sorry. It doesn't make sense, though. Zach and the cousins haven't mentioned her in years."

Delilah folded her arms across her chest. "Four attempts to kill me in three days says you're wrong. Were you part of the conspiracy to murder me and my mother?"

CHAPTER TWENTY-FIVE

On the street in front of Norris's office building minutes later, Matt wrapped his arm around Delilah's waist and tucked her against his side. "Are you all right?"

"I can't believe I've been afraid of that lowlife since high school." Disgust filled her voice. "He's not worth one night of lost sleep. I've had too many sweat-filled nightmares featuring Sebastian and he's a pitiful weasel."

"Maybe now the nightmares will come less frequently. Aside from him being spineless, what's your impression?"

"Pretty convenient alibi for the night I was attacked in Otter Creek. I think Trish would back him up no matter what he claimed. She appears to be head over heels for Sebastian. She should have better taste in men."

He slid her a pointed look. "I don't like to hear his name from your lips."

She laughed, the sound tugging at his heart. Delilah should always laugh. When she laughed, Delilah became a being of unearthly beauty. "Kind of hard to talk about him without using his name. There are too many male players to not identify the man we're talking about."

"Why don't we call him what he is? Pond scum."

Delilah rolled her eyes. "I'll try to remember that. Pond Scum has a nice alibi that no one can break if Trish doesn't turn on him. I don't believe he's behind the attacks, Matt."

He scowled. "Why not?"

"I know you want him to be, but like you said, he's spineless. He hides behind his father and plays the big, important man in Harmony. He doesn't have influence outside of this town. Why would anyone risk prison time to do him a favor? I don't believe he was in Otter Creek. You saw him. He's soft and out of shape. He wasn't the man who cracked my ribs."

"You didn't see the second man. Pond Scum could have been hiding in your bedroom, leaving his accomplice to attack you. He'd still have the pleasure of knowing he caused you pain without touching you." The idea made Matt seethe.

"Why bother with me after all these years? I haven't been an active threat nor did I give the impression I wanted payback since I didn't see him after high school."

"If he's still tied in to your brother and cousins, wouldn't Pond Scum jump at the chance to torture you more?"

Delilah flinched. "Good point."

He walked with her across the street to the coffee shop. "We need to stop by the bank. They need a copy of the lawyer's letter."

"Let's do that before we go to my mother's house. Randy should have moved by now."

"If he followed the stipulations in your mother's will."

"Oh, man. I hope he did. I don't relish the prospect of having him evicted from the property. Talk about being labeled as heartless. My reputation would never survive the onslaught of venom from Randy. Everybody in town thinks he's a lovable teddy bear."

They entered the coffee shop and headed for Cade and Sasha's table.

Cade placed a cup of coffee in front of him when Matt sat down. "You look like you can use this."

He needed to take a long, hot shower to wash the slime from his body after spending those minutes enclosed in Norris's office. A cup of coffee would have to do for now. "Thanks."

Sasha slid Delilah's tea across the table. "Tori refreshed the tea for you."

"What's next?" Cade asked.

"A trip to the bank to present the document proving I have signing privileges for Mom's accounts. After that, a visit to my childhood home to assess what needs to be done before I sell the place." Delilah sipped her tea.

"You don't want to keep the house and move back here?"

Matt's heart stuttered. Under the table, his hand gripped his thigh, his emotions chaotic and dark despite the cheerful atmosphere of the coffee shop. He'd never considered she would want to move back to Harmony, especially after her experiences as a teenager in this town. Instead of building a new life in Otter Creek, she could resume the old one on her terms. An old life without him.

Delilah shook her head. "My home is in Otter Creek. I love my store and the life I've built." Her gaze skated to Matt. "I don't want to leave my store, my friends or Matt. As soon as I'm able, I'll leave Harmony. Unless Zach needs me, I won't come back."

Relief flooded Matt. He was invested in this relationship with Delilah. He would have kept their relationship alive by commuting to Harmony as often as work permitted. Long distance relationships were tough and his schedule was erratic. The weeks when Bravo was on call, Matt couldn't leave Otter Creek. The Fortress units were on deployment rotation for a month at a time. Worse, if Bravo deployed, he didn't know how long he'd be in the field.

He didn't want to be separated from Delilah that long. He already knew he'd have a hard time leaving her during his deployments. Good thing he'd be able to text and call during downtimes on missions.

Cade's eyebrows rose. "You plan to mail large checks to your family every year for the next five years?"

"I'll pay them off today if I talk to them. I don't want that burden hanging over my head. They can do what they want with the check as long as they understand the money train has officially dried up after this payment."

He studied her a moment. "And you're hoping to take the target off your back."

"That, too."

"I don't think Holloway and the Frosts will be satisfied with the payoff."

Matt didn't think so, either. Not when so many millions of dollars were at stake.

"Want us to stay on Norris?" Cade asked him.

"No. If he takes off, you won't be able to follow him without a vehicle anyway." A slight smile curved his lips. "Besides, I doubt he's anxious to leave his office."

Sasha tilted her head, a puzzled look on her face. "Too much work to do?"

"He was more interested in his assistant than his work. In fact, his desk didn't have anything on it except a phone and his computer."

"The phone wasn't ringing and his computer was off." Delilah's expression reflected her disgust.

Sasha's eyes widened. "Oh."

"And get this," Matt said. "Norris runs a foundation benefiting children."

Cade snorted. "Ironic."

"I can use two more sets of eyes in the Holloway house. If anything connects Randy to Michelle's death or

179

the attacks on Delilah, I want to find it and notify Russell."
To protect Delilah, Matt would play nice with the local
police. "Once we finish with Michelle's house, we'll find a
place for lunch, maybe meet with the rest of Bravo."

After finishing their drinks and taking the
documentation of Delilah's right to legally access
Michelle's accounts to the bank, Matt drove the SUV from
the center of town, following Delilah's directions to her
childhood home. Ten minutes later, he parked in front of a
brick one-story house with elaborate landscaping in the
yard.

Delilah's jaw dropped. "What in the world?"

He looked closer, hoping to see what had surprised her.
Nothing. "What is it?"

"The yard. It never looked like this when I lived here.
We received notices all the time about letting our grass
grow too tall. Zach wouldn't keep the yard mowed. Mom
never planted flowers. This looks like a fairytale house. I
can't believe the difference."

"The house has great curb appeal," Sasha said. "You
should get a good price for it if the inside is attractive as the
outside."

Matt and Cade exited the vehicle and opened doors for
the women. "You still have a key to the house?"

Delilah nodded. "I can't wait to see what Mom did
with the backyard and the inside of the house. This is
incredible."

At the front door, Matt held out his hand for the key.
He unlocked the door and stood back for her to move past
him into the darkened interior.

She turned on the lights and stood in the entryway,
staring. "Wow."

Matt threaded his fingers through hers. "What's
different?"

"Everything. The furniture, carpet, paint, curtains. The
only thing the same are the pictures on the walls." She

wandered from room to room, pointing out the changes in each one except for the two closed doors of bedrooms at the end of the hall.

Looked like Michelle had used some of her lottery winnings to redecorate the house. If this was her handiwork, Delilah's mother had been gifted at interior decorating. While the house looked like something out of a magazine, Michelle had managed to make the home comfortable as well as beautiful.

"I always wanted our house to look like this." Delilah leaned against the wall in the hallway. "But we lived hand to mouth. With interior decorating, it was feast or famine, and Dad's job as an elementary school teacher didn't pay well. We didn't have money for the house to look like this, even after Mom married Randy."

Matt glanced at Cade. "You and Sasha start at the front of the house. Delilah and I will search back here. We'll meet in the living room."

With a nod, Cade led Sasha to the other side of the house.

Matt turned to Delilah. "Where do you want to start?"

"The guest bedroom."

"You don't want to start in your mother's bedroom?"

"I'd like to save that for last." She walked to one of the rooms. Delilah opened the door and pulled up short.

Matt eased her back into the hall. In stark contrast to the rest of the house, this room had been systematically destroyed. Lamps lay broken on the carpet. Pillows and the mattress on the king-size bed showed signs of knife work. A few worn articles of Randy's clothing were strewn around the room. The drywall showed signed of violent rage with multiple holes in the walls. Ugly epithets covered the walls, the air still smelling of spray paint. The carpet had dirt and manure ground into the fibers. The mirror lay in shards on the dresser and floor.

"Your stepfather wasn't happy."

Delilah gave a shaky laugh. "You think?"

He opened the closet door. Similar destruction in there, too, along with old shoes and more ragged clothes.

"Matt."

He turned to see Delilah had left the room. He went to the hall and peered inside the master bedroom. Delilah stood just inside the door with her arms wrapped around her middle.

More damage in here, worse than the destruction in the guest room. Anger knotted his stomach. "Don't touch anything. We'll take pictures and call Russell."

He pulled out his phone and snapped photos of everything in both rooms. From the clothes tossed around and shredded with a knife, the master bedroom belonged to Michelle alone. Nothing of Randy's was in the room while the guest room held remnants of Delilah's stepfather. Had Michelle found out about his cheating and consigned him to another bedroom or had she been so sick her husband voluntarily moved to the other room?

"Matt!"

Cade's shout had him swinging around. Matt's friend raced down the hall with Sasha in tow, her face white with fear.

"What's wrong?"

"Bomb attached to the water heater. Fifteen seconds."

CHAPTER TWENTY-SIX

Matt led Delilah to the window at the farthest point from the water heater while Cade shut the bedroom door and locked it. Matt opened the window and boosted Delilah to the sill. "Run!"

He reached back, lifted Sasha, and nudged her out. Matt motioned for Cade to follow his wife, then dived out the window himself. He bounded to his feet and sprinted after Delilah.

He and Cade caught up with the women within a few strides and urged them to run faster toward the opposite side of the street. He had to get them farther away from the pending explosion.

Two seconds later, Cade said, "Down."

Matt wrapped his arm around Delilah and took her to the ground, covering her body with his own, his arms surrounding her head.

Behind him, the house exploded, throwing shrapnel in every direction. Heat stung Matt's exposed skin and debris raining over them. His ears rang, but he was alive. A win, in his book.

When he was sure it was safe to move, Matt eased off Delilah. "You okay?"

She groaned. "In case you didn't know, the ground is hard and you're not a lightweight." Delilah glanced at him, lips curving. "But I'm fine, thanks to you."

"Matt!"

Sasha's shaky call had him glancing their direction. A spear of wood protruded from Cade's shoulder. Blood poured from the wound, staining Sasha's hands as she tried to stem the tide of red.

Matt leaped to his feet. "Delilah, call 911, then call Trent." He ran to his SUV, thankfully still intact aside from blistered paint, and grabbed his mike bag before returning to his teammate's side. "I can't take you anywhere, Cade."

"Who needed stitching on our last mission?"

Matt chuckled. He had a scar on the back of his thigh from Cade's not-so-delicate handiwork. He grasped Cade's shirt and ripped the material away from the wound, baring the injury.

"Get it out." Cade's jaw was tight. "Can't protect Sasha like this."

Matt understood his friend's worry. He was concerned about Delilah being exposed on the street with neighbors gathering around them. Although he didn't believe the neighbors were a threat, Matt couldn't rule them out and his attention was divided between Delilah, Cade, Sasha, and the crowd.

"It's going to hurt," he warned.

"Do it."

"On three." Matt counted down, grasped the wood, and pulled it free. He worked fast to staunch the blood flow, utilizing another compression bandage. "Hospital, Cade."

"No."

Matt scowled. "Listen, you stubborn mule. Your wife is terrified and at risk. You need to get her somewhere more secure. The police will be here any minute and they'll want to know what happened. I can't have my attention divided when Delilah has a target on her back." He leaned down. "If we were on the battlefield, I'd take care of you myself. We're not and there's a perfectly good hospital ten minutes from here. You'll be out in a few hours." Probably. The doc might want to keep Cade for a while.

"I have to watch your back."

"Bravo is a few minutes out. They'll watch both our backs."

"Please, Cade." Sasha pressed a kiss to her husband's forehead. "Going to the hospital will free Matt to protect Delilah. You might need antibiotics and the hospital can provide that in an IV. You'll be out in no time."

Matt didn't have the heart to tell Sasha he had the same ability. However, she'd be more comfortable if Cade used traditional American treatment as opposed to his brand of battlefield medicine.

Cade gave a short nod, giving Matt a good indication of how much pain his friend was in. Normally, he would have insisted Matt treat him anyway.

The fire crew arrived and rushed to douse the fire. Lost cause. The Holloway house was a total loss.

The ambulance arrived. Two EMTs hurried to Cade's side, equipment in hand. "What do we have?" the bald man asked.

"Shoulder wound caused from a two-inch piece of wood driven into his back by the blast that caused the fire across the street. He's allergic to sulfa drugs and his blood type is A+."

Baldy frowned. "You a doctor?"

"Medic. Have his wife checked out, too."

"Hey," Sasha protested. "I'm fine."

"You wanted to be sure Cade was all right. Now it's your turn to give him the same peace of mind about you."

"What about you and the other lady?" the second EMT asked. "Any injuries?"

Matt turned to Delilah. "Sweetheart?"

"I'm all right."

He'd keep an eye on her. Adrenaline could mask symptoms of injuries. "I'll take care of her," he told Baldy.

After the ambulance left with Cade and Sasha, Matt grabbed his mike bag and walked with Delilah to the porch of a nearby home. He could watch the activity across the street and keep Delilah from being an easy target.

He grabbed his cell phone and called Russell.

"Yeah, Russell. Make it fast."

"It's Matt Rainer. The Holloway house just blew up."

Muttered swearing reached his ear. "Where are you?"

"Across the street from the house. Ambulance just left with Cade and Sasha Ramsey. If you want to talk to me and Delilah, you better hurry. I'm not leaving her in the open long."

"Two minutes."

After texting Trent an update, Matt slid his phone away and wrapped his arm around Delilah's shoulders. "I'm sorry about the house."

"Me, too. Who would do this? What was the point?"

He didn't say anything. She couldn't handle the truth right now. As intelligent as Delilah was, she'd figure out the implication soon enough.

Wry laughter escaped her. "Guess I don't have to worry about selling the house now."

No, she'd have the headache of dealing with the insurance company. "The land is valuable. However, if you want to rebuild, you have a prime spot."

Delilah leaned her head against Matt's shoulder. "I hope Mom left the insurance papers in her safe deposit box or with the lawyer because I don't think there's anything left of the house. I'll call the agent she used when I was in high school. If he doesn't have the policy, he'll know who does."

She was quiet a while. "Did Randy do this? Did he try to kill me?"

Before he answered, a black sedan raced up the street and slid to a stop in front of them. Russell climbed out and jogged to the porch.

"You both okay?" he asked as his gaze took in the fight to save the Holloway house.

"We're fine. Ask your questions, Russell."

"Tell me what happened."

Matt ran down the events of the past few minutes.

The detective grimaced. "Your friend will be okay?"

"Might need surgery, but he'll be fine."

"Lucky. All of you."

So close. If Cade hadn't noticed the bomb, they would have been caught inside the house when it exploded. He shuddered thinking how close he came to losing the woman who held his heart in the palm of her hands. "We know."

"What were you doing in the house?"

"I wanted to see what needed to be done to prepare the house to sell," Delilah said. "Under the stipulations of Mom's will, Randy had to vacate the premises with only his personal belongings by this morning."

"Did he clear out his belongings?"

"He left a few old clothes." She glanced at Matt, eyebrows lifted.

"Tell him," he murmured.

"Tell me what?" Russell demanded.

"Someone trashed the bedroom we think Randy used along with the master bedroom." Matt pulled out his cell phone and let Russell scroll through the pictures he took of the damage.

A soft whistle from the detective. "Somebody was angry. The rest of the house like this?"

"Just these two rooms."

"But no proof Holloway did the damage."

"The damage was limited to their personal rooms. If a stranger broke in, the whole house would look the same."

"That still leaves the Frosts. I'm assuming you'll give Ms. Frost an alibi."

"Of course. Cade and Sasha were with us most of the morning."

"Why am I not surprised by that?" Russell rubbed his fingers over his jaw. "All right. I'd like a copy of the will."

Matt stood. "We have an extra copy in the SUV." He hoisted his mike bag and strode to his vehicle. After storing his medical supplies in the cargo area, he grabbed a copy of the will from his glove box and returned. "Have you brought Holloway in for questioning yet?"

"He's in an interrogation room, cooling his heels as we speak."

"Find out if he knows how to construct a bomb."

Russell's gaze sharpened. "You're sure it was a bomb?"

"Cade spotted it. He's trained in EOD."

The detective slid his notebook, pen, and the will into his pocket. "I'll have a word with the officers cordoning off the area, then talk to Holloway. I don't see him for this, but I've been surprised before." With a nod, he crossed the street to the nearest officer keeping the curious away from the emergency workers and equipment.

Matt helped Delilah stand. "I want to check on Cade and Sasha."

As he drove to the hospital, Matt remained alert for a tail. He didn't bother turning squares to avoid being followed. Wouldn't take a genius to know where he was going.

When he turned into the hospital parking lot, he noticed the black truck in his wake also turned into the lot. The back of Matt's neck burned. Not good.

With the sun glare on the truck's windshield, he couldn't see the occupants. Matt parked and stayed in place with the engine running, watching the truck pull into an empty slot four rows back.

Delilah rested her hand on his forearm. "What's wrong?"

"We picked up a tail. Let's wait a minute and see if someone gets out. You mind being used as camouflage?"

She grinned. "As long as it's you doing the using, I'll be happy to do my part."

Matt laughed and drew her into his arms. "I need to look out the back window."

"Ah. Does that mean I have permission to nibble on your neck and ears?"

"Go for it." He twisted to keep an eye on the truck and still appear to be engaged in making out with his girl. With his lips barely touching hers, he said, "Will this make you uncomfortable?"

"Being in the arms of the man I'm crazy about and stealing a kiss or two will make me want more kisses when we're not in public."

Matt threaded his fingers into her hair and tilted her head to press his lips more firmly to hers. "I'll be happy to fulfill that request."

Five minutes passed. Ten. No movement from the truck occupant. Matt, however, was having a difficult time staying focused. "You enjoy torturing me," he accused as he shivered at the love bite she pressed to his neck.

"Definitely."

"I'm not going to forget the scorecard."

"That's what I'm counting on."

After waiting another minute with no movement from the person in the truck, Matt levered himself away from Delilah, cupping her face with the palm of his hand. "He isn't taking the bait and I want to check on Cade. Wait for me to come get you."

He circled the hood and opened Delilah's door. Matt tucked her against his side and guided her to the emergency room entrance. As they threaded their way through the vehicles between their position and the entrance, he used mirrors and reflections on windshields to maintain surveillance on the truck.

Nothing. He must be settling in to wait until Delilah and Matt returned to the SUV. Zane might pick up the license plate from traffic cams. Matt wanted to know who owned the truck on their tail. If he knew that information, he might have a better idea who wanted to hurt Delilah.

CHAPTER TWENTY-SEVEN

Delilah walked with Matt into the hospital's emergency room waiting area. Sasha sat in a chair at the back of the room with Simon on one side and Liam on the other. "Sasha."

Her friend rushed into Delilah's open arms. "Any news?"

"The doctor is working on him now. He kicked me out of the treatment room so I don't know what's going on."

"I'll see what I can find out. This is a good time to flash my EMT credentials." Matt squeezed Delilah's hand and strode from the room.

Sasha released Delilah. "Do you think Matt will learn anything?"

"I'd put my money on him any day. Where's Trent?"

"At the door of the treatment room." Liam got up. "Sasha, you need a soft drink. Do you have a favorite?"

"Nothing with orange or grape flavor."

He looked at Delilah. "Stay with Simon. I won't be long."

Bemused over Liam's protectiveness, she wrapped her arm around Sasha's shoulders and led her friend back to her chair. "Cade will be fine."

"How do you know?"

"If he'd been critical, Matt would have gone with him to the hospital."

Most of the tension left her friend's shoulders. "You're right. I should have realized Matt wouldn't have let Cade go without him if he was critical. I know my husband's work is dangerous and he's the best, but this isn't a mission. He shouldn't have been injured."

Guilt assailed Delilah. Perhaps she should have insisted Cade and Sasha stay in Otter Creek. But Cade was Matt's best friend. They stuck together.

Simon laid his hand over Sasha's. "Unexpected things happen every day. You could be injured in a car wreck or fall off a ladder at Perk. At least Matt was on hand and Cade was at a hospital within minutes of the explosion. Another thing to keep in mind, Sasha. If Cade hadn't been at the Holloway house, Matt and Delilah would have been inside the house when it exploded. They're alive because of your husband."

"What if Cade had been injured like this when your team was on the battlefield?"

"Matt would treat him. He has almost as much medical training as a doctor, Sasha, and he's constantly studying and learning more. I trust Matt more than any medical doctor. He knows what he's doing."

She leaned her head against his upper arm. "I'm sorry. I'm just worried about Cade."

"Remember, we have his back and yours."

In that moment, Delilah understood what she'd be facing if she and Matt stayed together. No. Not if. When she and Matt stayed together. And that's when she knew the truth. Delilah loved the handsome medic. She had to find a way to deal with the uncertainty and worry when Matt was deployed.

She knew the wives of the Durango team were close and supported each other when their husbands were gone. If the women needed something while the men were deployed, Bravo helped out. Maybe the Durango wives would share some insights. The only other option was to walk away from Matt, and that wasn't going to happen. She'd already lost her heart to him.

Matt returned to the waiting room and crouched in front of Sasha. "The doctor is flushing out Cade's wound and will stitch him up shortly. Cade's grousing about the doc's terrible bedside manner and having to put up with an IV. They're administering antibiotics and a pain killer." He smiled. "In other words, he'll be fine."

Sasha wrapped her arms around Matt's neck. "Thanks." Her voice sounded choked.

He held her for a minute. "He wouldn't cooperate with the doctor until he knew Bravo was here to watch over you both. That's why there's been a delay in his treatment."

She gave a watery laugh. "Sounds like him."

"Can't fault him. He adores you and will do anything to make sure you're safe."

Sasha released Matt and wiped the tears from her face. "I don't know what I would do without him."

"That's not going to happen." Liam handed Sasha one of the soft drink bottles he'd brought back and gave Delilah the other. "I know you don't normally drink this, Delilah, but make an exception today."

She eyed the green bottle with distaste. She couldn't remember the last time she'd had a carbonated drink other than sparkling water.

Matt took her bottle and broke the seal before handing it back. "One quarter of the bottle, okay? We'll take a walk later and burn off the calories. The sugar helps combat shock."

A few hours later, Bravo left the hospital with a woozy Cade and a relieved Sasha. Matt turned to Trent. "The black truck four rows behind my SUV followed us here from the Holloway house and has stayed for five hours. Take Cade and Sasha back to the hotel while the rest of us take different routes. I want to lose this clown if I can."

"Know who's tailing you?"

Matt shook his head. "Haven't been able to catch a license plate or see a face. While we lead him away from you and the Ramseys, I'll call Zane and see if he can identify the truck and driver."

"We'll see you at the hotel." Trent guided Cade and Sasha to his SUV, then drove from the lot.

"Will they be all right?" Delilah asked.

"Liam and Simon will take alternate routes back to the hotel, but they won't be far. If Trent needs an assist, he'll have backup in minutes. So far, no one appears to be interested in Trent and the others. The black truck is still in the same place."

"What will we do?"

"Find a place for lunch. I'm starving. Bravo will order room service. They won't leave the Ramseys alone."

Delilah checked the time. "It's dinner time now."

"Do you have recommendations? I want a restaurant away from Harmony and West Fork."

When Matt climbed behind the wheel, Delilah asked, "Are you in the mood for Mexican?"

"Always. It's my favorite."

"Great. I know just the place." She gave him directions to Castle Springs, a town 30 miles in the opposite direction from West Fork.

While Matt drove away from Harmony, he contacted Zane on his Bluetooth.

"Murphy."

"It's Matt. You're on speaker with Delilah. I need you to do more hacking for me."

"I live to outsmart the law. What do you need?"

"Hack into the traffic and security cameras around the Holloway house, starting from eight this morning to one this afternoon."

"What am I looking for?"

"Black pickup tailing my SUV. I haven't been able to get a look at the license plate or the driver."

"Is it behind you now?"

"Yeah, but I'm on Highway 219. I haven't seen traffic cams. Delilah and I are driving to Castle Springs for lunch and leading our tail away from our hotel and Cade."

A slight pause, then, "What happened?"

Matt brought his friend up to date. "Cade will be fine, but he's out of commission for a few weeks while he heals. I've already alerted Nate Armstrong. If Bravo is deployed, he'll cover for Cade."

"I'll inform Maddox and get back to you about your tail. Might take a while. The Texas unit is in a hotspot at the moment."

Texas unit? Delilah twisted to stare at Matt. How many units worked for Fortress?

"I understand."

"If I can't do the search in the next few minutes, I'll hand it off to one of the tech geeks."

"Thanks, Z."

"Yep. Delilah, how are you?"

"Grateful to be alive and blessed to have Matt in my life." Understatement of the year.

"I'm sorry about your childhood home. Were you able to save anything?"

"We had fifteen seconds to get out of the house. The fire department was still working the fire when we left. Based on what I saw, I think the house is a total loss."

"Let us know if we can help. Matt, we'll be in touch soon."

Twenty minutes later, Matt parked in front of *Tres Amigos* restaurant.

"Perfect." Delilah smiled. "We're here before the dinner crowd. Do we still have a tail?"

"Oh, yeah. I wasn't trying to lose him." He sent a text and slid his phone away. "We'll eat and let Zane identify the truck's owner."

Ninety minutes later, they were back on the sidewalk in front of the restaurant. Matt scanned the parking lot as he pressed his hand to Delilah's back as he guided her toward the SUV. "Still have our tail. Good. Bravo should be back at the hotel and have the Ramseys settled by now. Time to lose the truck and check on Cade."

After helping Delilah into the SUV, Matt drove from the lot and headed for Highway 219 and Harmony. Ten miles later, he exited the highway in Waynesboro and turned squares as soon as they drove downtown.

The pursuer fell back as Matt increased the distance between them. He glanced in the rearview mirror and sped up. "Hold on." At the next corner, Matt turned, stomped on the gas pedal, and raced to one of four parking garages on this block.

He whipped into the farthest one and zoomed up the ramp until they were no longer in sight of the street. On the top floor of the garage, Matt parked and opened his door. "Stay here."

He got out and jogged to a concrete pillar at the front of the garage. Still in shadow, he eased closer to the edge and waited. The minutes stretched out while Matt remained motionless at his post.

Delilah wanted to see for herself what was going on. She wrangled herself under control. If she was caught in the open, Matt would risk his life to protect her.

Matt pulled out his cell phone and checked the screen. His expression turned grim.

Delilah's stomach knotted. Not a good sign. What now? Was Cade worse or had something else happened?

After another perusal of the street below, Matt returned to the SUV.

"Did we lose the truck?"

"Yeah, we did."

She wrapped her hand around his. "I know something is wrong. Talk to me."

"Zane hacked into traffic cams and captured the truck's license plate." He kissed her knuckles. "I'm sorry, sweetheart, but the truck is registered to your brother."

CHAPTER TWENTY-EIGHT

Matt drove from the garage and turned squares on his way back to the highway, frequently checking his mirrors. No sign of Zach or anyone else.

When he was sure they were clear, Matt activated his navigation system and drove toward West Fork. "You okay?" He glanced at Delilah, expecting to see distress or, God forbid, tears.

Instead, Delilah looked puzzled. "I assume Zane didn't make a mistake."

"No." Z didn't make mistakes like that.

"If my brother meant us harm, why didn't he force the SUV off the road or shoot us when we were in the open? Zach has a rifle with a scope and he's a good shot. Why is he following us around?"

"Good questions. We'll have to catch up with him and ask. Since he doesn't have a job, do you know where he hangs out during the day?"

"No idea."

"Who would know?"

"Shane and Evan, maybe Randy."

"Randy will be tied up for a while. Once I check on Cade, we'll figure out what we want to do. Might be best to catch your brother tomorrow morning before he leaves home."

"You're right. I also think you should be on hand in case Cade has problems."

Matt squeezed her hand, glad she understood his need to watch over his best friend. Cade had strong reactions to most pain meds.

In less than an hour, Matt swiped his card through the reader and opened the suite door, mike bag slung over his shoulder. Bravo was ranged around the room with Trent keeping watch at the French doors.

Simon inclined his head toward Cade and Sasha's room. "He's woozy and pukey."

"One of you go find a soft drink with real ginger in it and bring back a bucket of ice."

Liam got to his feet. "I'll get it."

"How can I help?" Delilah asked.

"Find a plastic bag and make an ice pack. If you can't find one, I'll make do with a hand towel." He knocked on Cade's door and walked inside. "Heard you missed me, Sunshine."

Sasha laid a damp washcloth over his teammate's forehead.

Cade narrowed his eyes. "If I wasn't ready to hurl any second, I'd show you how much I've missed your ugly mug. Delilah okay?"

"She's fine. No new injuries from the house explosion, thanks to your quick thinking. I owe you." Matt set his mike bag against the wall within easy reach. "Pain meds going against you?"

"Yeah."

"We'll try ice and a soft drink first. If that doesn't work, I'll use a nausea patch."

Cade groaned, his face losing all trace of color.

Matt grabbed a nearby lined trash can and rolled his friend to his side. He held Cade steady while he threw up, careful to avoid his injured shoulder.

Delilah hurried into the room with a fistful of plastic bags and a bucket of ice with a green bottle nestled in the ice.

"Perfect. Fill one of those bags with enough ice to make a small ice pack. I'll need another ice pack in a minute." If Cade followed true to form, he would be nauseated for a few more hours. The trick was to make sure Cade didn't become dehydrated. That meant an IV. Good thing Matt always traveled with his fully stocked med kit since he doubted he could convince his friend to make another trip to the hospital.

He helped Cade sit up to sip the soft drink. "Delilah, see if there's a regular trash bag under the sink in the kitchen. If not, send one of Bravo to find some."

She handed him the ice pack she'd made before she left the room again.

"What can I do?" Sasha asked, her gaze filled with worry.

"Keep the ice pack draped over his neck. The cold knocks back the nausea." He created another ice pack and draped it over the side of Cade's head and his forehead. "Other than that, the best thing you can do for Cade is take care of yourself."

Matt tied off the soiled trash bag, set it aside, and lined the can with a fresh bag.

"I've never seen him like this." Sasha stroked her husband's hair.

"You haven't seen him in the early hours after an injury. Cade's a wuss when it comes to pain meds. Everything I've tried makes him sick to his stomach."

"Because you always poison me," his friend muttered with a hoarse voice. "You take manic glee in making me suffer."

"Huh. Thought I had you fooled." A soft snort brought a smile to Matt's mouth. "Reassure your bride you won't die on my watch."

"I'm okay, Sassy. This is normal for me when I'm injured. You can ask my teammates. In a few hours, I'll be fine. Promise."

Sasha didn't look convinced, but she subsided and pressed a kiss to the top of his head.

"Did you eat dinner, Sasha?" Matt asked as he checked Cade's pulse.

She shook her head.

"Have Trent order room service for you."

"I can wait."

"Go, baby." Cade wrapped his hand around Sasha's and kissed her fingers. "Take care of yourself. I'm not going anywhere."

When a stubborn look flooded her face, Matt said, "You need to keep up your strength to help me take care of Cade overnight."

"Come get me if there's any change."

"Absolutely."

After another kiss, this time to Cade's cheek, Sasha left the room.

"Thanks." Cade swallowed hard. "She refused to eat when the guys offered to order something for her."

"Be straight with me. How bad is the nausea?"

"About like the time I had the knife wound in the thigh in Costa Rica."

Matt flinched. He'd had to administer two IVs to replenish Cade's fluids during that operation. If Cade didn't improve in the next half hour, he'd use the anti-nausea patch. "We'll give the soft drink a few more minutes."

"Watch over Sasha."

"You don't have to ask."

"Matt."

Knowing his friend needed the words to allow his body to rest, Matt said, "I'll keep an eye on her."

A slight nod.

Delilah returned with a large black trash bag. "I found a maid at the end of the hall."

"Excellent. We convinced Sasha to order room service. Make sure she eats."

"Sure." She patted Cade's foot. "Don't worry. I'll stay with her."

"Thanks."

Matt spent the next twenty minutes alternately holding Cade steady as he puked and repositioning the ice packs. When the thirty-minute mark came and went with no signs of the nausea easing, Matt grabbed a patch from his mike bag.

After another bout of sickness, Cade quieted and his color improved. Exhausted, his friend fell into a light sleep. Matt slipped from the room, leaving the door ajar.

Sasha dropped her sandwich on her plate and stood. "Any change?"

"Finish your meal. Cade's better. He has an anti-nausea patch behind his ear and he's sleeping."

Liam poured a mug of coffee and handed it to Matt. "Prognosis?"

"Full recovery with an eight-week healing period. Nate's agreed to cover if we're deployed."

Trent turned away from the French doors. "You need room service for yourself?"

Matt shook his head. He turned to Delilah. "Did you tell them about the truck?"

His team leader straightened as Delilah shook her head. "You ran into trouble?"

"Zane hacked traffic cams and managed to catch the plate. The truck is registered to Delilah's brother."

Trent frowned. "That explains why I never saw him leave his house."

"House?" Delilah sat up straighter. "Zach owns a house?"

"A nice one outside of town. You didn't know?"

"The last time I heard, he lived in an apartment."

"I'll text you his address." Trent turned to Matt. "You confirm the brother was driving?"

"Nope. Tinting was too dark or the sun glared off the windshield. The odd thing was Zach never approached or threatened us. He just followed us around until I lost him."

"You plan to confront him tonight?"

"Zach will keep until tomorrow."

Sasha pushed her empty plate aside. "I'll sit with him. Finish your coffee, Matt."

Although he wanted to encourage Sasha to give herself a longer break, Matt didn't waste his breath. If the situation was reversed, he would be as anxious to return to Delilah's side. "I'll be in soon."

With a nod, Sasha returned to her husband's side.

"You're off night watch tonight." Trent turned back to the French doors. "Rest when you can. Simon, Liam, decide who gets the next watch and relieve me in four hours."

Thirty minutes later, Matt checked on Cade. His color had improved and he was still sleeping. If the nausea remained at bay, Cade might avoid another IV.

"How is he?" Sasha whispered.

"Better. If you're tired, lay beside him. He'll rest easier with you close. I'll be back in another hour."

"Thanks, Matt."

Throughout the night, Matt checked Cade every hour. Liam took over the watch at 1:00, his eyebrows rising when he spotted Delilah curled into a corner of the couch.

Matt shrugged. He'd tried to convince Delilah to go to bed, but she insisted he might need her and wanted to be available. She'd fallen asleep a few minutes past midnight.

When the sun peeked over the horizon with hints of a beautiful summer day to come, Sasha entered the living room. Matt rose, fatigue dragging at him.

"Cade's awake and hungry."

Simon turned from the French doors, a smile on his face. "Great news. I'll order room service while you help him shower, Matt."

He frowned. "Why do I get that duty, too?"

"Because you bully him into behaving better than the rest of us."

"I can do it," Sasha said.

"You can't hold him up because he's weak. Cade also won't want to show weakness in front of his wife." Matt squeezed her shoulder as he passed. "He'll feel better being able to gripe and complain all he wants without sacrificing his manhood."

Sasha rolled her eyes. "Men," she muttered.

Cade sat on the side of the bed, swaying. Matt steadied his friend. "Looks like you tied one on last night."

"Feels like it, too. Whatever the doc gave me for pain threw me for a loop."

He didn't have the heart to tell Cade the pain med was a mild one. "Want a shower?"

"Yeah, bad."

Thirty minutes later, Cade was clean and dressed with a new bandage on his shoulder. "Thanks, Matt."

"Yep. You would do the same for me."

A slight smile. "Maybe. I wouldn't be nearly as good at it as you are." He opened the door and walked into the living room. Cade caught Sasha against his uninjured side. "I'm better. It's time to stop worrying."

She buried her face against his neck. "Don't scare me like that again. I don't think my heart can take it."

"I'll do my best, Sassy."

Matt's gaze shifted to the empty couch. "Where's Delilah?"

"Shower. She'll be out in a few minutes." Sasha walked with Cade to the couch. "Breakfast will be here soon."

A knock sounded on the door.

"I've got it," Matt said.

A minute later, the room was filled with the scent of eggs, French toast, bagels, fruit, and a selection of herbal teas along with two carafes of coffee. Matt's mouth watered.

This was perfect after a sleepless night. A little food, coffee, and a shower, and Matt would be able to sleep a couple hours. He set aside one of the bananas and a small helping of eggs for Delilah as well as two packets of tea.

The second bedroom door opened. Delilah emerged dressed in jeans, a long-sleeved t-shirt, and running shoes.

Matt sighed. They weren't able to walk the night before. Maybe he could convince Delilah to purchase a swimsuit and use the hotel's pool tonight. If her ribs weren't too painful, she would feel more in control for resuming her exercise regimen.

He brushed his lips over hers. "Morning, beautiful."

"Hi."

"I set aside breakfast for you. How do you feel?"

"Not bad, considering. I should be asking you that question."

"A two-hour nap and I'll be good to go."

When Delilah was seated and eating her banana, Matt loaded his own plate. Within minutes, he and his teammates polished off breakfast except for the food they saved for Liam.

Delilah laid her hand on his. "Matt, go take a nap. I know you didn't sleep last night."

True enough. He'd watched over her and his teammate. "Okay if I use your bathroom?"

"Of course. Take the bed, too. I'll stay out here with whoever is on watch."

"Don't leave the suite. If there's trouble, come to me."

"I will."

He looked at Trent, who popped off a snappy salute with amusement glittering in his eyes. Smart aleck. After a quick shower, he fell onto the bed and dropped into sleep.

At eight, he woke up, alert. Time to get moving. He wanted to track down the other players in this mess and figure out who was targeting Delilah. The sooner he got her out of Harmony the better for his peace of mind.

CHAPTER TWENTY-NINE

Matt pounded on Zach's door. When the knock didn't bring a response, he rang the doorbell. Inside the house, something crashed to the floor and broke. More thumps. Swearing, growing more distinctive as Delilah's brother approached the door. "Zach isn't in a good mood."

Her brother fumbled with the locks, uttering blistering curses, and threw open the door. "Do you know what time it is?" He stopped complaining when his gaze focused on Matt and Delilah. "What are you doing here?"

"It's 9:30." Delilah shifted closer. "Why are you still in bed?"

"Sleeping, not that it's any business of yours. I was up late."

She fanned a hand in front of her face. "You smell like a brewery, bro."

"Don't like it? Get out of my face, Dee. You're the one who showed up without warning. Too freaking early to deal with you." He turned and attempted to close the door in their faces.

Matt's booted foot was on the threshold. "We need to talk. Go shower. You have coffee?"

"Buy your own. I'm not running a coffee shop."

"Get moving, Zach, or I'll dump you in a cold shower myself."

"Go, Zach." Delilah pushed past her brother. "We'll be in the kitchen."

"I should go back to bed and make you wait until I'm ready to get up," he muttered.

"Try it and I'll drag your lazy keister into the shower." Matt closed the front door and locked it.

"You can't talk to me that way. This is my house. You're here uninvited."

"If you want to see a penny of the money Mom left to you before this time next year, get in the shower." Delilah turned her back on Zach and stalked to the back of the house.

"Did you know the police took your stepfather in for questioning yesterday?"

Shock filled his eyes. "What?"

"We'll tell you the details when you shower and dress."

Zach staggered from the room as Matt tracked Delilah by the sound of slamming cabinet doors.

He stopped in the kitchen doorway and leaned against the frame. Watching Delilah in a temper was a new experience. Matt made a mental note to check the strength of his cabinet hinges at home. At some point, he'd make Delilah angry. Might be wise to make sure his kitchen would hold up to a show of temper from the woman he planned to marry as fast as he could talk her into it.

Telling Delilah he loved her would be a good first step in accomplishing that goal. Soon. This wasn't the time or place to bare his heart. "Want some help?"

"Measure the coffee. I'm tempted to double the amount of coffee required for spite."

He whistled softly. "You have a mean streak, love."

She glanced over her shoulder. "That's a new nickname."

"Do you like it?"

A smile flickered at the edges of her mouth, some of the temper fading from her eyes. "I do."

Matt opened the coffee container and scooped out the appropriate amount of coffee plus a little extra for the caffeine kick. Based on Zach's condition when he answered the door, he'd drunk himself into a stupor last night and still felt the results of his overindulgence.

Five minutes later, the shower kicked on. By the time Zach walked into the kitchen, he was steadier on his feet although his skin was still the color of paste.

Matt poured coffee into a large mug as Zach dropped into a chair and propped his head on his hands with a groan. He set the mug on the table along with over-the-counter pain meds he found in the cabinet. "Take these."

Delilah's brother opened his eyes to slits, tossed back the pills, and chased them down with sips of coffee. He shuddered. "Who made this? It's terrible."

"Drink it." When Zach finished the coffee, Matt refilled the mug. "Again."

Glaring at Matt, he managed to down the second mug. Zach shoved the mug aside. "No more unless you want to clean up after I barf. What's going on with Randy? Why did the cops take him in for questioning?"

"Answer a few questions, then we'll talk about your stepfather."

Zach slumped in his chair and motioned for Matt to get on with the questions.

"Why were you following us yesterday?"

"How can you ask me that? Our childhood home blew up yesterday. I wanted to make sure Dee was safe."

"What did you plan to do? Run interference and beat down any attempt to hurt her?"

"Well, yeah."

209

Matt stared. "I'm in private security. I'll take care of your sister."

Zach waved his statement aside. "I know what you said, but I don't know you, do I? You talk a good game. That's no guarantee you're capable of doing what you say."

Ouch. Much as he hated to admit it, Delilah's brother had a point. Zach was also Delilah's only relative. Matt didn't like the clod, but he could reassure him about Delilah's safety.

Matt called Zane and placed the phone on speaker.

"Yeah, Murphy."

"It's Matt. You're on speaker with Delilah and her brother, Zach."

"What do you need?"

"Zach is concerned I can't protect his sister."

"No worries, Zach. Matt Rainer is a decorated war hero, many times over. He's an Army Ranger with too many missions to count, all of them classified so I can't tell you what they were. The president honored him for his bravery four times. He's been employed by Fortress for five years. Our employees are invited to apply and the boss only issues invitations to the best in the business. We don't advertise our services, but never lack missions. Fortress specializes in rescuing hostages and combating terrorism. Matt is the medic for one of our best teams. You couldn't ask for a better man for Delilah."

Although scowling, grudging respect filled the man's eyes. "Will he put her safety first?"

"He'd take a bullet for her in a heartbeat and die for her without a second thought. Her safety will always be Matt's top priority."

"How do you know?"

"Because I would do the same for my wife. Matt cares deeply about Delilah and that makes him more dangerous to anyone who threatens her, including you. Do you have more questions?"

"Why can't you tell me about his missions? Don't you have access to them?"

Zane chuckled. "I know more than I tell anyone. The missions are classified which means the brass determined knowledge of his work is a threat to national security. I'm also military. I won't leak classified intel to satisfy your curiosity. If what I told you isn't enough, I'll transfer you to our boss. He'll confirm everything I said."

"No need."

"Matt, anything else I can do to help?"

"Find out who has the insurance policy on the Holloway house and nudge the evaluation process along."

"Will do. Later."

"You're a decorated war hero?" Delilah's eyes were wide.

Cheeks hot, Matt shrugged. "I just did my job." He shifted his gaze to Zach. "Satisfied?"

"Yeah. Sorry."

"Don't be. If I were in your shoes, I'd want the same reassurance. Any other reason you followed us besides concern for Delilah's safety?"

A snort. "Isn't that enough? Someone wants her dead."

"Would that someone be you?"

Zach's jaw dropped. "No!" He turned to Delilah. "Come on, Dee. We weren't close growing up, but you can't believe I would hurt you."

"I didn't believe I had an enemy before two people broke into my house and attacked me."

What little color Delilah's brother had in his face drained away. He buried his face in his hands. "This is my fault."

Matt's eyes narrowed. "Explain." If Zach had anything to do with Delilah's injuries, he would pay.

"I'm sorry, Dee."

"What have you done?"

A wry laugh escaped. "Better question is what haven't I done? Look, not everybody is as driven and successful as you are."

Delilah blinked. "My shop is in the black, but not by much, and that's only been in the past year. I'm not wealthy. I work hard, but I love my shop and community."

"Mom talked about you and your shop all the time."

Matt poured himself a mug of coffee. "How did she know Delilah's shop was doing well?"

"Hired a private investigator to poke around. She was proud of you, Dee."

"She never told me that."

The pain in Delilah's voice raked at Matt's insides. He sat beside her and wrapped his hand around hers. "Get back on point, Zach. Why are you blaming yourself for the attack on your sister?"

"I like to gamble." At Delilah's pained look, Zach scowled. "What? I'm an adult and I have the money. I can afford to lose a little here and there." He winced. "At least, I did have the money to lose."

Matt shook his head. "Gambling is a fool's game. The odds are in favor of the house. Always. If you think you're responsible for what's happening to Delilah, then you lost a lot of money to someone calling in your marker."

Zach slumped in his chair. "Yeah, all right. I owe a lot of money. The guy I owe isn't keen on waiting for his payout."

"How much, Zach?" Delilah reached out her free hand to her brother. He grabbed hold as though gripping a lifeline.

"Fifty thousand. It wouldn't be a problem if Mom had given me the money before she died. This guy knows I'm good for it."

Matt snorted. "Get real. Joey Petrelli is a loan shark. He's not known for his patience."

Outrage filled the other man's face. "You had me investigated?"

"You're a threat to Delilah. You bet I looked into you and your financial situation."

"That's an invasion of privacy."

"Ask me if I care, Frost. No one matters to me more than your sister."

"You can't go on this way, Zach." Delilah squeezed his hand. "The gambling and alcohol will destroy your life if you don't stop."

"You don't know anything about it. How could you? Your life is perfect."

She burst into laughter. "Have you forgotten how much I weighed when I left Harmony?"

"Of course not. What does that have to do with me?"

"I had to take control of my life and my eating. I still fight that battle every day. Food is my addiction and I can't ever let down my guard."

"I don't think I'm as strong as you."

"If you're serious about breaking the addictions, you'll need help. You can't do it alone."

"I'll think about it after I get Petrelli off my back."

Delilah glanced at Matt.

He pressed a kiss to her temple. "Your choice," he murmured. Unless Zach wanted help, the money from Delilah would only be a temporary fix.

She reached into her pocket for the check she'd filled out before leaving the hotel and slid it across the table. "This is your five-year allotment from Mom. The money train stops right here, Zach. Mom made sure I didn't have the authority to give you more. Make good use of it, bro."

Zach stared at the check a moment, relief flooding his face. "I don't know how to thank you."

"Find something to do with your time that doesn't include gambling and alcohol. Get a job you love, Zach.

You're the only family I have left. I don't want to lose you, too."

He shoved the check into his pocket. "I'm mostly sober now. You promised answers. What's going on with Randy? Why did the police take him for questioning?"

"The autopsy results indicated your mother was murdered. Someone smothered her."

"That's crazy. Why would anyone murder Mom? She was dying with only hours to live."

"The person who killed her believed murdering Michelle was worth the risk."

Zach shook his head, winced as he pressed a hand to his forehead. "What does that have to do with Randy?"

"Delilah and I walked into your mother's hospital room with the alarms going off and Randy standing over her with a pillow in his hands."

Delilah's brother leaped to his feet, hands fisted. "He killed her? Randy killed Mom?"

"Sit down," Matt snapped. "We don't have proof your stepfather hurt Michelle. Detective Russell is investigating her death. He'll find the truth." And if he didn't, Matt would. He wouldn't stop until he eliminated the threat to Delilah.

"Why did you say you were to blame for the danger I'm in?" Delilah asked.

"Your boyfriend is right. Petrelli is a shark. When I was late paying back the money I owe, he threatened to go after my family."

Matt's muscles bunched. "Petrelli knows about Delilah?"

Zach swallowed hard.

"How does he know, Zach?"

Silence.

"You told him, didn't you?" He slammed a fist on the table. "How could you throw her under the bus? She would have no chance against scum like that."

"I didn't think he'd act on the knowledge because I intended to pay back the money."

Petrelli was a loose end Matt would have to tie up. He didn't believe for one minute that Zach was ready to seek help for his addictions. That meant he'd be returning to Petrelli for more money in the near future. Only this time Delilah's brother wouldn't have a ready source of cash to repay the loan. The shark would go hunting to get his money and that was a danger Matt wouldn't allow. He couldn't deploy with Bravo if he was worried about her safety. No matter the cost to himself, Matt would end the threat to Delilah.

"Be careful, Dee." Zach leaned closer. "Mom's lottery money brings out the worst in people."

CHAPTER THIRTY

Before climbing into the SUV, Delilah turned to Matt. "I don't want Zach to be the one targeting me." The idea that her brother might have tried to kill her more than once made her stomach knot. "Do you think he's guilty?" Delilah willed him to say no. Matt would tell her the truth whether she wanted to hear it or not.

The medic cupped her cheek with his palm. "I don't think he has the spine to hurt you."

"That doesn't exclude him from using someone else to do his dirty work." She'd just lost her mother. Would she lose her brother, too?

"No, it doesn't." Matt's thumb brushed across her cheekbone in a gentle caress. "I won't rule him out until I have proof, Delilah, but I don't think he's responsible for the attacks."

Some of her tension floated away. While she questioned her own judgment, Delilah trusted Matt's. His goal was to keep her safe, not protect a relationship which may be more wishful thinking than fact. "Who should we talk to next?"

"Your cousin, Evan." Matt keyed Evan's address into his navigation system. "Tell me about your cousin."

"He was a bully all through school, but since he was best friends with Pond Scum, no one dared call Evan down for his behavior. My aunt and uncle died in a car crash when my cousins were in middle school. Shane turned 11 and Evan 12 not long before their deaths."

"How did your mother and Randy end up with them?"

"They were such terrors no other family members would take them. Since Mom didn't want her nephews in the foster care system, she volunteered to take them. She was fragile, though, unable to care for herself or her family. Adding my cousins into the mix made the tension and stress in our household worse."

"Randy was agreeable to your cousins moving in?"

"Mom didn't give him a choice. The boys were family. As far as she was concerned, that was the end of the discussion."

"Did your stepfather resent being forced to take them on?"

"I'm embarrassed to admit I was so consumed by my grief over losing Dad I didn't pay attention to the rest of my family. My guess is Randy didn't care. He never disciplined Zach or me. I don't remember him correcting my cousins. Randy ignored us to pursue his own interests. He was good to Mom, though." Delilah frowned. "Except for his cheating. I had no idea he'd been doing that."

The knowledge made her heart ache for her mother. Had she known about the women? Maybe that's why she forced Randy out of the house with only his belongings and the promise of money for five years.

"Did Evan work before your mother started bankrolling the family?"

"Mom mentioned Evan working at the auto repair shop. He has a knack for fixing things, especially vehicles. He kept the family's fleet of cars running during the lean years." She smiled. "He might be a bully, but Evan works magic with engines of any kind."

"And now he doesn't work anywhere." Matt frowned. "Unemployment isn't good for anyone."

"Why do you say that?"

"Our self-worth is tied closely to our jobs. If we can't find work, we spiral into depression and discouragement."

"But Evan quit."

He slid a glance her direction. "He needs a purpose in life, Delilah. A reason to get up in the mornings besides the vices people fall into when they're bored or aimless. Volunteering counts as work and provides as much purpose as a paying job."

"I can't see Evan volunteering for anything except buying the next round of beer at one of the local watering holes. That was his favorite pastime from the day he earned his first dollar at the repair shop during high school. A philanthropist, he's not."

Matt turned right into a long, winding driveway and parked in front of a large Georgian home. "Nice."

Delilah goggled at the picturesque home and grounds. She met Matt at the front of his vehicle. "I don't know what to expect from Evan."

"I have a good idea. When he learns why you're here, he may settle down."

"And if he doesn't?" Matt didn't know Evan like she did. He was belligerent and cruel, purposely hurting people if he could get by with it. Sad to say, he was better with engines than people.

"I'll handle it. He's a homegrown terrorist. I hunt terrorists for a living."

She remembered the confrontation in the lawyer's office and the ball of ice in her stomach melted. Delilah didn't like conflict, but she wasn't a teenager without help. She had obligations. No one, including Evan, would stop her from carrying out her mother's wishes. Handing Evan his payout also meant she wouldn't have to deal with her cousin again after today.

Matt rang the doorbell. A minute later, he followed up with a hard knock and another punch to the doorbell.

"Hold your horses," a female voice called.

Delilah groaned. Evan had female company. He didn't care if the busybodies in Harmony knew about his flavor of the week. Delilah, however, didn't want to see irrefutable proof of his dalliances.

Someone fumbled with the locks and the door swung open to reveal a redhead with rumpled hair. She was dressed in a short, kimono-style robe in peacock blue, legs and feet bare.

"We need to speak to Evan," Matt said.

"He's still in bed. Come back later." Red started to close the door, but Matt shoved the door open.

"Hey!"

"Tell him Delilah is here to see him."

A scowl. "I'm not telling him some bimbo is here to see him. Evan's mine. I'm not into sharing. Buzz off."

"I'm his cousin." Delilah threaded her fingers through Matt's when she saw the muscles in his jaw twitch. "He'll want to see me."

"Cousin?" Red looked suspicious. "Well, all right. Just don't take long." Her lips curved. "I have plans for him that don't include visitors." Her gaze trailed over Matt. "Unless you want to join us. Could be fun."

"Get Evan up or I'll do it myself," Matt said. "He won't be a happy man if I drag him out of bed

With a huff, Red spun on her heel and stomped from the entryway, leaving the door wide open.

"I'll take that as an invitation." Delilah walked inside with Matt on her heels. She veered to the right to the living room. Glancing around, she spotted her mother's signature Bonsai tree.

"Your mother's handiwork?" Matt stayed by Delilah's side.

"Bonsai tree and her balance of design, color, and comfort. Her work improved after I left Harmony."

Heavy footsteps heralded Evan's approach. Delilah's cousin strode into the room dressed in boxers, an angry scowl on his face. "What do you want, Dee?"

"We need to talk."

"Later. I'm busy."

"If you want your payout before this time next year, you'll talk to me now."

Evan glowered and, hands fisted, stalked toward her.

Matt eased Delilah behind him.

"Hiding behind your boyfriend?" Her cousin sneered at Matt. "This is my turf, Rainer. You barged in here. I have a right to defend myself against intruders."

"Delilah, looks like your cousin isn't interested in money or your mother's murder. Let's not waste our time."

"Wait." Evan caught Matt's arm to prevent them from leaving. "Murder? What are you talking about?"

"Autopsy results are in on Michelle. She was suffocated."

"That's ridiculous. She would have croaked within a day or two at most. Why kill a dying woman?"

"You tell me," Delilah said.

"How should I know? You're the one holding the purse strings."

"That's right. What if something happens to me?"

He blinked. Seconds later, he surged toward Delilah only to find himself sprawled on the couch.

"Stay there," Matt warned.

Evan glared at Delilah. "You're accusing me of killing Aunt Michelle."

"Did you leave the restaurant and sneak into Mom's hospital room ahead of us?"

"Of course not. You saw us. We were at the bar for a couple hours before we went to the restaurant. I have a receipt somewhere for my meal with a time stamp on it. Or you can check with Daisy, the waitress. She'll know when I left the place. I gave her a big enough tip." Another frown. "I don't have to answer your questions. You're not a cop."

"Consider this practice for when the police question you."

He cursed. "They got no reason to question me. I didn't have nothing to do with Aunt Michelle's death. And if you spread around town that I did, my lawyer will contact you."

"The police took Randy in for questioning," Matt said. "Expect them to talk to you and the rest of your family."

"I already said I didn't have nothing to do with it and I got witnesses who will vouch for me. Zach and Shane were with me."

They were also drunk as skunks. Doubtful either would remember too many details about that night.

"I hear you're a good shot with a rifle. What do you have?"

"A .308. What's it to you?"

"A couple of your buddies shot up Baxter's with a .308. Later that night, a shooter with a scope shot at Delilah with the same type of rifle."

"It wasn't me."

"Hope you have an alibi for the time of the shooting, Frost. I'm sure Detective Russell will talk to you soon."

"You said you wanted to talk about money. So, talk."

Delilah handed Evan the check. "Your five-year allotment, paid in full."

Her cousin glanced at the check and tossed it on the coffee table. "Why?"

"You're an adult. Use the money however you want."

He snorted. "That's a drop in the bucket compared to my expenses every year. What am I supposed to do for money now?"

"Find a job."

"Get real. I don't want to work for old man Dixon, but it's the only job I'm qualified for. He cheats the customers."

"Open your own place." Delilah indicated the check he'd tossed aside. "There's the capital to start. You're a better mechanic than Dixon."

He was silent a moment. "Is that how you started your shop?"

"What do you mean?"

"Did Aunt Michelle front you the startup capital?"

"No, she didn't. I earned a business degree, worked long hours in candle shops, and worked second jobs while saving every penny I could spare to start my own business. Starting Wicks was the best decision I ever made besides losing weight."

Evan's gaze swept over her, his forehead furrowed. "Did you have surgery?"

Delilah shook her head. She'd explored that option. Ultimately, lack of money and fear of the surgery itself helped her decide against the procedure.

"I'm getting tired of waiting for you, Evan," a petulant female voice called from down the hall. "Hurry up."

"Shut up," Evan yelled. He turned back to Delilah and Matt. "I gotta go."

"We'll see ourselves out." Matt cupped Delilah's elbow and escorted her from the house.

As they drove away from Evan's home, she twisted to look at the medic. "Wonder how long the redhead will stick around when she figures out the waterfall of money is gone."

"Couldn't say."

"She was beautiful."

The corner of his lips tugging upward. "Was she? I didn't notice."

"How could you not? She propositioned you."

"She propositioned us. I didn't pay attention to her looks because I'm only interested in you. Aside from assessing other women as potential threats to your safety, they don't matter to me. No woman has caught my attention since the moment I saw you, Delilah."

Delilah's eyes stung. Good grief. Matt Rainer was a keeper.

"Your cousin, Shane, lives outside of town. According to Zane, he bought a cabin twenty miles away in the middle of a 200-acre wooded area. From the aerial pictures, the place is beautiful."

"He's a serious hunter."

"The woods will have plentiful game." His cell phone rang. Matt activated his Bluetooth. "Rainer."

"Matt, it's Kira. We need to talk."

CHAPTER THIRTY-ONE

Matt's grip on the steering wheel tightened. He knew that tone in Kira's voice. Trouble. "You're on speaker with Delilah Frost. Delilah, this is Kira Brody, the forensic accountant I asked to look into your mother's accounts." After the women greeted each other, he asked, "What did you find, Kira?"

"Oddities in Michelle Holloway's accounts being administered through Oliver Shannon's office. By the way, you didn't make a good impression on the lawyer. He gave me what I needed with great reluctance and many threats. Needless to say, he's not a fan of yours."

"I'm not surprised." Didn't hurt his feelings, especially since his precaution paid off. Matt hadn't expected to find issues with the accounts. Now that he had, he would pursue the lead.

She laughed. "And you're not bothered by it, either."

"Nope."

"What kind of oddities?" Delilah asked.

"Someone has been skimming money out of the accounts almost from the beginning. I have to report my findings to the authorities, Matt."

"Do it. The sooner, the better." Matt reached for Delilah's hand. "Do you know how much has been taken, Kira?"

"Five million and change. Considering how much Mrs. Holloway was worth, no one would have noticed if you hadn't asked for the audit."

"Can you trace where the money went?" Delilah asked.

"The initial deposits went to the Essex Corporation in an offshore account. It's a shell corporation with ties to the Cayman Islands. From there the money was routed all over the world into multiple holding companies and then transferred to a Swiss bank account. That's as far as I'll be able to track it. Zane might be able to do something further, but I can't guarantee that."

"Anything else?" Matt asked.

"Not right now. I'll keep digging, but I thought you'd like to know what I have so far."

"Great job, Kira. I owe you one."

She laughed. "Yes, you do, and I intend to collect."

Uh oh. That sounded expensive. "What's this going to cost me?"

"Your Nolan Ryan baseball card."

Matt flinched. "Sheesh, Kira. That hurts." He'd looked long and hard for that card and had been lucky to find one in mint condition.

"It's for my nephew."

That took some of the sting out of his loss. Jase was a great kid. "How is Jase doing?"

"He's hanging in there."

"Still waking at all hours of the night?"

"Unfortunately. He wakes up crying for my sister. I don't know how to help him, Matt." The forensic accountant's voice was rough.

"Talk to Marcus Lang. He might have some suggestions."

"That's a great idea. I don't know why I didn't think of that sooner. Thanks."

"Sure. I'm out of town with Delilah right now. I'll get the card to you as soon as I return to Otter Creek."

"Thanks, Matt. Jase will be thrilled."

Maybe the baseball card would lift the nine-year-old's spirits. Although he hadn't seen the boy in a while, Matt liked to spend time with the baseball fanatic whenever he was in Nashville. "Send me everything you have, Kira. I'll pass the information along to the detective working on Mrs. Holloway's murder."

"Will do. Best of luck to you and Delilah on sorting everything out. I've got another call. I have to go." She ended the call.

Matt accelerated onto the highway.

"What does this mean, Matt?"

"You're a target because you're the executor of your mother's estate and the missing money. Whoever is embezzling money from your mother's accounts is desperate to hide the theft."

She looked skeptical. "Oliver Shannon may have been stealing from my mother?"

"Wouldn't hurt to check his financial status."

"But he's been Mom's friend and lawyer for years. Mr. Shannon was the one who handled all the details when my father died. I can't see him doing this to Mom."

"We have to start somewhere. Look, I don't like this anymore than you do, but the fact is we're likely to learn the guilty culprit is someone you know."

"I hate the thought that someone who could be family or a friend is a snake in the grass, waiting to strike me down."

"I'm not fond of snakes."

She stared. "You hunt terrorists and yet you're afraid of snakes?"

Matt frowned, his face burning. "Hey, some of the deadliest snakes in the world are natural inhabitants of the places Fortress sends Bravo. I have to keep my mike bag stocked with anti-venom in case we're bitten on a mission. I'm not a fan."

"Want to know a secret?"

Disgruntled, he glanced her direction. "What?"

"I'm not a fan of snakes, either."

Some of his irritation vanished. "I won't discover you have a secret pet snake?"

"Good grief, no." She shuddered.

"Excellent. We're made for each other." He noted her quick glance his direction and wondered if she knew he meant what he said. Delilah was perfect for him.

When he parked in front of Shane's cabin, his mood had mellowed considerably. Might have had something to do with the company on the drive. After the snake discussion, Delilah asked him about his baseball card collection and how he'd started the hobby.

A fun way to spend the time. She seemed genuinely interested and Matt rarely had a chance to talk baseball with anyone. His teammates were football and NASCAR fans. "Hope you didn't mind me droning on about my secret vice."

"It's fascinating. I loved to watch baseball with my dad, but he wasn't a card collector. He took me to a professional game once. We enjoyed it."

Matt turned off the engine. "What team did you watch play?"

"Texas Rangers. They won the night we attended the game. I've been a fan of theirs since then."

He came around to her door. Matt clasped her hand and approached the porch. He knocked on the door, glancing in the large window into the living room.

He caught a glimpse of the back of a woman with long, dark hair as she broke out of an embrace with Shane Frost and hurried out of sight. A door slammed and a moment later a vehicle engine turned over. Was the woman or Shane leaving, or both of them?

The front door swung open. Shane frowned at Matt and Delilah. In unbuttoned jeans, an unbuttoned shirt, and bare feet, Shane stepped back. "I suppose you want to talk."

"Evan called." Delilah moved past her cousin, her hand still cradled in Matt's.

"And Zach. I hear you two have been stirring up trouble all over town." As he closed the door, a vehicle sped around the side of the house.

From the corner of his eye, Matt saw a silver SUV speed past. Guess the lady didn't want to stick around for the interrogation. "Sorry to chase off your visitor."

Shane shrugged. "She had to go back to work anyway. I need coffee. Want some?"

"Sounds good." People tended to relax more over food or drink. Maybe Shane would be more forthcoming than his brother or cousin.

He and Delilah followed in Shane's wake and sat at a round wooden table in the kitchen.

"Coffee, Dee?"

"No, thanks."

"What brings you by this early?"

Delilah laughed. "It's 10:30. Most of the workforce has been working for over two hours."

Shane set a mug of coffee front of Matt before pouring the last of the coffee for himself and joining them at the table. "Point taken." He sipped the steaming liquid. "I haven't had to worry about time for years." He sent her a pointed look. "Guess that's about to change."

Delilah shrugged. "I'm only carrying out Mom's instructions. It's nothing personal."

"Maybe not to you, cousin, but it's all kinds of personal to me. You're taking away my livelihood."

"Your livelihood doesn't consist of sleeping half the day away and staying up all night like a vampire. Will you go back to work now?"

"All things considered, I suppose I'll have to do something for money, won't I?"

Matt's eyes narrowed at the sharp edge to Shane's words. "Where did you work before Michelle won the lottery?"

"Hunting and fishing guide."

Made sense. "Think you'll go back to that?"

"Never stopped. I find some hunts are more challenging than others." Though he smiled, the sentiment didn't reach his eyes. "There's nothing more I love than a good challenge."

"What's your favorite weapon to use on a hunt?"

"Mossberg .308 Scout rifle with a Vortex scope."

Matt sipped his coffee. "Sweet rifle." Also, one capable of firing the rounds at Delilah at the hotel.

A slow nod. "It does the job."

"I hear you're part of an exclusive shooting club."

"That's not a crime."

"Guess you're good with a rifle."

He snorted. "I better be if I'm a hunting guide." Shane tilted his head. "What are you getting at, Rainer?"

"Your buddies, the Randolphs, shot up Baxter's with us in the restaurant. Later that night, someone shot at Delilah on the balcony of our hotel."

"What does that have to do with me?"

"The shooter left behind brass from a .308. You know anything about that?"

A scowl. "Why should I? Hope you're not accusing me of trying to kill my cousin. My lawyer might have something to say about that."

"I'm stating facts and asking questions, Frost. Wouldn't you do the same if your woman had a target on her back?"

Shane's gaze sharpened. "I would do anything it took to protect her."

"Then you understand why I have questions."

"Are you good at your job, Rainer?"

Where was he going with this? "If I wasn't, I'd be dead by now and so would my teammates."

"What exactly do you do for Fortress?"

"I'm a medic." Among other things. All Fortress operatives were cross-trained. Although Matt wasn't in the same league with Liam, he was also trained as a sharpshooter.

"You have the same training as your alpha teammates?"

Shane thought Matt had a beta personality? Unbelievable. "I'm as well-trained as my unit."

"Maybe one day I'll see you in action."

"Where were you two nights ago between nine and eleven?"

"With my lady friend. Don't ask her name. I won't tell you who she is." A smile. "She's shy."

Delilah huffed out a breath. "Harmony isn't a thriving metropolis. Do you really think you can keep her identity a secret?"

Shane laughed. "You'd be surprised what I can do, cousin. Where's my check?"

"Evan must have hit speed dial as soon as we left his house," she muttered. Delilah dug the check from her pocket and slid it across the table.

"You've fulfilled your obligation. Are you leaving town now, Dee?"

"Anxious to get rid of me?"

He lifted one shoulder in a lazy shrug. "Curious. We are related, after all."

Under the table, Matt squeezed Delilah's hand in warning. He didn't want to share too much information with her family. Better to keep them all guessing about Delilah's movements.

"I still have loose ends to tie up with Mom's estate."

"What's to tie up? You distributed the money to us poor saps who've been dependent on Aunt Michelle. Now you can take the remaining money and live in luxury. That's what I'd do if I were in your shoes. You must want to return to your home soon."

"Of course I do. I miss my store. I also have an obligation to Mom."

"She's gone. Aunt Michelle won't know if you follow her instructions to the letter or not."

"I'll know."

He inclined his head in acknowledgment, then turned his attention to Matt. "Next time you're in Harmony, stop by. We'll go hunting and test out your skills on the local wildlife."

Matt's face showed nothing of the revulsion he felt at the prospect of hunting with Delilah's cousin. He hunted enough two-legged predators and the occasional four-legged variety when on missions. He'd rather not kill for sport. "I don't have much down time. What I have, I'll be spending with Delilah."

"Admirable." Shane climbed to his feet. He pocketed the check before leading the way to the door. "I'll be seeing you, cousin."

The door closed behind them with a quiet snick.

As Matt walked with Delilah to his vehicle, he thought about Shane's last statement. Why did it sound like a threat?

CHAPTER THIRTY-TWO

As Matt drove away from Shane's cabin, he handed Delilah his cell phone. "Call Detective Russell." Perhaps the detective had more information he would share. If not, Zane would hack into the computer system and find the information.

"Russell," was the man's short greeting.

"This is Matt Rainer. Delilah and I need to talk to Randy Holloway. Is he still a guest of the police department?"

"We're about to cut him loose."

Matt's gut knotted. "You didn't find anything on the hospital security footage to hold him?"

"Hold a second." When Russell spoke again, the noise level in the background had dropped. "The security footage wasn't much help. Someone in scrubs and a surgical mask entered Mrs. Holloway's room five minutes before her husband arrived. That person left two minutes later. Can't identify the bozo in scrubs." Frustration rang in his voice.

"Did you see the hair color?"

"Surgical cap on the head. What do you want with Holloway?"

"To talk. Delilah's been away from home a long time. Randy knows more about Michelle than anyone else."

"Right."

Yeah, the excuse was lame, but he didn't owe the cop an explanation. "Did you or one of the patrolmen bring Randy to the station?"

"That's right. Why?"

"He'll need a ride to his girlfriend's place. Hold him for thirty minutes and we'll give him a lift. That will allow Delilah time to talk to him without interruption."

"I can lose his paperwork for another thirty minutes. What's your game plan, Rainer?"

"Same as you. Track leads and see where they go."

"In other words, you're using your girlfriend as bait."

He scowled. "I would never knowingly place Delilah in danger. She means everything to me."

"Got a funny way of showing it, pal. Word's out around town that you're talking to all the major players in Mrs. Holloway's murder."

"Most of them are beneficiaries of Michelle's will. I won't prevent Delilah from carrying out Michelle's last wishes. I'll be with her every minute. Anyone who wants to harm my woman will have to go through me first." He wouldn't hesitate to use deadly force to protect her.

"I hope you haven't overestimated your skills. You're pushing your luck, my friend. That's on you. Don't make it my problem by presenting me with another crime scene or victim. I'll hold Holloway until you get here."

"We're no closer to an answer than before." Delilah's head dropped back against the headrest. "What do we do now, Matt?"

"Keep moving forward. We stir the pot and see what rises to the top."

"From where I'm sitting, the only thing we're stirring up is trouble."

"We're making someone nervous. If we weren't, you wouldn't be a target."

"That doesn't make me feel better. I don't want either of us in the crosshairs of a shooter. I don't want to lose you."

"You won't."

"You can't guarantee that. What if the shooter's bullet had hit you instead of the French doors the other night?"

He captured her hand. "It didn't. We can't operate on what if's, Delilah. Dwelling on it will paralyze us."

"I can't lose you, Matt. I wouldn't survive."

Matt's head whipped her direction. Did she mean what he prayed she did? "What are you saying?"

"I can't survive without my heart," Delilah said softly.

Now? She had to do this now? Heart slamming against his ribs, Matt didn't say a word as he hunted for a place to pull off. He needed Delilah in his arms before he confessed his secret. Seconds later, he spotted what he was looking for.

He veered right and took the exit for a national park.

"What are we doing? I thought we were going to pick up Randy."

"He'll wait another few minutes. We need to talk." Two minutes later, he parked at the entrance to an easy walking trail with posted signs of many benches along the path.

Matt guided Delilah along the deserted path to the first bench. Perfect. The seat was situated a few feet off the main trail in the shadow of a stand of pine trees.

Hand on her lower back, Matt nudged her toward the bench. Once seated, he attempted to calm his racing heart to no avail. Matt captured her hand and raised it to his lips to press a kiss to her knuckles. "Say that again."

"Which part?"

He frowned. "Don't toy with me, woman. The heart thing."

A gentle smile curved her mouth. "I can't live without my heart, Matt. I love you with everything I am. If I lost you, my life would have no purpose."

Relief swept through him with the force of a tidal wave. "Thank God." He cupped Delilah's nape, tugged her against his chest, and slammed his lips against hers in an act of raw passion. When he raised his head minutes or hours later, they were both gasping for air. "I love you more than I've ever loved anyone in my life, Delilah. You walk into a room and the whole place lights up, including inside me. You're the light in my darkness. With you in my life, I can breathe again. You are my greatest miracle."

"Matt." Tears sparkled on her lashes. "I didn't know you had the soul of a poet."

"Don't spill my secret to my teammates, okay?"

She laughed. "I promise."

After a long, gentle kiss, Matt eased back. "Will you marry me, Delilah Frost?"

"I can't think of anything I want more than to be your wife."

Satisfaction and joy filled him at her quick response. "Soon?"

"How soon?"

"When we return to Otter Creek."

Delilah blinked. "That could be in a day or two."

"I know."

"But we don't know if the target on my back will be removed by then."

"All the more reason to marry now. I'll be able to protect you better if I'm beside you, day and night."

"What if you're deployed with Bravo?"

"If we're called in, I'll take a leave of absence until this is resolved. I won't be able to concentrate if I'm not positive you're safe. I'll be distracted, making me a liability on a mission."

"Your teammates need you. We'll think of some way to keep me protected if you're sent on a mission before this is resolved."

"You didn't answer my question." Matt's hands tightened on her upper arms. "Will you marry me when we return to Otter Creek?"

"As soon as you want."

He held her tight. "Thank you, baby. I swear you won't regret this. I'll do everything in my power to make you happy."

"We'll make each other happy. This isn't a one-way street. We're creating a life together. Your happiness matters as much to me as mine does to you."

Matt hugged her tighter. How could he have been so blessed to have this amazing woman agree to be a permanent part of his life, a partner, a lover, a wife, maybe one day a mother to his children? He longed to discuss a family with the woman of his dreams, but Russell would only be patient for so long. They needed to get going or the detective would cut Delilah's stepfather loose. "We need to go."

Delilah stood. "All I want to do is throw off responsibility for a while and spend every free minute with you."

Matt squeezed her hand as they retraced their steps. "We'll get there. Tonight, we celebrate our engagement with our friends, no matter what happens with the rest of your family."

"I'll hold you to that."

"After we drop off Randy, would you like to pick out a ring?"

"You don't want to wait until we return to Otter Creek?"

"I want everyone to know you belong to me. The sooner, the better."

She stopped in the middle of the path to face him. "You can't be worried about another man stealing me away."

"You don't see yourself the way men do, Delilah. You're gorgeous, successful, and kind. You care about people. That's quite a draw. You bet I want to warn off the competition."

"There is no one but you and hasn't been since you arrived in Otter Creek."

"Good to know. I still want the outward symbol on your finger. I want everyone to know how much I adore you."

"How can I argue with that logic?"

"You can't." He urged her toward the SUV. "Is there a jewelry store you like in Harmony?"

"I used to window shop at O'Shea's Jewelry. They had the most amazing jewelry." Her cheeks flushed. "They were kind to me. It was obvious I couldn't afford to buy anything, yet the shop workers let me try on anything that caught my eye and answered every question. Believe me, I had a million of them."

"We'll go to O'Shea's, then."

By the time they walked into the police station and were admitted to the bullpen, Russell was pacing beside his desk. He scowled at them. "I expected you thirty minutes ago. Where have you been?"

"Unavoidably detained." Matt studied the detective's expression and body language. "What happened?"

"Harrison Norris is bending the ear of the police chief as we speak. It seems his son, Sebastian, whined to his old man about Ms. Frost and her thug boyfriend. You'll be lucky if I don't have to bring you up on charges."

Matt snorted. "For what? There's not a bruise on him." Too bad, that. He wanted to leave the slimy creep with painful reminders that Delilah was no longer alone and helpless.

The detective looked skeptical. "You expect me to believe that?"

"Hunt him down and look at him. When you do, remind Norris that I'm watching him."

"Why do you have it out for him? I can't say I like the man, but I don't understand your animosity toward someone you just met."

Beside Matt, Delilah stiffened. Much as he longed to tell the detective the truth, he didn't want to break a confidence. "He was one of a pack of boys who bullied Delilah in school."

"So, you're waging psychological warfare." The corner of Russell's lips curled upward. "I like it. Think the tactic will work?"

"For his sake, it better."

"I heard from the arson investigator right after you called. I'm sorry, Ms. Frost. The house is a total loss and he confirmed a bomb started the fire."

"I'm not surprised. The house was engulfed in flames when Matt and I left yesterday."

Matt rubbed Delilah's back. "You ready to kick Randy loose, Russell?"

"Oh, yeah. He's been making a nuisance of himself, whining about the injustice of being brought into the station and mistreated by officers with no respect for authority."

Matt rolled his eyes.

"Sounds like him," Delilah said. "We'll take him to his girlfriend's place and get him out of your hair."

"You'll earn the thanks of every officer on Harmony's police force," he muttered. Russell strode away and returned ten minutes later with Randy Holloway dogging his steps, lips flapping as he groused.

"Zip it, Holloway." Matt slid his arm around Delilah's shoulders.

"What are you doing here?"

"Giving you a ride. Let's go unless you want to walk to your girlfriend's place."

"What's the hurry?" Randy lumbered after them, his breath coming in puffs by the time they reached the lobby door.

"We have plans."

"In a rush to spend all my wife's money, Dee?" was the bitter response from Delilah's stepfather.

As soon as they were clear of the police station lobby, Matt spun around to face him. "Do you remember what I told you at the hospital, Randy?"

The man stumbled back a couple steps. "Sorry," he muttered although it was obvious he wasn't the least bit sorry.

"Don't insult her again." Matt inclined his head toward his black SUV. "That's my ride. You walking or riding to your girlfriend's place?"

Another glare at Matt and Delilah, but Randy kept his mouth shut and walked to the vehicle, giving Matt a wide berth.

Smart man. After helping his future wife into the shotgun seat, Matt climbed behind the wheel and cranked the engine. "Where to, Holloway?"

"258 Tulip Grove Road."

"Take a right on Main," Delilah said. "Tulip Grove Road is about five miles away. You'll turn left into the Tulip Grove Estates."

With a nod, Matt drove from the police station parking lot.

"What are you planning to do with the money?" Randy asked Delilah from the backseat.

"I don't know yet."

"I've been thinking."

Matt's eyes narrowed. This ought to be good.

Delilah turned to look at her stepfather. "About what? The fact that you cheated on my mother for years and blew through her money like there was no tomorrow?"

He scowled. "Your mother understood how our marriage worked. Michelle accepted my preferences."

"I don't believe that for a minute. I'd care a great deal if Matt had an affair."

"Never going to happen, sweetheart." Matt kissed the back of her hand. "Why would I settle for less than perfection?"

She flashed him a blinding smile before looking at her stepfather. "What's your point, Randy?"

"I know you can't divide the lottery winnings because of Michelle's ridiculous will. That doesn't prevent you from giving gifts to your family."

"Gifts?"

"Cars, houses, trips, vacations, boats. Gifts."

Matt glared at the slimy worm in the rearview mirror. "Forget it, Holloway. You've had your fun. Michelle cut you off permanently. If she loved you so much, why did she change her will?"

"How should I know? It's not fair. I'm tempted to seek out a lawyer. What have I got to lose?"

"Money you don't have. Lawyers are expensive. If you take Delilah to court and the ruling goes against you, that empty bank account of yours will go into the red. Do you really want to gamble a good portion of the money Michelle left you on breaking an air-tight will?"

"Why bother to give me a ride? Did you just come to gloat about your good fortune, Dee?"

"Two reasons. One, I wanted to give you this." Delilah handed him the check.

Randy's eyes widened. "The whole amount. Why?"

"I thought you and the rest of the family might need the whole amount while you all decide what jobs to pursue."

"And the second reason?"

"Do you know anything about the attacks on Delilah?" Matt asked.

The other man frowned. "What attacks?"

"The Randolphs shot up Baxter's with us inside. Later that night, a sniper fired at Delilah when she sat on the balcony of our hotel. Yesterday afternoon, someone detonated a bomb in Michelle's house."

"I don't know anything about . . ." Randy's voice petered off. "Did you say a bomb?"

"That's right. Somebody planted a bomb and set it off with Delilah inside the house. Know anything about that?"

"Are you insane? Of course I don't. I've been at the police station for more than a day. I had nothing to do with any of that." He turned to Delilah. "Is the damage bad?"

"Total loss. What the bomb didn't take out, the fire finished. I hope you removed everything from the house, Randy. If you didn't, your belongings are now ash."

Matt turned left into Tulip Grove Estates and followed Randy's directions to his girlfriend's place. He parked in front of a two-story brick house with flowers blooming in abundance in the yard and an agate walkway that led to the porch steps. White posts, slats, and railing enclosed the large porch.

"We need to ask you some questions about Zach and the cousins." Matt unbuckled his seatbelt and climbed out. He met Delilah at the front of the SUV and waited for Randy to heave himself out of the backseat. They followed a few feet behind her stepfather.

At the door, Randy dug into his pocket and pulled out a key.

As he slid the key into the lock, Matt noticed a red dot on his back. "Randy, get down!" At the same time, he grabbed Delilah and took her to the ground, flipping at the last second so he took the brunt of the hit with the ground, then rolled to cover her body with his.

Randy turned. A rifle fired. Delilah's stepfather fell back against the front door, shock on his face. He slid to the ground, a red stain spreading over his white shirt.

CHAPTER THIRTY-THREE

"Randy!" Delilah pushed against Matt's heavy weight. "We have to help him."

Matt hauled Delilah to her feet, tucked her close to his side and rushed her to the SUV. He pushed her inside the SUV. "Stay here where you'll be safe. Call 911 and get an ambulance here." He ran to the back of the SUV and grabbed his medical bag before sprinting to the porch again and dragging Randy behind the dubious protection of the porch rails.

Delilah's hands shook as she grabbed her cell phone and called for help. She gave the address and as many details as she could about Randy and the injury. As she talked to the dispatcher, Delilah watched Matt work frantically on her stepfather. He'd ripped Randy's shirt down the middle, exposing a chest covered with blood. He dug into his bag and applied some type of bandage. The medic checked the pulse in Randy's neck and started CPR.

"Delilah, is the victim breathing on his own?" the dispatcher asked.

"I don't think so. My boyfriend is doing CPR. Tell the ambulance to hurry."

"They're one minute away."

Matt was still working on Randy when the EMTs arrived and took over. He moved his medical bag out of the way as he talked to the men. After a moment, he jogged to the SUV. "There's a bottle of water in the console. Would you get it for me?" He tugged his shirt over his head and tossed it aside.

Delilah found the bottle and waited until Matt finished cleaning his hands with alcohol wipes before handing him the bottle. He broke the seal and poured the water over his hands.

"How is he?"

Matt found a clean shirt in the cargo area and tugged it on. "Doesn't look good. I think the bullet nicked an artery. He's lost a lot of blood and his pulse is weak. I did what I could, but he needs a top-flight surgeon, fast."

Delilah wrapped her arms around his neck and held on tight.

"Are you okay?"

She nodded. Delilah adored this man and admired his strength and courage. After getting her to safety, he'd returned to help Randy despite the danger to himself. The shooter could have shot Matt when he ran back to help her stepfather. He wasn't wearing his protective gear. He would have been as vulnerable as Randy to a sniper's bullet. Matt still didn't hesitate to step up and offer aid to a man he didn't like.

"Did I hurt you when I took you to the ground?"

A head shake. "I was terrified for you. The shooter had a clear shot at you."

His arms tightened around her. "He or she sped off when I grabbed the mike bag."

"How do you know?" Was he trying to pacify her?

"An engine started and tires squealed as someone sped away on the next block. Since there were no more shots fired, the shooter either hit his target or was scared off and left. Didn't you hear the commotion?"

"All I heard was the sound of my heart pounding in my ears." And that's when her body began the horrific shaking. Ticked her off royally. "Oh, brother. I hate this."

"It will pass soon." Matt kissed her. "I'll get a blanket. The warmth will help. Unfortunately, I don't have a soft drink in the vehicle and we can't leave. The police will want to talk to us."

"Again. Detective Russell won't be happy when he hears about this."

They watched as the ambulance pulled away from the house with Randy on board. Would this be the last time they saw her stepfather alive? Matt retrieved the blanket and wrapped the warm material around her shoulders.

An unmarked police car skidded to a stop behind them and Detective Russell strode toward them, his expression grim. "What happened?"

Between them, she and Matt conveyed the events of the past few minutes to the detective. When they were finished, he dragged a hand down his face. "I told you not to give me another crime scene."

"Not intentional," Matt said.

"Did you see the shooter?"

"No. I heard a vehicle start up and race away on the next block a couple minutes after the shot was fired."

"One shot? You're sure?"

"Positive. Shooter had a laser on the rifle."

"Was Delilah the target again?"

"The laser stayed on Randy. If Delilah was the target, the sniper would have fired shots at her. The shooter hit what he aimed for."

"What are Randy's chances of survival?"

"Not good. He suffered substantial blood loss. His life depends on the skill of the trauma surgeon and a boatload of luck."

"I don't like the guy, but he doesn't deserve this." Russell speared Delilah with a pointed glance. "Why did you and Rainer offer Holloway a ride? Did you set him up for this?"

Matt stiffened, his gaze hard.

Delilah gripped Matt's hand. She didn't want the medic punching the police detective. "I wanted to give Randy the money my mother left him in her will. You'll find the check I wrote in his wallet."

"What about you, Rainer? You haven't denied being willing to kill to protect your girlfriend. Is this your handiwork?"

Matt scoffed. "You must think I can be in two places at once. Again, the shot was fired from across the street with a rifle. Delilah and I were ten feet behind Holloway. I didn't shoot him."

"A couple officers reported a confrontation between you and Holloway outside the station. Maybe this is a case of payback."

"Holloway insulted Delilah. I called his hand on it. He apologized. That was the end of it."

"And if it hadn't been the end?"

"He would have gotten a black eye, not a bullet in the chest."

"What about your teammate, Cade? I'm sure he's more than capable of making the shot."

"He's in our hotel room with his wife, recovering from his shoulder injury. You're barking up the wrong tree, Detective. Don't waste your time and ours trying to pin this on us."

"This is a quiet neighborhood with several retirees and stay-at-home moms. Someone will have seen something. If you're lying to me, I'll find out."

"The neighbors will corroborate our story. Are we free to go? Delilah and I need to check on Holloway and we have some errands to run."

The detective moved back a step. "Stay available. I will have more questions."

Matt helped Delilah with her seatbelt and circled to climb behind the wheel. As he turned at the corner, Delilah glanced in the side mirror to see Detective Russell watching them leave, suspicion clear on his face.

"He doesn't believe us."

"Would you? We've been involved in too many incidents in the past few days and cops are naturally suspicious."

"Detective Russell can't seriously think we're to blame. I have no motive. According to Mom's will, I inherit everything. Why do I need to kill Randy or the rest of my family?"

"People kill for more reasons than money." He glanced at her. "Your family bullied and verbally abused you. Some would take this opportunity to make the abusers pay."

"My mother is punishing them where they'll feel it the most. In their wallets." As angry as she had been at their unfair and cruel treatment, Delilah had never wished them ill. Despite everything, she still loved her brother and mother. The cousins, she tolerated.

"Let's check on Randy first, then we'll go to O'Shea's." He called Trent for an update on Cade and reported Randy's injury. "Delilah and I are on the way to the hospital. We have an errand to run, then I'll take Delilah to lunch and talk to the lawyer. He has some explaining to do."

"Watch your back. I don't want to be down two team members."

"Yes, sir."

Minutes later, they walked into the emergency room and approached the information desk. "We're here for Randy Holloway," Matt said.

"Are you family?"

"I'm his stepdaughter," Delilah said. She should have called Zach and her cousins. Everything had happened so fast.

"Have a seat in the waiting room and I'll check his status for you."

Matt escorted Delilah to seats against the wall where he could watch the nurse at the desk as well as the exits. The action made her smile. This would be her life. Matt and his teammates were always prepared for the worst. A good thing. He'd saved her life more than once since this crazy journey began.

He wrapped his arm around her and drew her close. "Still cold?"

Delilah shook her head. "The blanket did the trick."

The nurse walked into the waiting room. "Mr. Holloway is in surgery. The doctor will update you when the surgery is complete."

Or if Randy died on the operating table. "Thanks for checking."

"We're likely to be here a while." Matt patted his shoulder. "Rest for a few minutes."

"After I let Zach and the others know about Randy." She sent a text to her brother and cousins, then slid her phone away and leaned her head against Matt's shoulder. "I don't know if any of them will show up."

"All you can do is give them information. What they do with it is on them." He pressed a soft kiss to her temple. "Sleep if you can."

"I should be offering you my shoulder. You're the one who was up all night."

He chuckled. "I'll take you up on that offer after we're married."

With a smile on her face, Delilah closed her eyes and relaxed against the love of her life. She woke with a start sometime later when Matt rubbed her arm and said her name. "What?"

"The surgeon is here."

Delilah sat up to see a man dressed in scrubs waiting nearby. She and Matt stood. "I'm Randy's stepdaughter, Delilah Frost."

"Dr. Rosenthal. I'm sorry, Ms. Frost. We did everything we could, but Mr. Holloway didn't survive the surgery."

Matt slid his arm around her waist.

"Do you know if he had other family who should be notified?"

"I never heard him mention anyone, but I know who probably does. We'll make sure his relatives are notified."

"Give the nurse at the desk information about what should be done with Mr. Holloway's remains. Again, I'm sorry for your loss."

As the surgeon hurried away, Delilah turned to bury her face against Matt's chest, reveling in the security of his embrace. Would the danger and fallout never stop? Worse, she felt guilty because she was grateful Randy was gone and Matt was still alive and well.

"Dee." Zach ran into the waiting room. "What's happening? How is Randy?"

"The doctor just left. Randy's gone. There was too much damage from the bullet."

Delilah's brother ran his hands through his hair, leaving the strands mussed. "I don't understand. How could this happen? You're a medic, Rainer. Didn't you try to help him?"

"I did everything I could. The bullet did a lot of damage and your stepfather lost too much blood. Within two minutes of the shot, Holloway no longer had a pulse. I performed CPR until the EMTs arrived. The medical personnel did their best. Sometimes, it's just not enough no matter how good you are and how fast the victim receives medical help. This is one of those times. I'm sorry, Zach."

"It's not right. Randy didn't deserve to die. He wasn't shot by accident?"

Matt shook his head. "The bullet was fired from a rifle with a laser. The red dot never moved from your stepfather. This time, Delilah wasn't the target. Randy was."

"Why? He was harmless." Zach swallowed hard. "Do you think Joey Petrelli was behind this?"

"It's possible. When is your deadline to repay the money?"

"Tomorrow at noon."

"Chances are it wasn't your bookie. He'd wait to the deadline before making his point by harming your family members." Matt tilted his head. "Unless there's something else you're not telling us, something that will shed light on this whole mess."

"There's nothing." As he spoke, Zach's gaze darted down and to the left.

Delilah recognized the tell from childhood. Her brother was lying. "Yes, there is, Zach. Spill it."

Looking sick, her brother said, "I slept with his daughter."

Cold chills raced up her spine. "Zach."

"What else?" Matt snapped.

"She's pregnant."

CHAPTER THIRTY-FOUR

Matt scowled at Delilah's brother. "There's nothing more you can do for Randy. You can, however, protect your sister. Pay off your debt immediately. If Delilah gets so much as a tiny scratch on her body from Petrelli's goons and I find out you're to blame, I'll take you apart with my bare hands."

What little color Zach had in his cheeks drained away at Matt's threat. "Are you serious?"

"Try me."

"Yeah, all right. I'll take care of it right away." Zach looked at Delilah. "You okay, Dee?"

"It's a tossup as to whether I'm more angry or afraid. Other than that, I'm peachy."

A small smile tugged at her brother's lips. "I can see that."

"I sent a text to the cousins about Randy. Should we wait here for them to arrive?"

"They aren't coming. Evan and Shane tolerated Randy, but there was no love lost between them. Do what you need to do, Dee." He turned to leave and stopped. "Will you let me know when you're leaving town?"

"Sure."

"Zach." Matt waited until Delilah's brother focused on him. "Get help for that gambling addiction, for your sake and Delilah's. If Petrelli stays after you because of his daughter and the baby, let me know. I'll see what I can do."

With a nod, Zach strode away, hands shoved into his front pockets.

"I need to tell the nurse the arrangements for Randy."

"Have the hospital release the body to the same funeral home your mother chose. The funeral home will wait for your instructions. In the meantime, the lawyer may be able to shed some light on whether or not Randy had relatives. Besides, since Randy's death was a homicide, the ME won't be releasing the body immediately."

He threaded his fingers through hers and walked with Delilah to the nurses' desk. After conveying the necessary information, they left the hospital. On the way to O'Shea's, Matt called the detective and reported Holloway's death. "The hospital has Holloway's personal items. Make sure you confiscate the check Delilah wrote. I don't want that floating around."

"I'll take care of it. Holloway's girlfriend arrived a few minutes ago. She's understandably upset and says Holloway didn't have an enemy in the world."

"Does she know if he has any family members we should notify?"

"I'll ask her and leave a message with Fortress."

When Matt parked in front of O'Shea's, he caught Delilah's hand and kissed her palm. "Choose whatever you want."

She looked skeptical. "Why don't I choose several that I like, and you make the final selection? That way, you can balance my tastes against your bank account. I don't want to cause you hardship."

"I'm not as wealthy as you are, but I do pretty well for myself. Brent Maddox is a generous employer. What we do is dangerous and he compensates us accordingly. I can afford the ring you want, sweetheart."

Delilah froze with her hand on the door latch. "Will Mom's money be a problem between us?"

"No, ma'am. I like the fact my future wife has a bundle of money at her disposal. Makes me happy that you can have some fun and lose the stress about keeping Wicks afloat."

The stiffness left her shoulders. She flashed him a bright smile and opened the door.

Matt escorted her inside the store. The sales assistants greeted them, the male staring at Delilah with a puzzled expression.

"I'm sorry, but do I know you from somewhere? You look familiar."

Delilah smiled. "My name is Delilah Frost. I used to come into your store all the time when I was in high school. You were kind enough to let me browse for hours and answer questions."

The middle-aged man smiled, his eyes twinkling. "Of course. I apologize, Delilah. I didn't recognize you."

She laughed. "I'm not surprised. I've changed quite a bit since those days."

"You look wonderful, my dear. I heard you had left town. What brings you back? Visiting family?"

"My mother passed away a few days ago. I'm here to handle her estate."

"I'm sorry to hear that."

"Thanks."

"Is there something I can help you with or would you like to browse around like in the old days? I'll be happy to answer more questions for you."

Matt threaded his fingers through Delilah's. "Delilah and I are interested in engagement rings and wedding bands."

"Congratulations. Follow me." He led them to the right side of the room with a long display case of solitaires, wraps, and wedding bands. "Any preference or should I select a few things to get you started?"

Delilah darted a look at Matt.

"You spent a lot of time dreaming in this store. Choose a ring that makes you happy." Matt remained quiet as she and the sales associate discussed different looks and cuts of stones.

When they left the store an hour later, Delilah was wearing an oval-cut sapphire surrounded by diamonds on a wide gold band. Matt helped her into the SUV and kissed her. "The ring is perfect for you."

"It's more beautiful than I ever imagined having on my finger."

"Is this one of the rings you chose while window shopping during high school?"

Her cheeks turned pink as she nodded.

"I'm glad. I'll spend the rest of my life making the rest of your dreams come true."

On the way to a restaurant for lunch, Matt smiled when he caught Delilah sneaking peeks at the glittering gems on her finger. It eased something in him to give her a gift that brought such happiness in a week filled with fear, sorrow, and loss.

Following their meal, Matt and Delilah drove to Oliver Shannon's office, hoping to catch him between appointments. He didn't want to give the lawyer time to come up with excuses to avoid seeing them.

As he held the door open for Delilah to enter the building, Matt noticed a man walking rapidly down the street. He frowned. What was Shane doing here? Maybe he consulted with the lawyer about the stipulations in Michelle's will.

Matt trailed Delilah to Shannon's office. The assistant glanced up at their entrance. Matt's eyebrows rose. Ms. Walters's dark hair was mussed and her lipstick smudged. Her cheeks were flushed and her breaths rapid.

"May I help you?" she asked, her tone rapier sharp.

"Delilah needs to see Mr. Shannon."

"Do you have an appointment?"

"If he's not in a meeting or in court, I need to see him."

"He's a busy man, Ms. Frost. You'll have to make an appointment and come back later."

Delilah glanced at Matt. "Guess we'll be announcing ourselves."

They turned away from the desk and walked to the lawyer's closed door.

"Hey, you can't do that."

"Watch me." Delilah pounded on the door and twisted the knob.

Startled, Oliver Shannon glanced up from a document he'd been reading. He scowled at Delilah and Matt. "Did we have an appointment?"

"No, but you'll want to hear what we have to say." Matt laid his hand against Delilah's lower back and urged her inside the office.

"I'm sorry, Mr. Shannon. I told them you were busy today, but they barged in anyway." Ms. Walters shot them an angry glare. "Should I call security and have them escorted out?"

Matt snorted. As if a rent-a-cop stood a chance at making him leave if he didn't want to go.

"It's all right, Lisa. They won't be here long. Will you, Mr. Rainer?"

"That's up to you."

The assistant hovered in the doorway. "Would you like more coffee, Mr. Shannon?"

He smiled. "Thank you."

She left without offering refreshment to Delilah and Matt, leaving the door open. Yeah, Matt's feelings were hurt over that. Not. The angry glare she'd sent his way would have made him uneasy about accepting any type of refreshment from her hand.

Shannon waved them to the chairs in front of his desk. "What was so urgent you couldn't make an appointment with my assistant?"

"Randy Holloway is dead, shot to death two hours ago."

Blood drained from the older man's face. "He was murdered?"

"That's right. I guess you don't know anything about that."

"Of course not. Why would I?"

"You have a good reason to reduce the number of people looking into Michelle Holloway's dealings with your office."

"I had nothing to do with Holloway's death. I haven't left this office since I arrived at 9:00 this morning."

Lisa Walters returned with a steaming mug of coffee in her hands. She, too, looked pale. Interesting considering she'd been flushed and out of breath minutes ago. Perhaps the accusations against her boss upset her.

"What did you mean about reducing the number of people looking into Mrs. Holloway's business with my office?"

"At least one person in your firm has been skimming money from Michelle's accounts almost from the day she put you in charge of them."

"That's outrageous. Are you accusing me of embezzling funds, Mr. Rainer?"

"Someone is guilty as sin. I don't know if it's you or someone else. I won't quit digging until I know who's responsible for the theft."

"You have proof?"

"The forensic accountant I asked to check Michelle's accounts found evidence to back up her findings."

"I see. What will you do now?"

"The authorities have been notified. I want the name of every person authorized to handle those accounts."

"It's a limited list."

"All the better. I want the list now. I'm sure you understand the urgency of the matter."

"Of course," Shannon said, his words stilted. He turned away to his computer.

Shannon's assistant returned. She had pasted a smile on her trembling mouth. "There's a phone call for Ms. Frost."

Matt frowned. "Who is it?"

"Her brother. He says it's important he speaks with her."

Something to do with Petrelli? He straightened.

Delilah motioned for him to stay. "I'll find out what he wants. Get what you need from Mr. Shannon. I won't be gone long."

He didn't like having her out of his sight. "I don't think that's a good idea."

"I'll be in the next room. Two minutes at most."

He gave a reluctant nod. "Don't leave the office for any reason."

Delilah kissed him lightly and preceded Ms. Walters from the room. The assistant closed the door. Matt took a step toward the door to open it again.

"Can we get on with this?" Shannon snapped. "I have court in an hour."

He turned back, determined to get the list and spirit his girl from this place. Matt's skin crawled, never a good sign. Someone in this place was dirty and desperate enough to attempt kidnapping and murder to protect a money trail. "Print the list and we'll be out of your hair."

The lawyer didn't appear to know his computer system well because he used the hunt-and-peck method of typing, squinting at the screen and muttering curses when he made mistakes and had to backtrack.

Good grief. Matt dragged a hand down his face. If Shannon didn't get a move on, Matt would shove him aside and find the information himself. He didn't have Zane Murphy's mad computer skills, but he could navigate the system better than Shannon.

Two minutes later, the lawyer twisted his char around to grab the single sheet of paper spit out by the printer. "If that's all, I'd appreciate you leaving my office so I can prepare for court."

"I'll be back, Shannon. Be available to answer questions."

The older man drew himself up as though affronted.

Matt didn't have time to soothe ruffled feathers. His instincts were screaming at him to get to Delilah. She'd been gone too long. Something was wrong.

He flung open the door and moved into the outer office where all was quiet. No sign of Delilah or Lisa. "Delilah?" No response. He quickly searched the rest of the suite of offices. Other than several startled law associates and assistants who denied seeing Lisa or Delilah, Matt came up empty.

Pulling out his cell phone, he called her number. A cell phone rang close by. A ball of ice formed in his stomach as he followed the sound to the trashcan beneath Lisa Walters' desk. Under a mountain of paperwork dumped in the container rested the Fortress-issued cell phone.

He barged into Shannon's office again. Striding to his desk, Matt slammed his palms on the flat surface. "Where is she?"

Shannon eased his chair further away from the desk. "Who are you talking about?"

"Delilah. She's gone."

The lawyer blinked. "I don't understand."

"What don't you get? My woman is missing and so is your assistant."

"You must be mistaken." Shannon grabbed his desk phone and punched in a number. "I'm sure this will be cleared up shortly. Perhaps they went for coffee or a quick bite to eat."

"She wouldn't go against my instructions unless someone forced her to go."

Several long seconds later, Shannon dropped the phone handset in the cradle, concern filling his gaze. "Lisa isn't answering her phone. I don't understand this. She always answers when I call. My assistant knows how important my job is."

Matt circled the desk and yanked the man up by his lapels until his face was even with the lawyer's. "I'll explain it to you in simple terms. Your assistant kidnapped the woman I love." He gave Shannon a hard shake. "If anything happens to Delilah, you won't be able to find a hole deep enough to hide in to escape me."

CHAPTER THIRTY-FIVE

Delilah's heart slammed against her ribcage. Although she tried to focus on the asphalt ribbon they drove on, her gaze kept shifting to the gun Lisa Walters pointed at her from the passenger seat of her silver SUV. "This isn't a good idea, Lisa."

Harsh laughter escaped from the other woman. "It's a great idea. With you missing, the cops will be more interested in your disappearance than they will in Michelle's money."

Not a half-bad plan except for one thing. "Matt isn't a cop and his focus will be on tracking me."

"He won't find you. You don't have a phone which means he can't track your cell signal. By the time anyone finds you, it will be much too late. If they find your body at all."

Cold chills swept over her despite the soaring temperature of the day. "Matt will never stop looking. He'll tear Harmony apart and interrogate every person connected to my disappearance. That includes you. He'll know I left Shannon's office with you."

Lisa scoffed, her gun steady. "Like I care about that. I'm a good actress. He won't learn anything from me."

"You're fooling yourself, lady. Matt is a trained Special Forces soldier and Fortress honed his skills even further. He knows interrogation techniques that will make you scream and beg to tell him every secret you've ever had." At least, she assumed that was true. If he didn't know the techniques himself, Delilah had a feeling one or more of his teammates would step in to obtain information.

"He's a medic. All they do is slap on bandages. Rainer isn't an alpha like my man. I don't like liars, Delilah."

She shrugged as though she didn't care if the crazy lady believed her. "It's your funeral. Literally. He might be a medic, but he's a trained elite soldier like his teammates."

For a few seconds, Lisa appeared worried, then the lines of concern on her face smoothed out. "His teammates aren't here. I don't have anything to worry about. Besides, my boyfriend will take care of them if they show up. He'll do anything I tell him. All I have to do is point him at the medic and his buddies, and he'll kill them all."

"Your boyfriend can't take on a group of Special Forces soldiers the government spent millions of dollars training in war tactics."

"He's better than any government stooge," she bragged.

The woman was nuts. "Where are we going, Lisa?"

"Keep driving. I'll tell you when to turn." Lisa pulled out her cell phone and cursed. "Shannon's called me four times."

Hope blossomed in Delilah's heart. Matt knew she was missing. She and Lisa didn't have much of a head start. She had to stall for time. Matt would find her. Of that she had no doubt. How to stall was the question? Could she overpower the crazy lady with the gun and steal her phone?

REBECCA DEEL

Not for the first time since she was kidnapped from the lawyer's office, Delilah wished Matt had trained her in self-defense tactics. That would come in handy about now.

In the bright sunlight, Delilah's ring sparkled and sent another wave of determination through her to survive. She wanted the life she'd dreamed of during the darkest hours of the night since Matt Rainer arrived in Otter Creek. Against all hope, the most handsome man she'd ever met had fallen in love with her. She wanted that future and no crazy bimbo was going to steal her dream of loving the medic until they were both old and gray. "Who is your boyfriend?"

Lisa smirked. "You'll find out soon. For a supposedly smart woman, you're stupid, Delilah." Without shifting the weapon from Delilah, the woman punched in a number and pressed the phone to her ear. "Hi, baby. I got her. Everything went just like you said." A pause, then she smiled, a smile that froze Delilah to her bones. "You got everybody? Great. Shouldn't take long. She doesn't stand a chance of escaping us. I'll take her to the meeting point. See you soon."

That conversation meant nothing good for Delilah. As soon as Lisa slid the phone away, Delilah said, "It's not too late to stop this. Let me pull over. You'll be long gone before I get to a phone. If you move fast, the law will never find you or your boyfriend. You can skip the country and live like royalty."

"And live my life on the run? I don't think so. All I have to do is take care of you and play the sick assistant who ran home because I'm dealing with nausea from pregnancy."

Delilah stared at Lisa. "You're pregnant?"

"Two months. I'm so excited. I can't wait to be a mother."

She was horrified to think of this woman and her partner raising an innocent baby in a home filled with evil.

"Is your boyfriend happy about the news?" She didn't really care if the mysterious man was pleased or not, but it seemed wise to connect with Lisa on some level. It might save Delilah's life.

"I haven't told him yet. I'll tell him tonight when we celebrate the end of our trouble with you."

"What does that mean?"

Joyous laughter filled the SUV. "You'll see."

No matter how much she prodded Shannon's assistant, the woman refused to say anything more about what lay in store for Delilah. Maybe it was just as well. She'd rather not prepare herself for one thing only to find out Lisa lied and all Delilah's mental preparations were for nothing.

She tried to keep track of the turns to retrace her steps when she escaped. After taking multiple turns on back roads with no signs, Delilah was forced to concede defeat. Her best bet was to find a phone and call Matt for help. Thank goodness she'd memorized his cell phone number.

One hitch in her plan. For the last twenty minutes, she hadn't passed a dwelling or business. From all appearances, Delilah was driving into the middle of nowhere.

"Turn right at the dirt road." Excitement filled Lisa's voice. "Almost there. This will be so much fun."

For who? Delilah frowned and turned as directed. Once the wheels left the asphalt road, driving was more difficult. Potholes and deep ruts made keeping the SUV under control difficult. The last thing she wanted to do was jar Shannon's assistant enough that she pulled the trigger by accident.

When the dirt path ended at a thick stand of trees, Delilah put the vehicle in park and turned off the engine. "Now what?"

"Get out. If you run, I'll shoot you in the back. I'm an excellent shot. My boyfriend might be ticked off that I ruined his fun, but he'll understand I couldn't let you escape."

Although she longed to plunge into the thick tree cover, Delilah reminded herself the point was to survive until Matt found her. No matter what it took, she wouldn't give up. Praying for strength to face whatever challenge awaited her, she opened the door and moved to the front of the vehicle.

Lisa waved at the nearly invisible trail through the tree line with her gun. "That way."

She walked the trail for nearly fifteen minutes, stumbling and falling a few times over exposed tree roots, before hearing male laughter up ahead. A knot formed in Delilah's stomach.

When she hesitated at the edge of a clearing, Lisa jabbed the gun into her back.

"Move, Delilah. We don't want to keep your date with destiny waiting, do we?" When Delilah stood frozen in place, Lisa shoved her forward.

Stumbling, she fell to her hands and knees, her hair swinging forward to block her view. The fall jarred her cracked ribs, stealing her breath and bringing tears to her eyes. Delilah remained still, taking shallow breaths while the pain subsided. Thank goodness Matt had taped her ribs. Otherwise, the pain would have been debilitating.

Three pair of hunting boots appeared in her field of vision.

"Just what I like to see," one male voice drawled. "A woman on her knees."

"I paid good money for this," a second male said, tone sharp and angry. "Don't tell me she doesn't have any spine."

"You disappoint me, Dee. I expected more fight from you."

Ice water ran through Delilah's veins as she raised her head. Before her stood Sebastian Norris, Donovan Cain, and her cousin, Shane. All three were dressed in fatigues and boots and carried rifles with scopes.

"Do you have my gear?" Lisa asked.

Shane inclined his head toward the duffel bag several feet away. "Go change, baby. We'll wait until you're ready." He turned back to Delilah, his eyes glittering with excitement. "Unless Little Cuz gives us trouble. You won't do that, will you?"

While Lisa grabbed the bag and disappeared into the trees, Delilah rose, grateful the pain in her ribs had eased. "What's going on, Shane?"

"Protecting what's mine."

"The money?"

An ugly smile curved his mouth. "That's a side benefit. I'm protecting my woman just like your boyfriend claims he'll do for you. He's not doing such a great job at that, by the way. You were easy pickings." He chuckled. "So much for his extraordinary training. He let a simple hunting guide steal you from right under his nose."

"Lisa stole money from Mom's accounts?"

"She's a smart woman. Knows all about burying money trails. We have a good nest egg. All that money Aunt Michelle was kind enough to hand over to me every month has gone into accounts overseas."

"You must have made good money with your hunting business. Why would you jeopardize everything you've worked for?"

"I can set up my business elsewhere. By the time anyone knows we're gone, Michelle's money will be in my accounts. I won't ever have to wonder where the next dime is coming from. I'll be able to do whatever I want. Oh, I have big plans, Dee. None of them include handing over that money to you."

"I thought you were doing this for Lisa. Sounds to me like you're planning to take the money for yourself."

"We love each other," Lisa said as she left the tree line. She, too, was dressed in hunting fatigues, boots, and a rifle with a scope. "We're lovers and partners. I protect him and he protects me. Mates for life." She grinned as she tossed the duffel bag aside.

"Can we get on with this?" Donovan Cain said, his gaze sweeping over Delilah. "I want my chance at this one."

"She's mine," Sebastian Norris snapped. "I called dibs on her in high school."

Delilah's stomach lurched as memories from those horrible minutes in the bathroom assailed her.

"My rules." Shane scowled at both men. "Whoever finds her first can do what they want with her."

Oh, man. That didn't sound good, especially not considering the gleam in Donovan and Sebastian's eyes. She needed an escape plan. Fast. "You don't want to do this, Shane." A pack of people dressed in hunting gear and carrying rifles told her these creeps were planning to hunt and she was the prey. "Matt knows I'm gone."

"That's what I'm counting on. Makes the game more challenging."

"What's the game?"

"Capturing you and making off with the prize before your stupid boyfriend figures out where you are." He smirked. "Shouldn't be hard. He doesn't have a clue where you went."

"And when he does find me?"

The smile widened. "Oh, I hope he does. Sebastian and I have a bet going as to who will kill the not-so-super soldier."

A snort from Sebastian. "Should be easy pickings. He patches injuries."

Shane swung his gaze back to Delilah. "Time to run, Dee."

She stared. "Run?"

Shane lifted his rifle to his shoulder and pointed the muzzle at her. "To be fair, I'll give you a twenty-minute head start. Run as fast as you can, Little Cuz, because we're coming for you. Run!"

Delilah spun on her heel and sprinted for the tree line.

CHAPTER THIRTY-SIX

Matt ran from the lawyer's office to his SUV. Inside, he called Zane. "I need help," he said as soon as his friend picked up.

"Talk to me."

"Delilah's been kidnapped."

"Want me to ping her phone?"

"She was forced to leave the phone behind. I have it with me. I think Delilah was taken by Lisa Walters, Shannon's assistant, because she disappeared as well and isn't answering calls. I don't care how many laws you have to break. Find Lisa."

"Do you have her cell phone number?"

Matt told him the number and waited impatiently while Z worked his magic.

"Sorry, Matt. The phone is off. I can't track her that way. What does she drive?"

"Silver Lexus SUV. It looks like last year's model."

"Excellent. I'll need a few minutes to locate the vehicle. In the meantime, one of the geeks will check traffic cams in the area. We'll start you in the right direction and cut down on some time. Do you have your gear?"

"Of course."

"Find somewhere safe to gear up. Want me to call Bravo and alert them?"

Matt cranked the engine and backed away from the curb. "I'll take care of it. Hurry, Zane. Someone wants Delilah dead and I don't know how long they'll keep her alive."

"Copy that. I'll update you in five minutes." Zane ended the call as Matt raced out of town.

Once he reached an abandoned building at the edge of town, Matt parked behind the structure, opened his Go bag, and suited up. That done, he climbed back into his vehicle and called Trent.

"St. Claire."

"Lisa Walters kidnapped Delilah."

"Where do we meet?"

"Don't know yet. Zane's trying to locate Lisa's SUV. In the meantime, one of the geeks is checking traffic cams so I'll have a direction to start."

"We're gearing up now. We'll head for Harmony. When you have coordinates, we'll decide on a rendezvous point."

"Get there when you can. I'm not waiting."

"Rainer."

"No. Would you wait if Grace was missing?"

A growl from his team leader. "No, I wouldn't. Use your head. If you go in without a plan, you'll get yourself killed. You need Bravo and Delilah needs you."

"Cade is down. He needs to stay down." As terrified as he was for Delilah, Matt couldn't forget Cade's compromised health.

"Forget it," his best friend snapped.

Matt scowled. Trent must have put the call on speaker. "If you have to fight in close quarters, you'll be at a serious disadvantage and undo all the work the doctor did on your shoulder."

"I'll be fine. Besides, if I need repair work, you can do the honors while you nag me for not listening to you. Just shut up about it. I'm not staying here."

"Give it up, Rainer," Liam said. "We're ready to roll and Cade hasn't popped any heavy-duty pain pills for hours. Even wounded he's worth ten wannabe terrorists."

Worry for Cade still gnawed at him, but he would have done the same if the situations were reversed. "Yeah, all right. Just be careful, Cade. I don't want to break in a new partner."

"Yeah, yeah. Same here, Matt. Watch your back."

Trent broke in. "As soon as Zane contacts you, call us."

"Yes, sir."

A call came in through Matt's Bluetooth. "Rainer."

"This is Cam Jennings. I'm with Fortress research. I hacked into the traffic cams around the law office. One silver SUV tore out of the parking lot ten minutes before you called Zane. I tracked the vehicle as far as I could. The women took East Main out of town to the north side of Harmony."

"Women?"

"Yes, sir. Both had dark hair. I can probably clean up a picture of them and forward it to your phone."

"Do it. Where did they head, Jennings?"

"I tracked them up Highway 122 for 20 miles. At that point, they turned off onto a side road on the right and disappeared. No traffic cams in that area. I'm sorry."

"You did great. Transfer me to Zane."

"Yes, sir."

Silence, then Zane said, "I'm still working on locating the SUV. I need another five to ten minutes."

"Jennings gave me a starting direction. She said the women took Highway 122 for 20 miles and took a right onto a side road. Can you tap into a satellite?"

"You bet. Hold."

The sound of Zane's rapid typing brought a brief smile to Matt's lips. The only other person he knew who could make a computer almost sit up and beg was a Navy SEAL who was also a top-flight sniper and a friend.

"Got it. I sent you the link for the still shot of the area and another link for the sequenced shots. The satellite is almost out of range. I have backdoor access to a military satellite that will be in position in twenty minutes. I'll have the link ready at the twenty-minute mark if we need it."

"Send the same information to the rest of Bravo. They'll converge on my location." Matt sped onto the entrance ramp to Highway 122. "Can you work on the SUV's location and feed me information about the area in the satellite stills as I drive?" The mission clock ticked in his head, counting down the last minutes of Delilah's life. He knew in his gut if he didn't find her in the next hour, he'd lose the love of his life.

More keys clicked. "The road they took leads into a large forested area that butts up against a wildlife preserve and a river."

"Who owns the property?" Matt weaved his way through traffic on the highway, urgency riding him hard.

"Hold." A moment later, Zane returned. "A business called Into The Wild owns the property."

Anger simmered in Matt's gut. "Find out who owns the business. I also need to know the whereabouts of all the members of that exclusive gun club Sebastian Norris established."

"Copy that. I'll touch base with you in two minutes." Zane ended the call.

Sebastian Norris was in on this. Somehow, Matt knew that scumbag had a role to play in Delilah's disappearance. Whether the mayor's son had anything to do with the rest of the attempts on Delilah's life and the murders remained to be seen. One way or another, Matt would find out everything Norris knew.

He darted around a truck pulling a trailer loaded with hay and placed another call, this time to Miles Russell.

"Russell."

"It's Matt Rainer. Delilah was kidnapped from Oliver Shannon's office."

"When?"

"Twenty minutes ago. Fortress is helping me track a late-model Silver Lexus SUV that was seen racing from the office parking lot at the time Delilah disappeared."

"Any idea where they're headed?"

"I'm racing up Highway 122 toward the land held by Into The Wild."

A few seconds of silence was followed by, "That's the hunting business Shane Frost owns."

The confirmation increased Matt's sense of urgency. "My teammates are en route to that location. I know you have to mobilize your officers and respond. I'm asking you to hold them at the perimeter of the property. I don't want your people to fire on my team."

"That's a huge area to search for your girlfriend, if she's even there. The more manpower you have in those woods, the quicker you'll find her or eliminate the possibility she's on site."

"Bravo will handle the search. Stay out of our way. Lisa Walters is also missing. She told Delilah Zach had called to talk to her. That was the last time I saw either of them."

"Have you talked to Zach?"

"Not since early this morning."

"I'll try to track him down while we mobilize."

"Delilah and I also talked to Shane this morning. When we walked into the house, a woman with long dark hair left by back door and took off in a silver SUV."

"You see her face?"

"No."

"I may know someone who can help connect the woman with Shane."

"Once I confirm with Fortress that Lisa took Delilah to Shane's property, I'll let you know. Other than that, I won't contact you again. I'm trusting you to keep the perimeter of the property secure. Based on what I know to this point, I think Shane is involved in this mess up to his neck with Lisa and Sebastian Norris. There may be others involved as well. We already know about the Randolphs. Whatever you do, don't let them off the property. I want them wrapped up tight."

"And if I don't?"

Matt's hands tightened around the steering wheel. "We'll hunt them down and take care of them ourselves. If these homegrown terrorists hurt Delilah, they will be my unit's next mission. We never give up on an objective. None of them will escape."

"You're not cops, Rainer."

"Exactly. You have to follow the rules. We don't."

"You can't just execute them."

"Then you better hope they don't harm Delilah. If she dies, all bets are off."

"You're a professional soldier. Don't tell me you can't incapacitate without killing."

"If they give us the option to take them alive, we will. If not, we'll do what we're trained to do." He ended the call and pulled up his email as he sped through a straight stretch of highway. Taking the coordinates Zane included with the satellite images, he keyed them into his navigation system. The last thing Matt wanted to do was miss the turnoff and have to backtrack.

Seconds later, Zane called. "Into The Wild is owned by Shane Frost. I checked on the other members of Norris's gun club. Lisa, Shane, Sebastian, and a guy named Donovan Cain are missing or not answering their phones. Delilah's brother, Zach, was on his way to Atlantic City to pay off his gambling debt. When I told him Delilah was missing, he said he was returning to Harmony immediately."

"How soon will the satellite be in position?"

"Five more minutes."

Matt slowed for the turn off the highway and plunged ahead. "Run the sequential photos from our satellite. I'm on the dirt road now."

"No need. I've located Lisa Walters's vehicle. I'm sending you the coordinates."

"Where is it?"

"In the heart of Frost's property."

"Send the same information to Bravo. I need to know what's happening in that forest, Zane."

"I'll contact you as soon as I get anything."

Matt keyed the new coordinates into his navigation system. Fifteen, twenty minutes max before he'd find the silver SUV. He prayed he didn't find Delilah's body as well.

CHAPTER THIRTY-SEVEN

Delilah stopped behind a large outcropping of rocks, hand pressed to her side and gasping for air. She was in good shape after so many hours of swimming, but this pace was grueling, especially with cracked ribs.

She glanced at her watch. The creepy foursome should be on the move now. Would they split up or come after her as a group? Separately, she decided. Shane had promised her as a prize to whoever caught her first.

How could her own kin turn against her? She wasn't a prize horse to be auctioned off to the highest bidder, but that's what she felt like. Once she caught her breath, Delilah turned her attention to her top priority.

She needed a plan. Running blind through the woods wouldn't help her escape experienced hunters. The four people tracking her through the woods were familiar with the terrain.

Delilah studied the area and chose the hardest packed dirt and rocks to walk on. She didn't want to leave a trail a mile wide pointing to her location.

She started off again, grim determination filling her. She wouldn't make this easy for them. The less of a trail she left behind, the better her chances of survival. Although Delilah knew Matt was coming, she had to find a way to save herself in case Shane and his cronies found her first.

Ten minutes later, Delilah darted into a thick stand of trees and hid behind the largest tree trunk. She struggled to quiet her breathing, ears straining to listen for a repeat of the noise she'd heard.

Delilah prayed the noise indicated a deer or something innocent. Better yet, she hoped Matt was behind her. Zero chance of that, though. Bravo didn't make any noise unless they wanted you to know they were near.

At her feet lay a tree limb the thickness and size of a baseball bat and nearly the same length. With careful, slow movements, Delilah lifted the stick. Relief filled her. Perfect. Solid and strong. Although she longed for a gun, Delilah didn't know how to shoot a gun anyway. She'd probably end up shooting herself by accident. Another skill she needed to learn from Matt. She just had to survive to learn those skills.

Footsteps drew near. Delilah pressed her back against the tree. She waited, gaze glued to the area on her right. Leaves rattled and a branch snapped. Terror swept through her. Not Matt. Animal or one of her pursuers?

She tightened her grip as Lisa moved into view. The other woman paused fifteen feet away, studying the ground with a puzzled frown. Would she pass by and search elsewhere?

Lisa held the rifle loosely in her hands as she moved further into the stand of trees and closer to Delilah.

Not good. Delilah tensed, prepared to fight for her life. Lisa kept coming, her gaze focused on the ground. Cheeks flushing, she swore, frustration evident in her voice.

When the other woman drew even with Delilah, she glanced up. Excitement flared and she started to raise the rifle.

Delilah swung the stick and hit the side of Lisa's head. The other woman flew back and slammed into a nearby tree trunk. She fell to the ground, unmoving.

Afraid the other woman was faking unconsciousness, Delilah kept her stick ready as she kicked the rifle away from Lisa's slack hands. No response.

Delilah needed to search Lisa for a phone. She prayed Shannon's assistant had kept her cell phone with her. She would want to brag to her buddies that she'd found Delilah.

A cell phone was in Lisa's shirt pocket. Thank God. She turned on the phone and breathed a sigh of relief that Lisa hadn't bothered to use a screen lock.

Delilah called Matt's cell phone.

He answered with a whispered, "Yeah?"

"It's Delilah," she murmured, worried one of the other hunters was in the area.

"Are you okay?"

Not even close. "Lisa Walters kidnapped me at gunpoint and forced me to drive into a heavily wooded area. Shane, Sebastian, and Donovan Cain along with Lisa turned me loose in the woods and they're hunting me. I knocked out Lisa and took her phone. I don't know where I am, Matt. I'm somewhere off Highway 122."

"You're on Shane's property. Leave the phone on. I'll find you. I'm entering the woods now and the rest of Bravo is five minutes out."

"Do I keep moving?"

"Are you in a secure location?"

"Not really. I'm in a thick stand of trees. I got lucky that Lisa found me first. I wouldn't have been able to knock out one of the men."

"Don't short-change yourself, sweetheart. Find a more secure place to hide. Look for a rock formation or a cave. If you go into the cave, stay out of sight near the mouth so I don't lose your signal."

Oh, man. Delilah hoped the big rock formation she was using as a guide was closer than it appeared. She didn't want to take shelter in a cave unless absolutely necessary. "Okay."

"Be as quiet as you can and stay aware of your surroundings. Listen to your instincts, Delilah. Once you find shelter, stay put. No matter what you hear, stay hidden. Come out of hiding only for me or one of Bravo. I'm going radio silent. Leave our phone connection open. I'll be here if you need me."

Delilah slid the phone into her jeans pocket and continued toward the rocks. She pushed herself to move faster despite pain in her ribs and a stitch in her side.

Somewhere behind her, a shout of pain cut off in mid-scream. Delilah spun, afraid for Matt. No. She made herself continue forward. Matt or his teammates would find her. Making herself more of a target by backtracking into the woods would endanger Matt and the rest of Bravo. If she was safe, they could focus on Shane and his friends.

Delilah pushed harder to reach the rocks. A few more yards and she could rest. At the edge of the clearing, she paused and glanced around. Twenty yards of open ground between her and the rock formation on the hillside. Might as well be 1,000 yards. The open space made her uneasy. Worse, those invisible spiders were racing over her skin now.

She didn't have a choice. Her safety was paramount. With her hand gripping the stick, Delilah moved into the clearing and headed for the rocks. Fifteen feet. Ten. Five.

"Uh uh. Not so fast, Delicious Delilah," a masculine voice drawled.

Delilah froze.

"Turn around and drop the stick."

After letting the stick fall from her hand, she spun to face Donovan Cain. The supreme satisfaction and unholy glee in his face and gaze made Delilah's stomach churn.

Donovan set aside his rifle. "You're mine now. My beautiful, sexy prize." His gaze drifted over Delilah. "I've looked forward to getting my hands on you again."

Again? A horrible certainty filled her. "You broke into my house in Otter Creek."

He flashed a smile at her. "Very good. Beautiful and smart."

"Who helped you?"

"The Randolphs."

"Shane asked you to kidnap me, didn't he?"

"Kidnap you?" Donovan's laughter ratcheted Delilah's terror to another level. "Oh, no, baby. Not kidnap. The plan was to spend some very private time doing whatever I wanted with you, then kill you. But you messed up my plan. You'll pay for that before I'm finished with you." He moved toward her.

Delilah ran. Before she'd gone ten feet, a heavy weight crashed into her back and took her to the ground. Agonizing pain in her ribs stole Delilah's breath and stunned her into immobility.

Donovan's hard hands flipped Delilah to face him. One large hand clamped around her throat, squeezing slightly in a silent warning to remain still. The other hand grabbed Delilah's shirt and tore it from her body.

"No!" Delilah struggled to break his hold on her throat, her nails digging into the back of his hand as she clawed at him.

"No woman tells me no," he growled. "But I love it when they fight." Donovan backhanded her, then reached for the button of her jeans.

CHAPTER THIRTY-EIGHT

Matt navigated the rocky terrain with ease, frequently checking Delilah's location on his phone. From her lack of movement in the past few minutes, she might have found shelter. He refused to dwell on the possibility one of the creeps stalking Delilah had caught up with her.

He moved fifteen feet deeper into the woods and stopped when he heard a low-voiced moan. Female. Delilah?

A male voice murmured to the woman. "She'll pay, baby. I swear to you. Dee won't get away with hurting you."

"I want her dead."

"She won't leave the woods alive. My cousin isn't trained. She has no chance against us."

Matt's jaw tightened. Shane and Lisa. Although his gut clawed at him to find Delilah, he wouldn't leave a known threat at his back. Resolved to deal with the couple as fast as possible, he moved into position. Matt spotted a rifle with a pink camouflage stock. Must be Lisa's. He hid the weapon and eased closer to two of the people who planned to harm Delilah.

A few feet from his targets, he took advantage of Shane's distraction with his girlfriend and tackled Delilah's cousin, knocking him away from the injured woman. Shane fought with ferocious intensity, anger glittering in his eyes. Although he landed a couple punches, Matt's training and skill in hand-to-hand combat quickly shifted the balance in his favor. He ended the fight with an elbow strike to Shane's temple, dropping the hunter in his tracks.

He glanced up to see Lisa swing his direction with a Smith & Wesson in her hand. She swayed, but the weapon in her hand would injure or kill him if she got lucky.

Not seeing another choice, Matt executed a leg sweep that ended with Lisa flat on her back. One punch to the face and she was out. He used zip ties to restrain her and Shane, then slapped duct tape over their mouths to keep them from calling out for assistance.

That done, he checked his phone for Delilah's location. Still no movement. Good. He jogged in her direction. She wasn't far away. Hopefully, his teammates would deal with the other two clowns hunting Delilah.

He froze a second when he heard a male voice taunting Delilah over the cell phone in Matt's hand. Fury engulfed him when he realized what would happen if he didn't reach Delilah in time. Matt ran, uncaring of being heard. He wouldn't let the man rape her. His gut knotted. If he hadn't already.

He came to the edge of a clearing. Delilah lay on the ground with a muscular man holding her down. Delilah's torn shirt lay on the ground. As Donovan Cain's free hand reached for her bra, Matt sprinted across the open area and slammed into the man, forcing him off Delilah.

Cain shoved Matt off him and grabbed his Ka-Bar. "Think you're such a tough guy, Rainer? Come get me. After I gut you like a fish, I'll take my time with your woman. I'll keep her alive a while before I kill her. She'll know what a real man is like instead of a wussy medic."

Matt tuned out the words and concentrated on Cain's body movements. If he allowed the other man to distract him, Matt and Delilah would both die.

Cain changed his hold on the Ka-Bar and rushed him. Matt blocked the knife strike and trapped the other man's arm against his side. He punched Cain in the throat with as much force as he could muster in close quarters.

His opponent's eyes widened in shock. He dropped the knife and jerked away from Matt, hands pawing his own throat as he fought to breathe. Not feeling charitable, Matt shoved him to the ground and bound his arms and legs with zip ties.

After confiscating Cain's weapons and tossing them aside, Matt turned to Delilah. She'd scrambled to her feet and leaned against the rocks, a large stick in her hand. He moved closer, afraid to move too fast and spook her. "Delilah, you're safe now."

"The others?" she whispered.

"I found Lisa and Shane and restrained them. Cain can't hurt you now. My teammates will have Norris wrapped up soon if they haven't already dealt with him. If he shows up here, I'll handle him like I did the others. Will you let me hold you?"

Delilah dropped the stick and raced into Matt's open arms. He hugged her tight against his chest, thankful to have her in his arms again. "Did Cain hurt you, baby?" She buried her face against his neck without replying. His jaw clenched. Cain had hurt her. "What did he do?"

"Backhanded me. I'm okay, though. Nothing an ice pack won't cure."

"I'm taking you to the hospital to be checked out."

She huffed out a short laugh. "You're a medic. Check me yourself."

Matt eased away to tilt her face toward a patch of sunlight. Matt gently probed Delilah's reddened cheek to check for fractures and breathed easier when he found nothing more than the beginning of a bruise.

"I'm sorry I didn't find you sooner." When Delilah refused to meet his gaze, alarm roared through him. "Sweetheart, look at me."

When she complied, he cupped her uninjured cheek with his palm. "Be honest with me no matter how uncomfortable you feel. Will you do that?"

"I'll try."

"Whatever your answer is to my next question, know that I love you. Nothing will change how much I adore you."

"I love you, too, Matt."

He drew in a deep breath and said, "For the sake of your health, I have to know if Norris or Cain raped you."

She shook her head. "They were more interested in hunting me like an animal. Shane said the person found me first could do anything he wanted with me. If you hadn't arrived when you did, Donovan would have raped me. He didn't have the chance. Your timing was perfect."

Relief swept through him like a tidal wave. He dropped a light kiss on her mouth before stepping back. He tugged off his t-shirt and helped her slip it on. He still wore his bulletproof vest with a t-shirt underneath.

Over the comm system, Matt's team leader said, "Norris is down. Report, Matt."

Matt activated his mic. "Copy. Bring Norris to the rendezvous point. Lisa, Shane, and Donovan Cain are down. I have Delilah."

"Copy that. Let me know if you need assistance. Russell is waiting for us, then he'll do cleanup. See you at the rendezvous point."

Matt's attention locked on the love of his life. "Let's get out of here. The cops are at the perimeter, waiting to pick up the garbage."

CHAPTER THIRTY-NINE

Matt kept a close eye on Delilah as they walked toward the perimeter the Harmony cops had established. The adrenaline rush was ebbing and she stumbled more than once. Finally, he stopped, scooped her into his arms, and set off for the rendezvous point again.

"I can walk," she protested.

"You can," he agreed. "I need to hold you, Delilah. I thought I would be too late." A true statement though his motivation was to give her body time to recuperate before Detective Russell began his interrogation.

Arms wrapped around his neck, Delilah relaxed against him. "I knew you would find me."

He squeezed her tighter for a moment. "Rest while you can. Russell will have questions for you."

"Cain was one of the men who broke into my house."

"He's the one who hit you?"

She nodded.

Matt regretted not killing the thug who hurt his woman. "Did he say who the second person was?"

"No. That's a job for Detective Russell. Matt, I must be heavy. Put me down."

"I'm enjoying myself. Relax and let me do what I want." He waited a few minutes after she'd settled against him again before broaching a new subject. "How soon will you marry me?"

Delilah laughed. "As soon as I find a dress. If I find what I want, we can get married the day after we return to Otter Creek."

Oh, yeah. He liked that plan. "Do you want a big wedding?" A major social event would be impossible to pull off in a super short time frame.

She shook her head. "I want Sasha and Cade in the wedding. I'm sure we can find her a dress."

"What about the reception?"

"I'll call Zoe tonight. She'll have suggestions. Will you talk to Marcus about performing the ceremony?"

He smiled. "I'll call him when we return to the hotel. He'll be happy to accommodate us. When do you want to go home?"

"As soon as we get out of these woods, but I think the Harmony police might have something to say about that plan."

He glanced down at her. "We'll be making trips back and forth to Harmony for months to give statements, be interviewed multiple times, and testify in the trials of the foursome."

"I wonder who killed Mom and Randy."

"We'll find out."

She lapsed into silence as he continued to stride toward the perimeter and his teammates. When he broke into the clearing where Bravo waited with a cursing Norris, Russell and a uniformed cop. His teammates straightened, their gazes locked on Delilah.

"She okay?" Cade asked.

"Adrenaline dump. I need an ice pack. Cain hit her."

"I'll get it." Simon caught the key fob Matt tossed to him after he set Delilah on her feet.

"This is all your fault, Delilah," Norris screamed. "I should have taken care of you years ago. No one will believe anything you say. I have more power than you can imagine in this town."

Matt scowled. He glanced at his best friend. With a lift of his chin, Cade walked to Delilah and took up position by her side.

Norris cursed and raged, fighting against Trent and Liam as Matt stalked to the man who had humiliated Delilah and would have done worse if he'd caught her in the woods. Matt shifted his weight to the balls of his feet and slammed his fist into Norris's jaw. The other man's head snapped to the side, eyes rolled back in his head. He sagged against Matt's teammates, out cold.

Liam snorted in disgust. "Glass jaw."

"Should have watched out for those exposed tree roots," Trent said. "Isn't that right, Detective Russell?"

A slow smile appeared on the detective's face. "There are a lot of them out here. He should have been more careful." His fellow cops smirked and nodded in agreement.

The detective turned his attention to Delilah. "We have an ambulance waiting around the curve. My questions can wait until you're checked out at the hospital."

"I don't need a hospital. I just need Matt."

Matt returned to her side with a nod of thanks to Cade. "I'll take her in myself if I'm not satisfied with how she's responding." Matt wouldn't allow anyone to separate them again. "If you question Delilah here, she needs to sit down. My SUV is in the trees about four hundred yards away." He wanted Delilah inside his vehicle where she would be safe if Shane had more cronies in the area.

"Tell Officer King the location of Lisa Walters, Shane Frost, and Donovan Cain first." After Matt gave the information, Russell said, "Lead the way, Rainer."

At the vehicle, Simon handed Matt the chemically-activated cold pack and moved a few feet away to keep watch. Russell climbed into the backseat, yanked out his notebook and pen, and asked Delilah to relay what happened from the time she and Matt arrived at Shannon's office that afternoon.

An hour later, the detective shook his head as he shoved the notebook and pen in his pocket. "Incredible. I'll contact Detective Kelter." He grinned. "Your detective will have to get in line with his B & E and assault charges. Attempted murder and rape trump those charges."

"As long as Cain and his buddies are off the streets and held accountable for their actions, Rod won't mind."

Russell turned to Delilah. "I know you want to leave Harmony behind in the dust, but I need you to stay until tomorrow morning at least. I'll have your statements ready by then and perhaps be able to answer more questions about Michelle and Randy's deaths and the attempts on your life."

Delilah frowned. "I want to go home, Detective Russell. I have wedding plans to finish."

The other man smiled. "Congratulations. When is the big day?"

"As soon as we can arrange it," Matt said. "I'm not letting an extra day pass without marrying Delilah. I almost lost her today. I don't want to wait."

The two men exchanged looks of understanding.

"I'll have your statements ready in the morning by 9:00. Stop on your way out of town. I'll send a message through Fortress when I need you for other steps in the legal process." He left the SUV.

Trent walked from the tree line with the rest of Bravo. "You're free to go?"

Matt nodded. "I need to take Delilah to the hotel. Cade, you want to ride with us?" His friend looked pale.

"I wouldn't turn down a ride."

Trent's eyes narrowed when Cade staggered and almost fell into the backseat. "We'll follow you, Matt."

With a nod, he cranked the engine and angled the air vents to blow toward Cade. Matt circled to the hatchback for over-the-counter pain meds and an unopened bottle of water.

Matt pressed both into Cade's hands. "Swallow these and take a nap. I don't want Sasha angry with me."

"Better you than me," his friend murmured. That he didn't argue against taking the meds told Matt how bad Cade felt. When they returned to the hotel, Matt would check his wound for signs of infection or broken stitches.

As Matt drove toward the hotel, he kept an eye on his surroundings and on his passengers. Cade stretched out across the seat. Delilah fell asleep with her hand gripping Matt's.

When he parked in the hotel's garage, the sun was beginning to set. "Delilah, Cade, we're at the hotel."

Trent parked in the slot next to his and Matt's teammates piled out of the SUV. Simon and Liam flanked Cade, engaging him in conversation while making sure he didn't hit the ground. Trent saluted Matt and followed the three men.

Delilah smiled at Matt. "A few more hours and we can go home."

"Do you have a preference which house we choose to live in?" He wanted to move Delilah into his place as soon as they married because his had the best security system Fortress offered.

"Your house. We'll decide what to do with mine once it's repaired."

He brushed his lips over hers. "Perfect. Come on. Let's go upstairs. I think we should order something decadent from room service to celebrate."

Her eyebrows rose. "Decadent?"

He winked at her. "A dessert with chocolate to top off dinner."

"Great plan."

Matt grabbed his mike bag and escorted Delilah upstairs to the suite. Sasha rushed to embrace Delilah.

"Are you all right? Cade told me what happened."

"I'm fine. A little bruised up, that's all."

"I can't believe your cousin was behind everything. Was your brother part of this?"

"No, he wasn't." Matt set aside his mike bag and sat with Delilah on the couch. "Zach was on his way to pay off his gambling debts when he learned Delilah had been kidnapped. He turned around and headed back to Harmony." He glanced at Delilah. "He'll want to know you're safe."

"Invite him to dinner." Sasha grabbed bottles of water from the refrigerator and passed them around. "I'm sure he'll want to see for himself that you're okay."

Delilah glanced at Matt, her eyebrows raised.

"It's up to you." He handed Delilah her cell phone.

"You found it."

"I called your phone when I couldn't find you at the lawyer's office. I found it in the trash."

Sasha gripped Delilah's left wrist and raised her hand for a closer inspection. "You're engaged! This is gorgeous, Delilah. Congratulations."

Liam grinned. "About time. Good job, Matt."

After the round of congratulations from Bravo, Delilah called her brother and invited him to their hotel for dinner. When Zach arrived an hour later, he wrapped Delilah in his arms. "I'm glad you're all right. I can't believe Shane would do this. Did he kill Mom?"

"We don't know yet. Matt and I plan to stop at the police station tomorrow morning before we go home."

"I don't blame you for leaving town. You've had nothing but trouble since you arrived."

"You said the deadline to pay your debt is noon tomorrow. Could you come to Otter Creek the day after?"

"Probably. Why?"

She grinned. "Matt and I are getting married if I can find a dress."

"Yes!" Sasha did a fist pump. "Don't worry, Delilah. We'll find your dress tomorrow. Please say you'll come, Zach."

Zach turned to Matt, an unasked question in his eyes.

Matt nodded. If this was what Delilah wanted, he'd give her brother the benefit of the doubt. Besides, with his teammates and friends from PSI in attendance, Zach wouldn't be able to cause trouble at the wedding.

"I'll be honored to come, Dee."

"Bring a suit, okay?"

He looked puzzled at the request but agreed.

A few hours later, Zach left with another promise to Delilah that he would see her in Otter Creek.

After Trent, Simon, and Liam returned to their rooms and Cade and Sasha went to bed, Matt gathered Delilah into his arms and held her for long minutes before walking her to the bedroom. "Get some rest. I'll be on the couch if you need me." After a soft, tender kiss, he nudged Delilah inside and closed the door.

When Delilah was asleep, Matt called Zane and updated his friend. "We'll return to Otter Creek tomorrow morning. I need time off, Z."

"I'm sure it won't be a problem. Is there a special reason?"

"Delilah and I hope to get married the day after tomorrow."

Zane laughed. "Great reason for a vacation. Congratulations, my friend. I'll pass the word along to the boss. We'll work around your honeymoon plans. Send Brent an email to let him know the dates you'll be unavailable."

"Thank you for your help in protecting Delilah."

"Glad to do it, Matt."

"That's good because I need another favor."

"Name it."

"I want a set of the GPS jewelry for Delilah and I need it overnighted to PSI."

"Everything will be waiting for you when you reach Otter Creek."

"I owe you, buddy."

"I'll remind you of that one day."

Too wired to sleep, Matt called Marcus Lang, the pastor of the church he and Delilah attended. After confirming Lang's willingness and availability to perform the ceremony in two days, Matt grabbed his laptop and planned the honeymoon.

CHAPTER FORTY

Miles Russell ushered Delilah and Matt into an interrogation room. He motioned for them to sit and slid papers across the table. "Read your statements. If they're accurate, sign them and we'll talk."

Delilah scanned the document and signed as did Matt. They slid the pages back to Russell. "Who killed my mother?"

"Donovan Cain confessed to killing her and Randy."

"Why?" Matt asked.

"An arrangement with Shane. If Donovan committed the murders, Shane would split the lottery proceeds three ways. He learned about the contents of Mrs. Holloway's will and Lisa's steady pilfering of the accounts from his girlfriend. He wanted to protect her. Since she was already stealing funds, Shane decided to take the rest of the money."

"Donovan planned to kill Delilah in Otter Creek, didn't he?"

Russell nodded. "If you and your teammates had arrived five minutes later, Delilah would have been abducted, raped, and murdered later that night on orders from Shane."

She shuddered at the vocalization of her cousin's plot. "Why does he hate me? I didn't do anything to him."

"You stood in the way of his goal. If Mrs. Holloway had split the lottery proceeds between you and the four men, he probably wouldn't have bothered with conspiracy plans. When he learned your mother gave you all the money except the bequests, he knew he couldn't protect Lisa for long. Shane was afraid Delilah would notice the missing money and discover Lisa was responsible."

"I should have killed him while I had the chance."

Delilah laid her hand on Matt's. He turned his hand over and threaded their fingers together.

A sharp look from the detective. "I'll pretend I didn't hear that although I'd feel the same if Shane had targeted my wife."

"Who was the second person who broke into Delilah's house?"

"Shane. He stayed out of sight in case Delilah recognized him, managed to escape Donovan, and ratted him out to the police before the plans were in place to handle Delilah and clean out the accounts."

"What about Zach and Evan?" Delilah frowned. "Were they part of this plan?" Delilah hoped she hadn't been wrong about her own brother.

"Shane broached the idea of knocking off anyone else who might be named in Mrs. Holloway's will, but treated it as a joke. Zach shoved Shane against a wall and told him not to even joke about it, that it wasn't funny. Evan agreed with Zach and told Shane not to be stupid. Shane, Lisa, and Donovan decided to cut Zach and Evan out of the plan. By the time Zach and Evan would have realized Shane had been serious, and he, Lisa, and Donovan were to blame for the empty accounts, they would have already gotten themselves new identities and left the country after transferring every penny to their offshore accounts. They were going to leave good old Sebastian to keep himself out of prison. He was never part of the money scheme, just a willing participant in hunting you. You're a lucky woman, Delilah."

She shook her head. "Not lucky. Blessed. I appreciate what you did to obtain justice for my mother and stepfather."

"Just doing my job." He shook their hands. "Here's hoping the rest of your lives are less eventful. I'll be in touch soon."

Matt and Delilah walked to the coffee shop where the Ramseys waited for them. Cade motioned to the to-go cups on the table.

"Coffee for you and tea for Delilah."

"Ready to go?

"More than ready."

Sasha stood with her own cup in hand. "We have a wedding to plan. Let's go home."

Five hours later, Matt parked in his driveway and helped Cade unload his and Sasha's gear. "Take OTC pain meds and sleep. I'll check on you tomorrow."

Cade smiled. "You're busy tomorrow, buddy. I'll sleep a few hours, then tell you where we're having your bachelor party."

Bachelor party? Delilah's mouth dropped. He was kidding, right? She'd never known Bravo to drink anything harder than soft drinks. They didn't want to be less than battle ready if Fortress contacted them.

Matt scowled. "When did you have time to plan a bachelor party?"

"I talked to the rest of Bravo each time we stopped to stretch our legs on the way home and Trent coordinated with Josh Cahill and the rest of Durango. You were too busy stealing kisses from Delilah to notice the phone calls."

"What kind of bachelor party?" Matt's eyes narrowed, suspicion growing.

"Our kind. Grilling out in my backyard with plenty of food and sweet tea. Nate will handle the food prep. Grace is planning a dinner party for Delilah, Sasha, and the wives of Durango at Trent's place."

Sasha grinned at Delilah. "This will be fun. Darcy is in charge of our food."

Delilah's stomach growled as if on cue. "Oh, man. I can't wait."

"You have to. We have a mission this afternoon."

Butterflies took flight in her stomach. Delilah needed to find a wedding dress in the next few hours and confirm reception details with Zoe and Darcy. The latter had volunteered to create platters of pinwheels and wraps for the reception while Zoe planned to serve a variety of cookies and cupcakes instead of a traditional wedding cake.

She glanced at Matt whose intense gaze was locked on her. "Nothing will stop me from marrying you tomorrow even if I can't find a wedding dress, Matt Rainer. I'll find something that works."

He cupped her cheek. "Meet me at the county clerk's office at four o'clock. We both need to be there to apply for a marriage license."

"Come on." Sasha nudged Delilah toward Cade's vehicle. "I'll drive Cade home to rest for a few hours, then you and I will go shopping."

The next three hours passed in a blur. By the time Sasha dropped her off in front of the court house to meet Matt, Delilah had purchased a wedding dress and finalized details with Darcy, Zoe, and the florist. She'd also stopped by Wicks to check in with Piper and tell her assistant the plans for the next day.

Matt dropped a quick kiss on her lips when she walked to him. "Did you find anything?"

Delilah nodded. "The dress is perfect. I hope you like it."

"As long as you're wearing it, I will. After we get the license, we're going to PSI to pick up a package from Zane."

Thirty minutes later, they left the clerk's office with the marriage license in hand and drove to PSI. By the time Delilah had fastened each piece of GPS jewelry in place, it was time for the parties planned by their friends.

When Matt walked her to Grace's door, Delilah asked, "When will you pick me up?"

"According to a text from Cade, I won't see you until tomorrow for the ceremony. Our friends have been busy. You'll stay with Sasha and Cade tonight."

Before he rang the bell, Matt wrapped his arms around Delilah and pulled her tight against his chest. "Tomorrow, you become Delilah Rainer and I can't wait to slide my wedding band on your finger. One more night to be separated from you. You don't know how much I want to fall asleep with you in my arms and wake with your beautiful face beside mine."

She gave a soft laugh. "Can't be more than how much I want the same thing. I love you, Matt."

"I love you, too, sweetheart." He captured her lips in a deep, intense kiss. When he lifted his head, Matt's cheeks were flushed and his breathing erratic. He pressed the doorbell. When Grace opened the door, Matt squeezed Delilah's hand and stepped back. "Enjoy yourself, Delilah. I'll be waiting for you at the altar tomorrow."

Grace drew Delilah inside and closed the door. "The others are here. We're so happy for you and Matt. He's an amazing man."

"I think so, too."

Sasha greeted her as she entered the large kitchen and brought Delilah into the circle of women who were married to members of Durango. As Del Cahill, Josh's wife, released Delilah from a hug, she flinched.

"Del, are you okay?"

"I'm fine."

Ivy, her cousin, moved closer with her newborn, Savannah, sleeping on Ivy's shoulder. "Are you in labor?"

"Maybe. I'm not sure. If the contractions continue, I'll ask Josh to come get me."

"How far apart are the contractions?" Grace asked.

"Five or six minutes."

Delilah relaxed. Grace was a nurse. She would know what to do and when Del needed to head for the hospital.

"Are they consistent?"

"For the last hour, yes. Come on. Let's eat while I have a chance and have Delilah open her gifts. If I'm in labor, I want something happy to think about later. Knowing that hunky Matt Rainer finally fell hard for a fantastic woman who happens to be a friend makes me happy."

As the women laughed, she noticed Stella, Nate's wife, slipping her phone from her pocket and firing off a text. Delilah hoped the Otter Creek detective was giving her husband, Nate, an update about Del. Since Bravo had invited the Durango to Matt's bachelor party, Josh was with them and only minutes from Grace's house.

Two hours later, Grace said, "Del, we have to call Josh. You need to go to the hospital."

Del nodded as she clutched her stomach. "I think you're right."

"Looks like both parties are moving to the hospital," Darcy said. "I'll put the food away. Del, do you have your hospital bag ready?"

"It's in the back bedroom. Josh makes me take it everywhere."

"Turns out it was a smart move," Quinn's wife, Heidi, commented. "Wonder how many laws our favorite patrol cop will break to get here?"

That set off another round of laughter.

Del grabbed her cell phone and called Josh. "I need you to pick me up, honey. Grace thinks I'm in labor." She rolled her eyes. "I don't need an ambulance, Josh. Grace is right here and we're only ten minutes from the hospital. I won't move, I promise."

She slid her phone away, her laughter dissolving into a groan. "Oh, man. You didn't tell me how much labor hurts, Ivy."

"Because it was worth every minute of the pain I endured. Savannah is the joy of our lives. You won't care about the labor when you hold your baby in your arms for the first time."

Instead of spending a sleepless night being anxious about her wedding, Delilah spent the rest of the evening and the early hours of the morning in a waiting room full of anxious operatives and their wives along with Josh's sisters, Serena, Madison, and Megan, and their husbands and Josh's parents, Aaron and Liz, waiting for word on Del and the baby.

At four o'clock, Josh walked into the waiting room, a blank look on his face.

Delilah gripped Matt's hand. Had something gone wrong?

Aaron Cahill got to his feet and gripped his son's shoulders. "Josh?"

He blinked. "What?"

"Is Del all right?"

"She's fine."

Delilah held her breath.

"What about the baby, son?" Liz asked.

"They're fine."

Silence fell on the room.

"They?" His mother moved a step closer.

"Twin girls."

Ethan Blackhawk burst into laughter. "Oh, man. This will be fun to watch."

Rod Kelter dragged a hand down his face, then turned to look at his wife, Megan. "We may have to revisit the idea of having kids. They're coming in batches now. Our luck, we'll have triplets."

Meg scowled. "Bite your tongue, Kelter. Serena, Maddie, and I terrorized Josh when we were growing up. I'm not riding herd on a pack of girls like us."

Nick Santana shook his head, a wide grin on his face. "I feel sorry for Josh's daughters' boyfriends. I bet he runs background checks on the boys."

Josh scowled. "There won't be any boys until my daughters are 30 years old."

After the general laughter died down and everyone congratulated Josh, Cade and Sasha took Delilah home with them. When Delilah crawled into bed in Sasha's guest room, she fell asleep immediately.

Sasha woke her at nine with breakfast in bed.

Delilah shoved her hair away from her face. "You didn't have to do this."

"You deserve to be spoiled today."

"Have you heard anything about Del and the babies?"

Her friend grinned. "They're all doing great."

"Do you know the names of the girls?"

"Erin Amaryllis and Eve Camellia."

Delilah's jaw dropped. "Wow. Big names for little girls."

"Del kept the family tradition of giving her daughters flower names."

"She and Josh are going to call them Erin and Eve, right? I can't imagine being in first grade and trying to spell Amaryllis and Camellia."

"That's the plan. Matt called a few minutes ago to check on you. He said to tell you he loves you and can't wait to see you this afternoon." Sasha handed Delilah a mug of tea. "That man is crazy about you."

"The feeling is mutual. The next five hours are going to drag."

Another smile from her friend. "I don't think so. Hurry up and eat. We have an appointment at the spa on the outskirts of town in thirty minutes."

"Are you kidding? That place has a waiting list a mile long."

"The owner is obsessed with my coffee and was happy to work us in." Sasha tapped her finger on the plate with the banana and one Hershey's kiss. "Your breakfast is courtesy of Matt including the tea. He dropped it by earlier this morning."

"Did he sleep at all?"

She shrugged. "He said he slept enough. I don't question the Fortress operatives. They know what they need to do to keep themselves in peak physical condition. Eat your breakfast and dress. We'll leave as soon as you're ready."

Delilah ate, showered, and dressed in ten minutes flat. She and Sasha were escorted to a treatment room as soon as they walked in the front door of the exclusive spa.

For the next three hours, Delilah and her friend were pampered and polished and emerged from the spa refreshed and ready for the next part of the day. Courtesy of the spa's owner, a makeup artist and hair stylist prepared each of them for the wedding.

Back in the SUV, Delilah said, "The owner must be obsessed with your coffee to treat us like this."

"I think her coffee will be comped from now on. This was beyond anything I asked her to do. Did you have fun?"

"I did. Thanks for arranging this, Sasha."

They returned to the house to pick up everything they needed to dress for the wedding and drove to the church.

After making sure Matt was nowhere in sight, Sasha helped Delilah carry their bags into the building.

Thirty minutes before the wedding, a knock sounded on the door of the room where Delilah and Sasha waited. Liz Cahill peered inside. "Delilah, your brother is here. He'd like to see you if you have a minute."

"Sure. Send him in."

"You look beautiful, honey. You'll take Matt's breath away when he sees you."

Delilah pressed her trembling fingers against her stomach. She hoped Liz was correct. Now that the wedding was due to start soon, Delilah worried he wouldn't approve of the dress or might back out altogether. Stupid. Everyone was right. Matt was as crazy about her as she was about him.

A moment later, the door opened again and her brother slipped inside the room. His eyes widened when he saw her. "Dee, you look incredible."

She glanced down at the white sheath dress and ran her hand over the silky material. "Thanks." Although she'd tried on several princess-style dresses with miles of skirt and long trains, none of them suited her as well as this one.

"I brought you a gift. I hoped you would wear it today."

Curious, she accepted the wrapped box Zach handed her. Tearing off the paper, she opened the oblong box to see a single strand of delicate white pearls. "Zach, they're beautiful." She hugged him. "Thank you for thinking of me."

"I think Mom would have approved of Matt and this marriage. She developed a fondness for pearls during the past two years. I went to the same store where she purchased all her jewelry and bought the sister strand to the one she owned. She would have liked for you to have hers if they would have survived the fire. If you won't take them from me, think of them as having come from Mom."

"Because the necklace is from both of you, it means even more." She motioned to a group of chairs. "Sit with me until it's time to go."

"Sure. Um, I paid off that debt. I'm free and clear, Dee. You won't have to look over your shoulder." He gave a small smile. "And your husband won't have to kill me."

Sasha grinned as she handed both of them small bottles of water.

"Zach, since Dad's not here, would you mind walking me down the aisle?"

He smiled. "I'm glad to stand in for him today."

They spent the next minutes becoming reacquainted. When Liz returned to announce it was time to go, Zach helped Delilah to her feet and held out his arm.

"Let's not keep your medic waiting. I have a feeling he'll track you down if you're late."

Delilah laughed, joy exploding in her heart as butterflies fluttered in her stomach. All the nervousness, however, disappeared the moment she saw Matt Rainer dressed in his military uniform waiting at the altar for her. The love in his eyes and the broad smile were all she saw. Nothing else registered until Zach kissed her cheek and placed her hand in Matt's.

Matt kissed the back of her hand and murmured, "You're the most beautiful woman I've ever seen, baby."

Marcus Lang cleared his throat, his eyes twinkling, and began the ceremony. Within minutes, he pronounced them husband and wife, and Matt's lips were on hers.

After a long, deep kiss, he turned with her to face the audience. Shock rolled through Delilah. Cornerstone Church was packed. Some of the guests she didn't recognize. Must be Matt's co-workers from Nashville.

Behind them, the pastor said, "I'm happy to present Matthew and Delilah Rainer."

Applause broke out as she and Matt walked down the aisle to piano music played by Rio's wife, Darcy.

Friends and family congratulated them, including Matt parents and his sister and her family. Such a sweet family, Delilah thought. She looked forward to spending time with them after the honeymoon.

At the end of the reception line, a buzz-cut blond with a beautiful woman and child beside him gave Matt a hug. "Congratulations, Matt."

"Thanks. Brent, this is Delilah. Sweetheart, meet my boss, Brent Maddox, his wife, Rowan, and their daughter, Alexis."

Delilah smiled. "It's great to meet you. Thanks for coming."

"As my wedding gift to you, a Fortress jet is fueled and ready to take you to your honeymoon destination. When you plan to return home, Zane will arrange a pickup. Matt, I don't want to hear from you for two weeks."

"I asked for one week, sir. I know you're short staffed because Durango is on leave from missions."

"We'll manage. Medics from other teams have agreed to cover for you. Enjoy the time with your wife, buddy. You've more than earned it." He escorted his family into the reception hall.

"Did you eat lunch, Delilah?" Matt asked.

She shook her head. "I was too nervous."

He kissed her. "We'll eat and visit with friends for a few minutes. In an hour, I'm stealing you from the reception. We have a plane to catch, Mrs. Rainer."

"Where are we going?" She didn't really care. Nothing mattered except that she had Matt to herself for a few days.

"The Bahamas. Nothing but sun, sand, and surf on a private beach. Best of all, I get to spend every minute with the woman I need more than my next breath. I love you, Delilah. You've made me the happiest man on the planet. Thank you for giving me the best gift I've ever received. You."

Delilah wrapped her arms around his neck and drew his head down for a series of kisses.

"Hey, you have two weeks to do that. The rest of us are waiting for you so we can eat. Get a move on."

They laughed and followed Cade into the reception hall. Her gaze swept over the people gathered in the large room. This was what life should be like. A life filled with joy, laughter, and friends who were now part of her family.

She and Matt managed to eat a few bites between conversations. At the hour mark, Matt stood and held out his hand to Delilah. The hall's occupants quieted down.

"Folks, thank you for sharing in our wedding day. We love you guys, but I want this beautiful woman all to myself. We're out of here."

Amid the laughter, Matt led Delilah from the hall and out to his SUV.

"Wait. What about my clothes?"

"Simon and Liam transferred everything to the SUV." He opened the passenger door, lifted her inside, and leaned in for a blazing kiss. "I have plans for you, Mrs. Rainer."

"Is that so?"

"Oh, yeah. I'm going to adore you and spoil you every day for the rest of our lives."

Delilah's heart melted. In his eyes, she saw their future. There would be difficulties ahead, but those times would be tempered by the strength and abundance of their love. She was ready to leave the past behind and walk hand-in-hand with her husband into their future.

REBECCA DEEL

ABOUT THE AUTHOR

Rebecca Deel is a preacher's kid with a black belt in karate. She teaches business classes at a private four-year college outside Nashville, Tennessee. She plays the piano at church, writes freelance articles, and runs interference for the family dogs. She's been married to her amazing husband for more than 25 years and is the proud mom of two grown sons. She delivers occasional devotions to the women's group at her church and conducts seminars in personal safety, money management, and writing. Her articles have been published in *ONE Magazine*, *Contact*, and *Co-Laborer*, and she was profiled in the June 2010 Williamson edition of *Nashville Christian Family* magazine. Rebeca completed her Doctor of Arts degree in Economics and wears her favorite Dallas Cowboys sweatshirt when life turns ugly.

For more information on Rebecca . . .
Sign up for Rebecca's newsletter: http://eepurl.com/_B6w9
Visit Rebecca's website: www.rebeccadeelbooks.com

Printed in Great Britain
by Amazon

38385964R00179